S/A

D0095426

WITHDRAWN

TIGER CRUISE

TIGER CRUISE

DOUGLAS MORGAN

A TOM DOHERTY ASSOCIATES BOOK
NEW YORK

TIGER CRUISE

Copyright © 2000 by Douglas Morgan

All rights reserved, including the right to reproduce this book, or portions thereof, in any form.

This book is printed on acid-free paper.

Edited by Leigh Grossman and Teresa Nielsen Hayden

Ship diagram by Precision Graphics

Map by Mark Stein Studios

Special thanks to LCDR Duncan J. Macdonald, USN.

Based on a storyline and characters created by Pamela Wallace and Susan Feiles.

A Forge Book
Published by Tom Doherty Associates, LLC
175 Fifth Avenue
New York, NY 10010

www.tor.com

Forge® is a registered trademark of Tom Doherty Associates, LLC.

Library of Congress Cataloging-in-Publication Data

Morgan, Douglas.
Tiger cruise / Douglas Morgan.—1st ed.
    p. cm.
"A Tom Doherty Associates book."
ISBN 0-312-87042-6 (acid-free paper)
    1. Destroyers (Warships)—Fiction. 2. Malacca, Strait of—Fiction. 3. Nuclear weapons—Fiction. 4. Typhoons—Fiction. 5. Pirates—Fiction. I. Title.

PS3563.O8265 T5 2000
813'.6—dc21   00-054172

First Edition: December 2000

Printed in the United States of America

0 9 8 7 6 5 4 3 2 1

To the sailors of the US Navy,
and all those who fight terrorism
or piracy worldwide

DISCLAIMER

Some elements in this story are deliberately inaccurate. I have not given, nor do I intend to give, instructions on how to seize a Navy ship on the high seas.

—*DM*

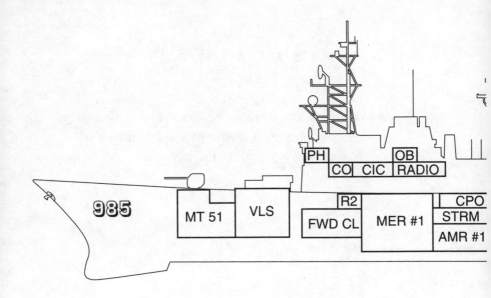

AMR— Auxiliary Machinery Room
CIC— Combat Information Center
CL— Crew Living Space
CM— Crew's Mess
CO— Captain's Sea Cabin
CPO— Chief's Mess/Lounge/Quarters
GEN— Emergency Generator Room
MER 1— Main Engine Room #1 (Main Control)
MT 51— Gun Mount 51
MT 52— Gun Mount 52

USS Cushing

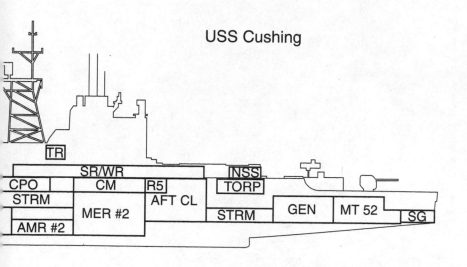

NSS—NATO Sea Sparrow Magazine
OB—Outboard Intelligence
PH—Pilot House
R2—Repair 2
R5—Repair 5
SG—Steering Gear (After Steering)
SR/WR—Officers Staterooms and Wardroom
STRM—Storerooms
TORP—Torpedo Magazine (Port/Stbd)
TR—Torpedo Ready Service Locker
VLS—Vertical Launch System
 (missile spaces)

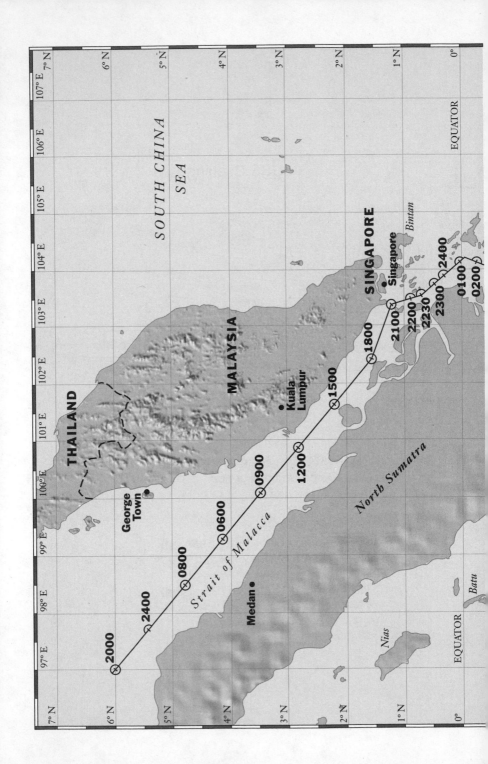

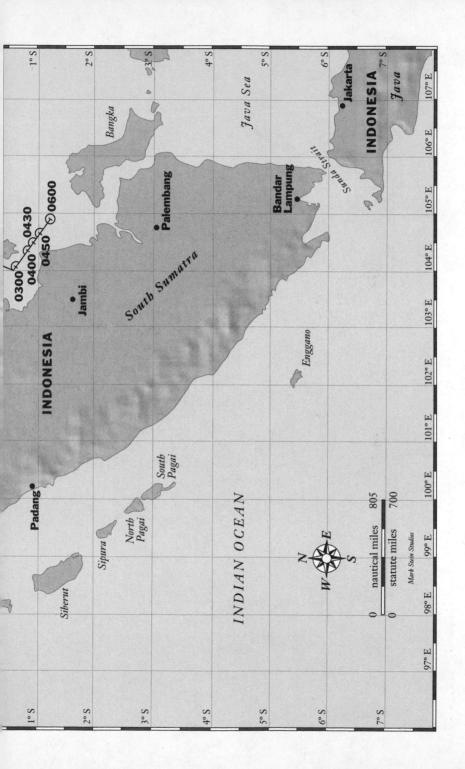

TIGER CRUISE

PROLOGUE

Nighttime, dark. Thin wisps of cloud. The groundswell was from nor-nor-east, waves from the east, propelled by a light air. A small launch powered by an outboard motor lay broadside to the seas, rolling, no lights showing.

Away to the west the moon was setting into the Java Sea. In the boat, low, wearing dark clothing, sat a group of men. They spoke Indonesian to one another when they needed to speak. They seldom needed to speak. Their leader, a young man, had a pair of ex-Soviet 8x30 binoculars. He swept the area to the west—where the crescent moon lit the water, where ships would be silhouetted. This was a shipping lane. A ship would be along sooner or later.

The launch was pointed generally to the south. The slender young man watched mostly to the northwest, though he often scanned all the way around the compass. He was a hunter. He did not wish to become prey, or to miss prey that came from an unexpected direction.

Away to the northwest a single white light appeared on the horizon.

"There." He took a bearing with a handheld compass.

Time passed. A second white light, lower than the first and to its left, appeared out of the sea.

"Fire it up. Come right."

The man at the stern of the launch got the outboard going. It coughed once then quieted. Its exhaust was underwater for muffling. He pulled the tiller port; the launch turned to starboard.

"Steady."

The man at the stern bought the tiller to centerline. The lights on the horizon were higher now, with a single red light glimmering below and a bit to the right of the higher of the two white running lights.

The young man looked through his binoculars. Someone un-used to the sea might not see anything. Where others might see black-on-black, a horizon undifferentiated from the sky, he made out hair-fine strokes of darker darkness. The ship's superstructure. The configuration of masts and booms told him that this was a coastwise merchant. He took another mark with his compass.

"More speed."

The wind of their passage picked up. The launch cut the waves at an angle, slapping the water with a whump-whump sound. He could taste the salt. Here in the tropics the air was always heavy with moisture. He took out a triangle of cloth printed in camouflage pattern and tied it around his head, partly to keep his hair out of his eyes, partly to soak up his sweat, and partly because it looked piratical. He had been to school in the West, and knew how im-portant image could be.

The lights on the ship did not change their angle, though they got closer.

"Lock and load. No one fires without my permission."

The response was a rattle of metal as magazines were inserted in a motley variety of weapons and rounds racked into chambers.

Close enough now that binoculars weren't needed to make out the ship they were pursuing. Three miles and closing. With the wind at their backs they had to be careful of sound. It would carry toward the target.

"Laddermen, stand by."

Now they were forward of the ship. "Cut power. Glide alongside." The merchant was making perhaps seven knots. Idling along through the warm night. Even that speed brought on the stempost and the slab-like sides high overhead. "Match speed! Do it now!" Parallel, staying out of the pressure wave just ahead of the screws. Here, at the waist, Venturi effect held the small craft tight against the merchant's side.

"Ladders up. Go!"

Two aluminum ladders, painted black, hooks at their tops, swung up from the launch and over the rail of the merchant.

The young man was the first one up. Once up he turned to his right. The superstructure was located aft on this vessel, and he needed to get there in a hurry. His men would be behind him. He wore athletic shoes, Nikes. He was quiet. He was fast. Speed counted here.

Up the external ladder to the Bridge. One level. Two. Bridgewing. This side was shadowed. A glance inside. Dim lights of radar repeaters. A glow from the binnacle. One man at the wheel, watching the autopilot work.

The young man was aware of another of his men arriving on the Bridgewing behind him. The rest would be close. He unholsterd his pistol, a largeframe 9mm, and dashed into the Pilothouse. Two paces, the man at the autopilot turning toward him, seeing nothing, weapon high, bringing it down, the man crumpling to the deck, not breaking stride, through the Pilothouse to the opposite Bridgewing.

An officer stood there, white cap with a black bill and a gold chinstrap glowing in the moonlight. The officer would have been touring the ship, checking that all was well. Perhaps he'd thought it was. If so, he'd been wrong.

The young man raised his pistol and pointed it between the man's eyes. The officer would see nothing but the muzzle.

"Tell me quickly," the young man said, speaking English now, "How many on board?" He took a step back, out of the officer's arm's reach, and brought the pistol close to his body. Perhaps this officer knew, or thought he knew, the unarmed moves to use against a man with a pistol. No sense taking chances.

"Seven," the officer said. In English. English was always a good first-guess language to use on ships' officers.

"Are you sure?" The young man looked quickly to the inside of the Pilothouse. In the darker darkness there he could make out one of his men, Tansil, perhaps, bending over the fallen sailor, ripping out the man's pockets, searching for weapons, money, keys.

"My men will search the ship. If you are wrong, if there are six, or eight, I will kill you. Now: How many on board?"

"Seven," the officer repeated. "Counting me and the man in there." The officer nodded toward the Pilothouse. His face was nothing but a pale oval under his white hat. The young man could imagine that the officer's eyes were filled with terror. Not that it mattered. "Seven men onboard," he called back into the Pilothouse, in Indonesian. "Find them. Let's move." Then he turned back to the officer. "The manifest is on the Bridge here, in a safe. Open it for me. I wish to inspect your papers."

"You don't look like a bloody customs laddie," the officer muttered.

The young man laughed. "My friend," he said. "One of the bullets I carry is worth thirty-eight cents. At the moment your life is worth thirty-seven cents. Don't make me waste money. Now open the safe."

A week later, *Sasago Maru* was posted overdue. Two months later a vessel that answered to her description turned up alongside a pier in Taipei, though the name on the sternboard was different, and the cargo of Japanese circuitboards and Malasian hemp had gone into markets gray and black. It took the ship's owners two years in Admiralty court to win the return of their vessel.

No member of the crew was every heard from again.

All that remained was a whisper of one name, a pirate known for his boldness even in waters renowned for their bold pirates. A young Indonesian named Michael Prasetyo.

USS *Cushing* (DD985)
Diego Garcia, British Indian Ocean Territory
73° 22' E/7° 16' S
1600 Local/1000 Zulu

From the air, the island of Diego Garcia looks like a gigantic human footprint set in the blue water of the Indian Ocean. A group of islets to the north make up the toes, and the ring of coral surrounding the central lagoon forms the instep, arch, and heel. The airstrip lies on Diego's western side, on the ball of the foot just underneath the big toe.

USS *Cushing* lay tied up pierside in the lagoon, outboard of a repair ship and a Military Sealift Command forward-deployed fast combat stores vessel. Captain Andrew Warner, *Cushing*'s Commanding Officer, sat working at the desk in his cabin, forward on the 01 level. Cabin bulkheads in this part of the 01 level were painted light blue—"babyshit blue," the sailors called it, in contrast to the "titty pink" of the passageway—to show that they were officers' country.

Warner had a private cabin with its own porthole, which in the cramped world of shipboard life meant that he rated. Junior officers on *Cushing* slept four to a cabin, and ordinary enlisted types berthed by division in six-by-two-foot bunks stacked four high.

The paperwork currently occupying most of Warner's attention was the pile of forms needed to give an administrative discharge to Fireman Thomas James Raveneau—"for the good of the service," Raveneau's aptitude for life in the modern military being somewhere between substandard and nonexistent. Getting Fireman Raveneau out of the Navy and back into civilian life had already generated a stack of paper several inches thick: Raveneau's complete service record, from enlistment up through the present; counseling forms from his division officer, attesting that Ensign Somers had talked with him repeatedly about his problems and performance; a sheaf of recommendations for discharge coming from, variously, Raveneau's leading petty officer, his chief, his division officer, his department head, and the XO; and records of all Raveneau's disciplinary appearances at Captain's Mast.

Raveneau's most recent offense had finally started him on his way out of the service. For reasons Warner didn't claim to understand, Raveneau, Thomas J., had first stolen and then attempted to conceal the baseball trophy *Cushing*'s team had won in a hard-fought game against the team from USS *Blue Ridge* on one of *Blue Ridge*'s rare deployments away from Yokosuka. Given the considerable size and heft of the trophy, he hadn't succeeded for very long. The trophy was back in its place of honor in the gedunk—the ship's store—and Thomas James Raveneau was at the head of the line for an admin.

With a sense of relief, Warner turned from Raveneau's stack of paperwork to the slightly thinner stack of paper that represented *Cushing*'s daily message traffic. Reading the traffic—mostly fuel expenditure reports for the rest of the task group, intelligence summaries that boiled down to "nothing new under the sun," and Local Notices to Mariners—wasn't the most exciting part of a captain's job, but it wasn't one that could be neglected. Even the most in-

nocuous of messages, in Captain Warner's experience, could come
back and bite the ass of the CO who ignored it, and Warner intended to preserve his own ass in its current unbitten state.

All of the sheets in the folder marked "CO Afternoon Traffic"
had initials in green ink in the upper right-hand corner—the XO's
chop, meaning that Executive Officer Ted Flandry had thought this
stuff important enough for *Cushing*'s commanding officer to see.
Warner could have gotten the full slug of message traffic down at
Radio Central, or off one of the wardroom clipboards where everything not eyes-only would be filed, but this way he only had three-
quarters of an inch of paper to go through, instead of three inches.

Today's excitement, such as it was, came in the form of a
weather summary reporting a tropical depression west of Indonesia.
Nothing dangerous as yet, but this was the typhoon season, and a
bad blow might cause trouble. *Cushing* would shortly be taking on
a contingent of Tigers—military dependents embarking at Diego
Garcia for the remainder of the voyage home—and some of them
might not be able to handle heavy weather.

Warner scribbled "NAV—our track?" on the weather summary
in red ink—red was reserved for the commanding officer's com-
ments, as green was for the XO's—and added that sheet to the pile
to his left, where action items went.

The summary was the next to last piece of paper in the stack.
Warner picked up the final item, a note from Rear Admiral David
Mayland congratulating everyone in the *Nimitz* battle group on a
successful rotation through the Persian Gulf.

So Davy Mayland gets one step closer to his third star, Warner
thought, as he read through the stock phrases of commendation and
recognition. Mayland had cherished high ambitions for as long as
Warner could remember, going back to when they were stationed
together in San Diego. Warner had been a lieutenant on board USS
Wallace Wood while Mayland was a "squad dog," a Lieutenant Com-

mander attached to DESRON—Destroyer Squadron—One. Even then, merely getting the job done right had never been enough for Davy Mayland. He had to be seen doing it right, and seen doing it by the right people at the right time.

This rotation was just the same. The lists for promotion from Rear Admiral (upper half) to Vice Admiral come out every year in the spring, but Congress considers the candidates for advancement in the fall—just about the time when David Mayland and the *Nimitz* would sail back into Pearl Harbor at the top of a successful cruise.

And not a moment too soon, either, Warner thought. *If Davy had to wait for it much longer, he'd probably burst.*

He initialed the Admiral's note, so that the XO would know that he'd seen it, and closed the folder.

Having dealt with the afternoon traffic, Warner turned to the sound-powered phone beside his desk. The 21MC, with its network of cables running throughout the ship, worked on the same general principle as a tin-can-and-string telephone. The system, not being dependent upon electricity for its operation, would function even if *Cushing* lost power completely.

Warner turned the selector to 12 for the wardroom and pressed the key. "XO, you down there?"

The amplified circuit gave two clicks, for "affirmative," as Flandry keyed his lever twice.

"I'm going ashore. Anything comes up, handle it."

Warner stood, picked up his hat, and left his cabin, heading aft. Although most of the officers aboard *Cushing* wore working khaki uniforms, today Warner had chosen to wear tropical white. He'd put on the crisply pressed uniform partly because he felt that being in port, even in Diego, deserved a little show, and partly because he'd be greeting the newly arrived Tigers at the airstrip, and they ought to be shown some respect.

But mostly he'd put on his trop whites because after 1600, working uniform wasn't allowed in the Officers' Club. He'd have to be in the Uniform of the Day if he wanted to take his wife to the O Club for a drink later.

Laura, he thought. He hadn't seen her for nine months—he sometimes worried that he'd forgotten the exact lines of her face, or the pitch and accent of her voice. But the prospect of seeing her again, so soon, brought the memories rushing in at full strength. The first time he'd come back to Laura after a long deployment, she'd been eight months pregnant, still finishing her graduate degree at UCLA, and he'd been deeply pessimistic about his chances of getting met at the pier.

He'd been a young Ensign then, on the forecastle of USS *Mc-Cloy*, coming into Bremerton Naval Shipyard in Puget Sound for a refit. The weather was gray and rainy. Laura was one of a couple of hundred people milling about on the pier, a swirling mass of color against the gray sky and drab wood and concrete of the dock; but his gaze went straight to her like compass turning to a magnetic north. He'd experienced a moment of disorientation—*who is this pregnant chick, anyhow?*—and then the Laura he'd left behind and the Laura at the pier coalesced again into one person. As the officer supervising the deck apes tying up the ship and securing her for the refit, he hadn't been able to get off the ship and close to Laura for almost an hour. By that time the rest of the crowd was gone, but Laura had still been there in the drizzle, waiting for him.

No matter how tense the homecomings sometimes got—and there'd been a few tense ones, especially as they both advanced in their careers and Chris grew from a baby to a teenager with a mind of his own—he'd always remembered that first time, and how she hadn't left.

Thinking of it, he walked a little faster now. On *Cushing*'s quarterdeck, he approached the Officer of the Deck, Ensign Luke Somers. The OOD was a tall blond kid from somewhere up in the hills of West-by-God Virginia—a high school and college basketball player who'd gone into the Navy through OCS after figuring out that a solid-but-not-stellar record didn't stand a chance with the NBA.

"Going over to the airstrip," Warner said.

"Yes, sir," Somers replied. He flipped the toggle on the Ashore Board from green to red, and stepped back.

Warner saluted Somers, who returned the salute. Then Warner saluted the flag and turned to go across the brow—the gangplank that spanned the gap between *Cushing* and her nearest neighbor, the repair ship *Ajax*. The Petty Officer of the Watch on *Cushing* rang four bells in groups of two—*ding ding, ding ding*—and passed the word, "*Cushing*, departing." As soon as Warner's foot touched the deck of *Ajax*, the Petty Officer of the Watch rang a final, single bell, to tell the signalmen aboard *Cushing* to hoist the absentee pennant— the black and white triangular pennant that let the world know *Cushing*'s commanding officer was no longer physically aboard.

At almost the same moment, the OOD on *Ajax* passed the word "*Cushing*, crossing," and rang four bells of his own. Compared to USS *Cushing*, *Ajax* was broader and higher above the water—a regular barge, from the viewpoint of a destroyer sailor—as well as being considerably older. Warner crossed via a wide through-decks passageway to the weather deck on the other side. Another brow led over from *Ajax* to the deck of the Military Sealift Command stores ship, where the Petty Officer of the Watch on the MSC vessel once again rang four bells and passed the word, "*Cushing*, crossing."

Thus heralded by announcements and bells, Warner made his way from one ship to the next, and down to the pier. At the foot of the pier, he found Master Chief Gunner's Mate Morrison, *Cushing*'s senior enlisted man.

"Good afternoon, sir," Morrison said, with a salute.

The Master Chief was a burly man of about Warner's own age, with a row of service ribbons as impressive as Warner's own. Twenty years in the Navy had muted his Tidewater accent; now it was only a somewhat softer version of the generalized Southern accent that eventually crept into the speech of everyone in the fleet.

Warner returned the Master Chief's salute. "Afternoon, Gunner. Off to meet and greet?"

"Yes sir. On my way to the strip right now."

The two men fell into easy step, heading for the landing field. The road, made of coral sand mixed with sea shells, crunched slightly under their feet. Except for bicycles and the occasional government vehicle, they didn't encounter any traffic—private automobiles didn't exist on the American side of the island.

The day was fair, the sky a deep blue with white cumulus clouds puffing up like kernels of popcorn. The crushed coral and shell walk glistened in the tropical sun, and the smell of hibiscus blossoms floated over the island on the breeze.

"Ship's vehicle is on its way already," Morrison said. "I have a working party standing by to pick up the luggage. We've found reliefs for all the sponsors during Sea and Anchor."

"Very well. Anything to carry the Tigers?"

"They'll want to stretch their legs, I think," the Master Chief said. "Any sick, lame, or lazy among 'em?"

"You're saying 'make 'em walk.' "

"Generally speaking, yes sir. But I do have a vehicle from the station standing by, just in case."

"I'll be taking my two to the club," Warner said. "Last chance for a drink until we hit Yokosuka."

"Mine will be doing laps all the way around Diego until we cast off," Morrison said.

Warner remembered the Master Chief's oldest from a ship's picnic back in Honolulu—an athletic-looking girl in her late teens, with short blonde hair and a killer volleyball serve. She'd had enough energy for any two ordinary people, and Morrison had been so proud of her he'd practically glowed.

"Running or swimming?" the Captain asked.

Morrison chuckled. "Both, if I know my Holly."

"What year's she in now?" Holly Lynne Morrison was a cadet at VMI, a fact which seemed to both please her father and leave him shaking his head in confusion.

"Just finished her second," the Master Chief said. "Your boy's about to graduate?"

"Yes. Cal State Long Beach. With a degree in philosophy, of all things." Warner shook his head. "Damned if I know what he's going to do with his life. I don't think he's figured it out himself yet."

"We were lucky; Uncle told us."

"You got that one right, Master Chief. All we have to do now is figure out what we're going to do when Uncle tells us it's time to say good-bye."

For a moment both men were quiet. Retirement from active duty could be a daunting prospect, coming as it usually did at an age when most civilians were barely in mid-career. Warner, as a Commander frocked to Captain—wearing the uniform of a four-striper and bearing the title, but still only getting a Commander's pay—could look forward to a promotion at the end of *Cushing*'s latest cruise. The formal rank would serve as a kind of good-bye present, since his pension would come in at half the base pay of his highest paygrade.

Warner knew that Laura worried about their future sometimes, and he wasn't sure that he blamed her for it. Put a man back on shore with a steady income and no obligations, and he was likely to do all sorts of strange things—take up hang-gliding, or poetry, or politics, or just a committed study of the bottom of a bottle. In her line of work, she saw all the worst cases.

The Master Chief was the first to break the silence. "Got something worked out for after your sunset cruise, Skipper?"

"When I transfer to COMNAVSIXPAC? I'm going to sit home for a while and handle the honeydew assignments. Laura's been after me to remodel the kitchen for a couple of years now, and I haven't had the time. After that, I think I'll travel some. Buy me something with two wheels, maybe, and ride it across the country, seeing the sights. No phone, no message traffic, no one calling me 'sir'. . . . How about you, Master Chief?"

"Look for a veterans'-preference job somewhere in civil service, probably," Morrison said. He didn't sound particularly enthusiastic about the prospect. "But tell you the truth, Skipper, sometimes I've thought real hard about chaining myself up in the middle of a field with a bale of wacky weed and seeing what I've been missing, all these years on the straight and narrow. Then I'm gonna go home and drink beer and watch TV and throw the empties out the back window. When I can walk out of the second-floor window on the cans, I'll go into town. People will say, 'Is he wearing a shirt?' and between my hair and my beard they won't be able to tell."

Warner chuckled. "Don't let the troops hear you say that."

"Hell, Captain," Morrison said. "If you and me weren't both getting out at the end of this cruise, I wouldn't've told *you*."

2

High over the island, a C-130 Hercules out of Guam began its initial approach. Pallets of supplies bound for Diego's Navy warehouses filled the cargo space in the center of the plane. The last pallet held a pile of suitcases—luggage belonging to the space-available passengers, two bags per person with a top limit of seventy pounds each, only loaded after all the important material had gone on board.

The wooden crates on their metal skids, stenciled with National Stock Numbers and draped with cargo nets, rose like a wall between the two rows of nylon web seats that ran down either side of the aircraft. The seats were red; everything else in the aircraft came in one shade or another of green or mustard.

Chris Warner sat all the way forward on the port side of the aircraft, strapped into the webbing with lap and shoulder belts. The seat hadn't been comfortable when the C-130 left Guam twelve hours before, and it hadn't improved any since. The four-engine turboprop wasn't particularly fast, but it made up for its lack of speed with plenty of shaking and noise.

The only soundproofing in the aircraft came from bright yellow earplugs that the crew chief had handed out to everyone before takeoff. The rattle and thrum of the C-130's metal body, the rush of wind across its wings, and the deep nonstop roar of its engines all went right past the earplugs as if they weren't there.

About a dozen passengers aboard the C-130 were bound for USS *Cushing*—Chris and his mother, a couple of older guys about the right age to be somebody's grandfathers or uncles, a handful of young-to-middle-aged men, a pair of twin kids who looked like they were busy thinking of ways to get into trouble on a plane in flight, and a blonde girl about Chris's own age. None of them looked as if they were enjoying the trip any more than he was.

The worst of it, he decided, was the boredom. The copies of *Outdoor Photography* and *Discover* he'd bought at a newsstand in Honolulu had long since lost their power to distract him. He had their contents memorized, all the way down to the ads for specialized lens filters and ecologically correct group tours of the Amazon Basin. In desperation, he'd turned to the college texts he'd brought along for the cruise from Diego Garcia back to Hawaii. He still had his senior thesis to finish, and the hours spent in transit would make a good time to work through the reading list.

Theoretically, at any rate. The noise and vibration of the C-130 had overcome all his good intentions, not to mention his ability to concentrate. He'd been trying to read the same paragraph in *The Critique of Pure Reason* for the last hour, without any luck.

It didn't help that Chris felt hungry as well as bored. The in-flight meal about six hours earlier had consisted of a bologna sandwich, an apple, a waxed carton of juice-substitute, and a packet of mustard, all served up in a white cardboard box. The Air Mobility Command didn't cater to tourists or business-class travelers, far less to members of the international jet set. AMC was for people who had to go from here to there at Uncle Sam's bidding—people who had no choice in the matter.

That's not me, Chris thought. He looked to his right, farther down the aircraft, to the place where his mother sat. Laura Warner had spent the long flight reading one or another of the professional psychiatric journals she'd brought aboard in her tote bag. *Maybe it's her. Maybe it's Dad. But it's definitely not me.*

He still wasn't sure why he'd agreed to come along on this so-called Tiger Cruise at all. Partly it was the collapse of his earlier vacation plans—the spelunking expedition to West Virginia hadn't survived his caving buddy's unexpected, and embarrassing, case of chicken pox—and partly it was the chance to take photographs of a part of the world he'd never seen before. But he had to admit, at least to himself, that the real reason he'd come along was because his mother had asked him to.

Come on, she'd said. *This is your last chance to observe your father in his natural habitat.*

Diego Garcia, BIOT
73° 22' E/7° 16' S
1631 Local/1031 Zulu

The Diego airstrip—a flattened and paved chunk of coral with a chain-link fence around it and a series of sheds to protect the equipment from rain—wasn't far to walk from the lagoon. Nothing on Diego Garcia, in fact, was very far from anything else. The entire island had a total area of something like ten square miles, about half of which was off-limits to US personnel.

A small group of officers and enlisted men—the sponsors of the arriving dependents—waited at the airport, scanning the clouds for a first glimpse of the plane that would bring the Tigers to Diego Garcia. Bursts of nervous conversation faded into silence, then started up again. Captain Warner stood with Master Chief Morrison and Lieutenant (junior grade) Drew Bailey, *Cushing*'s junior supply officer—the lambchop, in shipboard parlance, since supply officers in general were familiarly known as porkchops, from the shape of the stylized leaves on their insignia. Bailey himself was several years older than his rank implied. He was an OSVET, an Other Services Veteran, having done a hitch in the Army before finishing his college degree and joining the Navy's Supply Corps instead of continuing his career in the Green Machine.

"There's our Herky Bird now," Warner said as the C-130 Hercules lined up and came low over the lagoon, wheels down like a dragonfly settling onto a leaf. The plane touched the tarmac with a burst of white smoke from its tires and a whine of slowing engines.

The C-130 taxied to the arrival shed and began offloading cargo. The passengers came off last, walking down the plane's tail ramp after all the pallets had been taken away on trucks or trundled into the warehouses with forklifts. The aircraft's crew chief checked them off on a clipboard as they came. *Cushing*'s Tiger contingent looked about like Warner had expected—an even dozen civilians, mostly young and mostly male. They stayed close together, the only familiar things to each other, looking at the warehouses, the wispy clouds, then back to one another.

Lieutenant j.g. Bailey's twin sons broke away from the group first, followed at a more regular pace by a couple of older men, one black and one Italian—at a guess, Chief Willis's father and BM1 Dellamonica's grandfather, both of them retired sailors. The middle-aged trio coming after the two old salts were most likely MM1 Clay's uncle, ET2 Dixon's father, and Chief Turner's brother, which left the youngish Hispanic guy to be the brother of BM3 Esposito, and the other young man with the vaguely familiar face to be the half-brother—or maybe it was the cousin—of HT1 Frank Terrell. All Warner remembered at the moment was that two brothers from western Tennessee had married twin sisters and produced one or more children, possibly including the future HT1 Terrell and possibly not. Then, some time later, the two couples had played switch, divorcing and remarrying and (possibly) producing either HT1 Terrell or his cousin.

As long as the paperwork's in order, Warner thought, *it doesn't matter*. He turned his attention back to the arriving Tigers, now spreading out across the tarmac as their sponsors hurried forward to greet them. All of the Tigers looked worn out from the long flight and wilted by the tropical heat.

Almost all of them, anyhow. Laura wasn't wilting. Even from a distance, she looked cool and serene. Warner had asked her once how she did it, always turning up calm and unwrinkled no matter how bad the traveling got.

"You glide through things," he'd said—it had been late at night, with no one else nearby to hear him get sentimental. "Like a swan."

"It just looks that way," she said. "All the time I'm really paddling like hell, down underwater where it doesn't show."

He thought of the swan now, as Laura crossed the tarmac toward him with Chris following a step or two behind. Chris wore baggy jeans and a tee shirt advertising some band Warner had never heard of. He was festooned with an assortment of luggage that he hadn't entrusted to the ship's vehicle—his complete collection of photography gear, it looked like. He stopped twice in his way across the tarmac to raise his camera and take pictures.

Warner shook his head. If Laura was a swan, Chris was—what? *What* are *we going to do with that boy?*

Jakarta, Indonesia
105° 49' E/5° 10' S
1820 Local/1120 Zulu

The city of Jakarta had seen its share of riots and power strug-gles, from the dictatorship of Suharto to the chaos that followed his fall. Even now, years after, the scars remained. Half-built office towers, monuments to hubris and corruption, stood like skeletons in the midst of the city—the funds to complete them gone, the heavy equipment that would have built them rusting on the ground. Bamboo scaffolding looked down at empty lots where fast-growing vines covered the gaps left by burnt-out buildings.

Nuril Salladien's office window looked out past the urban decay to the sparkling water of the Java Sea, a golden-spangled expanse of blue dotted with ships. The phone on his desk rang, a harsh burr. Salladien picked up the receiver.

"Ministry of Defense," he said.

A moment.

"I see."

Another moment.

"Thank you."

Salladien replaced the receiver. He got up and walked to his window, where he stood watching the activity beyond it with his hands clasped behind his back. When he turned around, his expression had changed to one of determination.

He left the office and strode down the hall to the stairs. The electricity was not so reliable that he would use the lift.

The streets outside his office building were narrow, noisy, and mobbed with people on bicycles and on foot. Everywhere, the walls and billboards—with their advertisements for consumer goods like Coca-Cola and Ford cars—proclaimed the domination of the West.

The humid air made Salladien's white shirt cling to his body. He purchased a newspaper at a corner kiosk, then walked as quickly as he could to an outdoor tavern on a nearby street. The tavern was just a roofed-over corner—no exterior walls, only one pillar supporting the roof at the outer point—with a bar set against the inner wall. The tables inside spilled out onto the sidewalk. The customers themselves were a cheerful and varied lot, ranging from young executives on their way home from work to traders in drugs, sex, and black market currency. The bartender and the waiters accepted generous tips and asked no questions.

At the bar, Salladien called for two beers, one Tsingtao and the other Heineken, and went with them to sit at a table. He poured out beer from one of the bottles—the bartender had given him two glasses to go with the two beers—until one of the glasses was exactly half-full of Heineken. The bottle of Tsingtao he left alone, the empty glass inverted on its neck. Then he unfolded his newspaper and leaned back to wait.

An hour passed. The beer sat, its foam long gone. Nothing happened. The crowd in the tavern thinned out until only Salladien and two elderly Japanese men playing *go* remained at the tables. Salladien bought a skewer of grilled meat from a passing vendor and continued to read his newspaper. Another hour passed. The beer remained untouched. Salladien didn't rise from his chair.

At last, a shadow fell across the small table from the west. A man dressed, like Salladien, in a loose white shirt and trousers, approached and sat down across from him. Without a word, the newcomer took the empty glass and filled it half-full from the untouched bottle of Tsingtao.

Salladien folded up his newspaper. "Rain's coming," he said.

"It often is, this time of year," the other replied.

"Tell the captain that Tigerclaw is to happen," Salladien said. "Have him meet me here in one hour and I will give him all the information."

"One hour," the stranger said. He rose, not bothering to drink his beer, and walked away without looking back.

Diego Garcia, BIOT
73° 22' E/7° 16' S
1635 Local/1035 Zulu

Kyle and Tyson Bailey, otherwise known as the Terrible Twins, had been on their best behavior for long enough. Their mother—still muttering bad things about her ex-husband whenever she thought Kyle and Tyson weren't close enough to hear—had seen them aboard the Air Mobility Command flight in Honolulu, with instructions to keep quiet and do whatever the Captain's Wife told them to do.

The trip to Diego Garcia had been a long one, and Mrs. Warner hadn't been the kind of person you could mess around with. Worse—from Kyle and Tyson's point of view—Chris Warner, the Captain's son, was with her. Chris had taken one look at Kyle and Tyson and said, under his breath where Mrs. Warner couldn't hear him, "You guys screw around while we're on the airplane, and you're dead meat. And that goes double for messing with my camera stuff."

"We weren't going to, honest," said Tyson. Actually, he *had* been thinking about trying to sneak a look at one of Chris Warner's fancy cameras, but he wasn't planning to any more.

The whole trip had been like that. By the time the wheels of the big C-130 touched down on the Diego Garcia airstrip, Kyle and Tyson were as full of barely repressed excitement as a shaken-up Coke bottle is full of fizz. When they left the plane and spotted their father, LTJG Bailey, standing at the edge of the field, they abandoned their luggage and ran to meet him.

"Daddy!" Tyson got to Bailey first and grabbed him around the waist in an enthusiastic hug. Kyle did the same thing a few seconds later.

"Hello, boys," Bailey said, going down on one knee the better to embrace both twins at once. "Are you two ready to be Tigers for a while?"

"Yeah!" Kyle said, and Tyson echoed him, "Yeah!"

"Great," said Bailey. "First thing, let's get your luggage up onto the pickup truck. Then we can hike back to the ship."

"The whole way?"

"It's not far," Bailey said. "And it'll give you a chance to stretch your legs."

"My legs are already stretched," said Tyson. "I outgrew my school clothes two times last winter."

"No wonder you're so big."

"What about me?" Kyle asked. "I outgrew all *my* clothes last winter, too. *And* my shoes. I have bigger feet now than Tyson does."

"You do not!"

"I do, too!"

"You both have big enough feet to walk back to the ship," Bailey told them. "Let's go."

They loaded the boys' suitcases onto the truck and started out. The boys soon abandoned their squabbling in favor of eager questions.

"What makes the air smell so good?" Kyle asked.

"Flowers," Bailey said. "That's hibiscus you're smelling."

"What's hibiscus?"

"Those red flowers over there," Bailey said, pointing.

Tyson asked, "How big is the ship?"

"*Cushing*'s five hundred and sixty-three feet long," Bailey said, "and displaces about eight thousand tons fully loaded."

"What's 'displaces' mean?" asked Kyle.

"Don't they teach kids anything in science class anymore? That's how much water she'd slosh out of the bathtub, if you could find a bathtub big enough to drop a destroyer into."

"Wow. That's pretty big."

"Not really," Bailey said. "Aircraft carriers, now those are big—*Nimitz* is more than a thousand feet long."

"Wow," said Kyle again. "Do you wish *you* were on an aircraft carrier?"

Bailey laughed. "Not a chance. If I'd wanted to watch planes take off and land all day, I've have joined the Air Force. Give me a destroyer any time."

Diego Garcia, BIOT
73° 22' E/7° 16' S
1636 Local/1036 Zulu

Holly Lynne Morrison—"H. L." to her classmates and instructors, plus anybody else she could convince to call her that, which so far didn't include her father—stepped out of the shadowed interior of the C-130 Hercules and into the heat of the sun. The island air smelled of flowers, a welcome change from the jet-fuel stuffy interior of the C-130.

She squinted her eyes against the glare and scanned the landing field for her father's familiar broad-shouldered, stocky figure. As soon as she'd spotted him, she waved. He waved back, and she ran to join him.

"Daddy!" she said, dropping her carryall to the tarmac and wrapping her arms around him in an enthusiastic hug.

"How's my baby girl?" Her father gave her a hug in return, then stepped back again to look at her. "School's agreeing with you, I think."

"This year's been pretty good," she said, truthfully enough. The year before this one had been rough, though. She didn't ever intend to let her father know just *how* rough—it wouldn't have done any good at the time, and it was all past tense now anyway. "And I'm learning a whole lot."

"I'm proud of you." He reached down to pick up her carryall. She got to it before he did and slung the strap over her shoulder. He laughed. "Still 'me do it myself,' is it?"

"I don't need anybody taking care of me."

"Somebody might want to take care of you someday," he said as they began walking away from the landing field. "Wouldn't hurt to let 'em, once in a while."

"I'm not going to hold my breath waiting for them to show up, either. How was the Persian Gulf?"

"Boring. Even the seagulls yawned."

"I'll tell Mamma that," H. L. said. "She'll be happy."

"That's because she remembers when it wasn't boring."

H. L. remembered it, too. The Gulf War had taken place while she was still in elementary school, and she remembered her mother shushing the children at every CNN special report. H. L. had decided right then that if the grownup world was divided between the people who went out and saw places and did things and the ones who waited at home to find out what had happened, then no matter what else she did, she wasn't ever going to be one of the ones staying behind and waiting.

So far, nothing she'd seen of life had changed her mind.

3

Laura Warner was tired. The flight from Seattle had been long, the flight from Guam longer still, and now she'd have to play the part of the Captain's Wife for two straight weeks nonstop. No one would tell naughty jokes in her presence, because the Captain's Wife wouldn't like it. No one would gripe about shipboard life around her, regardless of the provocation, because the Captain's Wife might not approve. No one would even talk to the Captain's Wife like a human being.

Some wives got off on that kind of thing, but Laura didn't. Over the years she'd put a great deal of work into constructing an identity for herself—that of Laura Warner, Ph.D.—which wasn't dependent on the Navy for validation. She'd built up and maintained her own family counseling practice, although she still worked mostly with members of the military and their dependents, and she and Andrew had always tried to find off-base housing whenever possible.

To hear some of the other wives talk, Laura's lack of enthusiasm for the on-base social round was the main reason her husband was going to retire as a four-striper and never make Admiral. Had she been alone, she would have stuck out her tongue and wiggled her fingers in her ears at the phantom gossip-mongers. If Andrew wasn't going to make Admiral, it was because he'd never wanted to. Life at that level had too much politics, he'd said once, and not enough fun.

"Fun," she'd said. They'd been in the O Club at Pearl Harbor at the time, a last night out together before *Cushing* went on deployment. She would have preferred dinner and drinks in a real restaurant downtown, but Andrew couldn't leave the base. "As in, 'commanding a destroyer is fun'?"

He gave her his lopsided grin, the one that for a brief instant made him look scarcely older than the young Ensign she'd fallen into instant lust with, one evening in 1978. "Oh, yeah."

"Better than sex?"

"*Nothing* is better than sex," he said, with religious fervor. "But close."

"Just as well, 'cause *nothing* is what you'd better be getting on deployment," she'd replied.

Thinking back on that conversation brought another question into Laura's mind: Where was she going to be stashed while she was with *Cushing*? She'd be one of only two females aboard—which meant special berthing—and the other female wasn't an officer's wife, but an enlisted man's daughter. Socializing would be difficult; not for Laura, but for the girl. Assuming that a twenty-year-old girl wanted to talk with a forty-something matron at all.

At least tonight's dinner in the Diego Garcia Officers' Club was proving to be less of a strain than she'd anticipated. Laura had even managed to convince Chris to send his photographic equipment back to *Cushing* on the truck with the rest of the luggage. He'd grumbled about it, of course—he didn't like parting with his cameras and other gear, even for a little while—but she'd been firm. If

Andrew was going to take the trouble of wearing tropical whites and escorting both her and Chris to dinner, the least they could do in return was not look like a couple of footloose vagabonds.

Over the years, she'd developed a knack for picking out suits and dresses that would still look presentable after hours of travel. Chris didn't have the touch, or if he did he didn't bother to exercise it. His Korn tee-shirt and baggy, wide-legged jeans still bore the wrinkles and smudges of a long journey, and his hair plainly hadn't been cut for some months—in fact, not since Andrew had left home for this latest deployment.

She worried at first that Andrew would make some comment on Chris's appearance, or that Chris would decide to sulk after being deprived of his photographer's gear. Fortunately, the food in the Diego O Club was good, and so was her son's appetite; he was too busy devouring a large steak to be disagreeable. With relief, she applied herself to her own dinner, and listened to Andrew and Chris talk—somewhat guardedly; they seemed unwilling to upset the meal with an actual argument—about school and work.

"So. Any ideas yet about life after college?"

Chris finished chewing, and swallowed. "Sort of."

"What do you mean, 'sort of'? You either have an idea, or you don't."

"I sold some pictures a while back," Chris said, after pausing to deal with another bite of meat. "To a magazine."

Andrew nodded. "Your mother sent me the clippings. They looked pretty good."

"Thanks." Chris actually blushed a little, the fair skin reddening across his nose and cheekbones. Laura reminded herself that he'd always been more concerned about his father's opinions than he let on.

"That one photo of the bird's nest, though," Andrew said. "I still haven't figured out where you were standing when you took it."

"Um . . . I wasn't, exactly."

Laura put her fork down. Trust Andrew to spot something she'd missed—*Well, it takes one to know one.* "What do you mean, 'you weren't, exactly'?"

"We were rock climbing. There were ropes—it was perfectly safe."

"Nothing is ever perfectly safe," said Andrew. "And some things are downright stupid. Was this one of them?"

"We had the right gear. And we'd all been climbing before." Chris shook his hair out of his eyes and looked at him. "No, I don't think it was stupid."

Andrew regarded him thoughtfully for a moment, then nodded. "You were there; I wasn't. But do you seriously think you can make a living off of stuff like that?"

"I'm going to find out." Chris cut off another bite of steak. "What about you?"

Andrew's wince was so slight that she doubted anyone else would have noticed it. "Me?"

Chris impaled the bit of meat on the tines of his fork. "Uh-huh. You're getting out of the Navy after this tour. Got any plans?"

You have to admire an ambush like that one, Laura thought. With an effort, she kept herself from rushing in to fill the conversational gap before it could get awkward. *Andrew has to answer this question for himself.*

"I'm going to go back to college and get a master's degree in underwater basket weaving," Andrew said. "The world has a crying need for underwater baskets. Finish your dinner; it's almost time to go back to the ship."

Most of the Tigers had long since returned to *Cushing* in a group, accompanied by their sponsors, by the time Laura, Chris, and Andrew left the O Club and started walking back to the pier. The crew could go to Sea and Anchor without them. Their conversation, which had lagged for a while at the end of the meal, became animated once again as Andrew talked about his latest command.

Laura was glad to let him talk. From long experience, she knew that her first few hours—hell, her first few days—back together with Andrew would be difficult. The enforced separation would have made them into strangers with each other, but strangers with a certain intimacy assumed between them. They hadn't seen each other in nine months, hadn't spoken in six. The letters were few, brief, and long delayed. She'd grown used to it, over the years, grown accustomed to being a single parent and making all the decisions, then having to shift back into nuclear-family mode as soon as Andrew's latest deployment ended.

She spent a lot of her time counseling the junior wives on how to deal with similar situations. Being a trained therapist meant that she understood her own feelings. Understanding them didn't keep her from having them.

Andrew's coming retirement worried her. Worse than the separation of a long deployment, for many people, was the enforced togetherness of hanging around all the time. Men who had looked forward for twenty years to joining COMNAVSIXPAC would be driven bugfuck by a couple of months ashore. Divorces and deaths showed up in a big spike then. Deaths from heart disease, stroke, perforated ulcers, suicide—all the stress-related things you'd think they'd be immune to.

It's a hard life, she thought, *watching soap operas and drinking beer any time you feel like it, with no one to tell you when to shit, when to shower, and when to shave.*

Seeing the future through fatigue didn't make her any more able to handle Andrew. When their usual two-day fight came—the inevitable product of exhaustion, sexual tension, and the collision of fantasy with reality—it would have to be concealed from the crew.

Mustn't upset the children, after all.

So she smiled, and listened to Andrew telling her all about *Cush-*

ing's latest cruise. The unclassified details, that is, since he couldn't bring himself to reveal anything classified to anyone without access and a need to know. Neither of which she had.

They reached the pier, and there ahead of them, past the rusty coastal defense guns of WWII, lay the ship. As always, Laura found the actual sight of USS *Cushing* far less impressive than the image painted by Andrew's enthusiasm for his command.

The destroyer rode low in the water, its haze-gray shape dwarfed by the two larger vessels inboard along the pier. She knew all the details about how a *Spruance*-class destroyer was bigger than a World War II cruiser. The details only served to let her know how small World War II cruisers had really been.

"You have your choice of where to stay," Andrew said to her. "We could clear out a part of Chiefs' Berthing for you and Miss Morrison, or the two of you could share Forward Officers' Berthing. We'll put Chris in my cabin in any case, and I'll stay in my sea cabin off the Bridge."

Laura considered her options. Being the Captain's Wife meant having to consider the good of the ship as well as her own preferences—something she definitely wouldn't miss after Andrew's retirement. "Whoever we displace—the chiefs in the goat locker or the junior officers in Forward O—is going to get pissed off, right?"

Andrew didn't reply directly. "The other female is Morrison's kid. The chiefs are ready to do it."

The *if they have to* went unstated. The technicalities of commissioned versus noncommissioned rank aside, a wise Captain—and the wise Captain's Wife—understood the relative worth and importance of a barely-dry-behind-the-ears Ensign and a Chief Petty Officer with fifteen or twenty years under his belt.

"Better make it Forward O, then," Laura said. "Keep the chiefs happy."

4

USS *Cushing*
Diego Garcia, BIOT
073° 22' E/07° 16' S
1740 Local/1140 Zulu

Destroyers and frigates—the ships of the "Greyhound Navy,"
the eyes and ears of the fleet—exist to go looking for trouble. Of
all the vessels in the fleet, they live the closest to the cutting edge.

The carriers and battleships never go anywhere without a whole
screen of smaller escort vessels, but destroyers operate alone, often
far in advance of the main battle group. They're heavily armed for
their size, and fast enough to outrun anything they can't outshoot.
A destroyer at top speed can put up a rooster-tail of white foam ten
or twelve feet high, and lift her bow out of the water like a speedboat.

Destroyer sailors consider themselves a breed apart, marked by
initiative and élan and the legendary "destroyer dash." In time of
war, part of their business is to sail ahead into danger and send back
word to the fleet, often at the cost of their own lives—for the hard
truth is that destroyers, like the tin cans which give them their nick-
name in the fleet, are expendable.

In time of peace, fortunately, the danger is usually more theo-
retical than real. Nobody, for example, was expecting much trouble
from the passage of the *Nimitz* carrier group through the Strait of
Malacca. True, the Strait had a bad reputation for piracy, at least as
far as small craft and cargo ships were concerned; but *Nimitz* and
her sisters made too big a mouthful for even the most determined
freebooter to swallow.

Now *Cushing*'s Bridge was full of purposeful activity as the destroyer made ready to leave port. Executive Officer Ted Flandry
and Lieutenant Ernie Gilano were handling the detail.

Captain Warner went straight to the Bridge on his arrival. Part
of his mind followed the familiar litany of orders and responses even
while he was absorbed in idle conversation with Master Chief Petty
Officer Morrison. The two men were discussing the sale of cigarettes in the ship's store, a subject of amicable disagreement between
them ever since the beginning of the cruise.

"I've got half a mind to go ahead and take cigarettes off the
shelves altogether," Warner said. "It's not like we've got a whole
lot of smokers left on board any more."

The Boatswain's Mate of the Watch for Sea and Anchor detail
went to the 1MC on the aft bulkhead, took the mike and piped
attention. Then he turned back to await the next command. The
BMOW had a checklist on a clipboard, but he knew the routine for
getting underway well enough that he didn't need to consult it.
Warner followed the process with half an ear, and continued his
low-voiced conversation with the Master Chief.

"The younger enlisted and the junior officers don't smoke much
these days," he said, warming to his topic, "and all the senior officers
who used to smoke have quit now that Uncle doesn't approve of us
filling our lungs with tar and nicotine. So what are we doing selling
cigarettes in the gedunk, anyhow?"

"They sell candy in the gedunk," Morrison said.

"Cigarettes aren't candy."

"Candy makes you fat and rots your teeth," said Morrison. "The Nav doesn't approve of that, either."

The work on the Bridge continued as they talked. The sailors appeared so intent on the process that they had no attention to spare for the conversation between the Captain and the Master Chief, but Warner knew that this was an illusion. By nightfall, every man on board would know that the Captain had been talking again about banning cigarettes in the gedunk.

The helmsman and lee helmsman for Sea and Anchor, two of the most experienced seamen on board, took their places at the wheel and at the Engine Order Telegraph, and the status board talker and the 1JV talker plugged in their sound-powered phones. The status board talker's phone was connected on the JL circuit to the lookouts and to CIC—the Combat Information Center, sometimes known as "Christ, I'm Confused"—where the scope dopes hung out. The 1JV talker's phone was Primary Maneuvering and Docking, connecting Main Control, After Steering, the Forecastle, and the fantail.

"Main Control reports standing by to answer all bells," the 1JV talker said.

"Very well," said the XO. Ted Flandry was a brisk, squared-away type; he already had his orders for PCO—Pre-Commanding Officer—School, and would go there as soon as the ship docked back in Hawaii. Warner knew him for a protégé of Admiral Mayland's, but didn't hold it against him. Davy Mayland liked his own career too well to risk it by playing sea daddy to anybody who wasn't a hot runner. "Mr. Gilano, ready to take it?"

"Yes sir," said Lieutenant Gilano. Ernie Gilano, from Port-chester, New York, was dark-haired and wiry, and a great teller of sea stories on a long midwatch. Gilano was also a fine shiphandler, something required for the exacting process of getting underway.

"Pass the word, 'the Officer of the Deck is shifting his watch from the quarterdeck to the Bridge,' " the XO said.

The boatswain's mate did so. Shortly afterward, the Messenger of the Watch arrived from the quarterdeck, carrying the log.

"First entry, 'Assumed the watch, tied up as before,' " said Lieutenant Gilano, now the Officer of the Deck.

The Quartermaster of the Watch made the notation in his rough log. He would keep a running tally of all the orders given, with their times. A few feet away, Warner and Master Chief Morrison continued their talk.

"If we're selling cigarettes," Warner said, "it beats me why we shouldn't sell rolling papers in the gedunk, too."

Morrison said, "If we made 'em emblematic rolling papers, we could make a buck for the rec fund at the same time."

"That's an idea." Warner narrowed his eyes speculatively, as if pondering the merits of gummed rolling papers imprinted with the ship's seal and motto. Then he shook his head. "They'd never go for it back home. Drug paraphernalia and all that."

"Damned if I know why everyone thinks rolling papers are only good for that one thing," Morrison said. "I knew a boatswain's mate once who used to roll his own tobacco ciggies. Everyone called him Pappy, he was so old—he only had two teeth in his head . . ."

"Probably because of all the candy he bought from the gedunk."

Lieutenant Gilano had steadfastly ignored the talk going on a few feet away from him all this time. He walked over to the starboard Bridgewing and surveyed the ship's side, looking up and back. The water was clear; no small craft or obstructions visible. Then he walked to the port side, nearest *Ajax*.

"Single up all lines," he said.

The 1JV talker passed the word to the Forecastle and fantail. A moment later, the crew on the Bridge could hear the boatswain's mates fore and aft shouting "Single up!" a ghost of the order floating to the 03 level. Forward and aft, in response to the order, sailors from First Division took in the doubled portions of the mooring lines, heaving the lengths of five-inch-thick nylon back aboard hand over hand. When they were done, only six single strands connected *Cushing* to the vessel alongside her.

The process of unmooring continued, at once stately and delicate. Captain Warner abandoned his conversation with Master Chief Morrison and keyed the mike on the 1MC at the after bulkhead.

"This is the Captain. I'd like to welcome all the Tigers aboard. We'll be getting underway in a few minutes. If you'd like to watch the evolution, please go to the 01 level with your sponsor. That is all."

"Singled up forward," the 1JV talker reported. "Singled up aft."

Lieutenant Gilano gave the next order. "Cast off all lines forward. Cast off four."

The sailors of First Division hauled aboard the three lines that connected *Cushing*'s bow to the neighboring ship, then did the same for line four amidships. The 1JV talker reported back to Gilano, "All lines forward cast off. Four cast off."

"Very well. Right full rudder. Port engine ahead one third. Starboard engine back one third."

Helm and lee helm—the sailor at the wheel and the sailor at the Engine Order Telegraph, transmitting Gilano's orders to the engine room—echoed the commands. There was a pause, while the scarcely felt vibration of *Cushing*'s engines passed through the deck. *Cushing* was now "pivoting on springs"; the destroyer's bow began to move away from the side of the neighboring ship, while her stern remained held in place by the two remaining single lines.

"All stop. Increase your rudder to right hard."

"All stop aye," lee helm responded. A few seconds later, the vibration of the engines stopped.

"Increase my rudder to right hard," the sailor at the helm echoed in his turn; and a moment later, "My rudder is right hard."

The ship's bow drifted right, pointing *Cushing* toward the open lagoon, and Lieutenant Gilano ordered, "Cast off all lines."

The Boatswain's Mate of the Watch stood on the port Bridge wing looking aft. At the moment the last of the three remaining lines fell away from *Ajax* to splash into the water, the boatswain blew his whistle into the 1MC and said, "Underway, shift colors."

At that moment the Messenger of the Watch and the Petty Officer of the Watch struck the flags from the flagstaff aft and the jackstaff forward while the skivvy-wavers—the signalmen—broke the ensign on the mast. *Cushing*'s crew members carried out the maneuver with practiced smoothness, so that the two smaller flags came down at the same time as the larger one snapped open and streamed free in the breeze.

The Quartermaster of the Watch logged the time carefully. It marked an important moment of transition—the point after which *Cushing* was no longer attached to any part of the earth, but floating freely on the deep. In addition, Warner knew, the participants in *Cushing*'s unofficial ship-wide mooring pool would be waiting to find out the logged time of unmooring.

The pool worked by means of a simple mechanism: two sheets of plain paper, each ruled into sixty squares, and one sheet of carbonless carbon scrounged from a special request chit. On one sheet of ruled paper, the sixty squares held numbers from 00 to 59, in random order. On the other, the squares remained empty. The crew member running the pool would staple the sheets into a paper sandwich, with numbered squares on the bottom, carbon paper in the middle, and blank squares on the top, and then sell chances. For a dollar—or two dollars, or five, or twenty, depending on how important the voyage, and how long since home—a man could put his initials in one of the empty boxes.

Later, after the time of mooring, unmooring, anchoring, or whatever had been logged, the sandwich would be opened. The man whose initials appeared in the box with the correct minute would take the money.

Gambling is against Navy regulations. Therefore officers were never asked to join the pools, and never officially knew about them. Warner wondered how much this particular pool had been for, and who had won.

Ted Flandry penciled in the time of unmooring on the Movement Report message blank and gave it to the Messenger of the Watch. The Messenger of the Watch took the report over to Captain Warner for his signature, then put it into a plastic canister and sent it rattling down to Radio Central by way of the pneumatic "bunny tube."

"Rudder amidships, all ahead one third," Lieutenant Gilano said, and the vibration of the ship's engines once again made itself felt. Gilano went out onto the Bridgewing and dropped a piece of scrap wood into the water between *Ajax* and *Cushing*. The wood would remain stationary, more or less, so he could see his own motion. When the wood appeared to drift aft, he'd know his ship was going forward.

"Left five degrees rudder." A moment later, "Rudder amidships."

The gap between *Cushing* and *Ajax* widened. Lieutenant Gilano took a sight from the telescopic alidade on the port wing to the dayshape on one of the small islands that formed the toes of Diego Garcia's foot. "Come left, steer zero one five."

"Come left, steer zero one five, aye," the helmsman echoed, spinning the small wheel.

Cushing steered for the open sea. On the Forecastle, a sailor with a sledgehammer stood beside the pelican hook that would release the anchor if anything happened—loss of power, loss of steering—that might endanger the ship while in a piloting situation.

"All ahead two thirds. Come left, steer zero zero four."

The edge of the lagoon approached them, then fell behind. *Cushing*'s motion changed from a choppy vibration to a steady roll as it came into the swell.

"Secure from Sea and Anchor Detail," the boatswain's mate

passed over the 1MC. "On deck, condition four, watch section one."

"Good work, Ernie," Warner said to Lieutenant Gilano. Behind them, the sun hung low on the horizon, the lower edge of its disk already out of sight. The sky was all pearl and mauve, and a ruddy light played on the waves. "Next stop Yokosuka. We're heading home."

5

On the island of Bangka, near Cape Samak, heavy rainfall pocked and roughened the surface of the river. A stiff wind lashed at the waves, and carried down the smell of jungle vegetation to mix with the rotten-fish odor of mud and wet. In spite of the bad weather, a man waited on the shore, a Chicom AK slung on his shoulder.

The rain didn't let up, even after the sun—still hidden behind gray clouds—slipped down toward the horizon and evening came on. The man on the shore kept waiting. Eventually, a small floatplane emerged from the clouds to set down on the choppy water.

The plane taxied to a wooden dock nestled amid the mangroves that lined the riverbank. Before the lookout had finished dropping a line around the cleats on top of the floatplane's near pontoon— even before the propellers had stopped turning—a second man stepped out of the plane and onto the rain-soaked boards of the pier.

Michael Prasetyo was lean and fit, with black hair and sharp, intense features. He wore an expensive white linen business suit, like a man from one of the big city offices, and he carried a leather case clasped tightly under his arm.

He paid no attention to the driving rain that hit him as soon as he emerged, plastering his linen jacket to his body and dulling the shiny perfection of his shoes. Instead he strode down the pier to a building nearby—a shed, really, a structure to keep the rain off, nothing more, with rough wooden walls and a corrugated metal roof.

Once inside the shed, Prasetyo stripped off his jacket and shirt and handed them, along with the leather case, to one of the men who waited there—dark, muscular men, dressed in tiger-striped camouflage mixed with tee shirts, colorful headbands, and Western jeans. Some of the men wore combat boots; others wore athletic shoes, cheap knockoffs of Nikes and Adidas made for the local market.

Prasetyo took a green tee shirt from the man who stood to the right of the door and used the shirt to mop the rain off of his face before pulling the garment on over his head. He accepted a pistol belt from another man, a large sidearm already holstered on it, and buckled it into place. All of this was done in silence; with each change, some of his rich city look dropped away.

His voice was the first to break the sound of rain drumming on the tin roof. "So—Tansil. Everything quiet here while I was gone?"

The man who had handed him the shirt nodded. "Yes, boss."

"That won't last long. I've got information here on the biggest score we've ever tried."

"What is it this time?" Kino Tansil asked. "A cargo ship? A tanker? Maybe a yacht with some rich white-asses on board?"

"Not a tanker," Prasetyo said. "And not a yacht. This time, we're going to do something no one else has ever tried. We're going after the United States Navy. We're going to take a destroyer."

"Where's the profit in this one, boss?" Tansil asked quietly, under cover of the exclamations and startled murmurs from the other men. "You're talking about taking on the whole United States."

"Only one ship," Prasetyo said. "Just like any other ship, only painted gray. And the time is finally right. She'll be traveling alone, at night, in our waters, in heavy weather. The forecast is for the typhoon and this ship to come together out there"—he jerked his head downstream—"two days and twenty hours from now. And what they carry is worth more than any Japanese circuit boards."

"How is the crew armed?"

"Clasp knives and marlinspikes," Prasetyo said. "All of the small arms are locked away. Once we get past the main gun, the rest is easy. We take the ship, then we strip it and sell off its weapons and electronics systems for a great deal of money."

Tansil looked uneasy. "If anything's going to make the Americans mad, that's it."

"A ship unfortunately sunk in a storm? They won't get mad; they'll mount a major search-and-rescue effort." Prasetyo laughed. "Who knows? Maybe we'll even show up to help them look."

"You're really going to do this, aren't you?"

"*We're* really going to do this." Prasetyo nodded toward the leather case. "Don't worry. The ship's name is USS *Cushing*, and I have all the information there is to get on her." Prasetyo put his arm around Tansil's shoulders. "Just stay close beside me, Kino. We'll have them anchored in the lagoon before this week is out, and sunk in deep water the week after that."

Or maybe not, he thought. A man who controlled the resources of a modern destroyer would no longer need to seek the backing of corrupt government officials like Nuril Salladien. He could become a power in his own right; not a politician—Prasetyo had no ambition in that regard—but a man whose wishes politicians had to take into account.

Better just to say that we've scuttled her, he decided. *And lie.*

The thought warmed him. He set it aside for later and unzipped the leather case he had brought with him from the floatplane. He pulled out a laptop computer, powered it on, and called up a pre-sentation package.

"Gentlemen," he said, "gather 'round." He pointed at the diagram now illuminated on the laptop screen. "Here are the command and control spaces on a *Spruance*-class destroyer, marked in blue."

He clicked a key on the laptop and the display changed. "Here is the 'welcome aboard' package that the ship has on the Web. Observe the Captain. If you see this man, do not shoot him without my orders." He clicked again. "As you can see, the publicly available information as to the vessel's internal layout is sketchy. For this reason, we will need to capture one or more sailors to act as guides. . . ."

USS *Nimitz* (CVN68)
70° 15' E/01° 15' S
1640 Local/1140 Zulu

Rear Admiral David Mayland, commanding officer of the Task Group containing USS *Cushing*, leafed through his message traffic. *Cushing*'s Movement Report, and others like it, occupied a folder marked Task Elements. According to the MOVREP, *Cushing* was off from Diego Garcia and proceeding generally east and north to the Strait of Malacca.

A MOVREP allows the Navy to keep track of when a particular ship has left port, where it's going and what track it's traveling on, and at what time it should reach its destination. Bad things happen at sea, and even at the turn of the twenty-first century it's possible for a ship to drop off the face of the ocean as thoroughly as one of Columbus's vessels might have done.

The Movement Report System got its start after the loss of USS

Indianapolis at the end of World War II, when the *Portland*-class heavy cruiser was sunk by a Japanese submarine in the Philippine Sea. Because of the heavy secrecy surrounding the mission—*Indianapolis* had just finished transporting the atomic bombs that would later fall on Hiroshima and Nagasaki—nobody at the ship's final destination knew when it was overdue. The survivors in the water lost over two-thirds of their number to heat, thirst, and shark attacks before being rescued five days later.

Mayland's staff had also flagged a weather report for his attention. The report mentioned a tropical depression west of Indonesia that looked like it might brew up into a full-scale typhoon. The task force would want to avoid that area. Memories were long in the fleet, and nobody wanted a repeat of the infamous typhoon of December 1944, when wind and water battered Admiral Halsey's Third Fleet so brutally that the destroyers *Hull*, *Spence*, and *Monaghan* were driven under and sunk by the storm.

Mayland drank another slug of coffee and turned to the intel assessment. The report spoke of unrest in Africa, and warned travelers to use caution in Timor. Nothing unusual there. In these waters, it wasn't always possible to distinguish between oceangoing terrorists with political motives and out-and-out pirates ready to board and loot merchant ships for commercial gain. Especially when rumor spoke of secret government backing for both groups: of disciplined attackers wearing Indonesian military battle gear; of ports in China giving safe harbor to stolen ships.

But what else was new? Pirates had infested the waters of Indonesia and Borneo for centuries, and—unless the local governments made up their minds to sweep them from the seas as Pompey the Great had swept the pirates from the ancient Mediterranean—would continue to infest them for centuries more.

In the meantime, Mayland reflected, the *Nimitz* battle group had managed to keep the peace in the Persian Gulf for six solid months. If the people in Washington who gave out admiral's stars didn't appreciate the difficulty of that, then there was no justice left in the world.

Sydney, Australia
151° 10' E/33° 56' S
2250 Local/1150 Zulu

"There you have it." Commander Dennis Weir, Royal Australian Navy, leaned back in his chair at Maritime Headquarters and ran his fingers through his thinning red hair. "Our contact in Jakarta's Ministry of Defense reports that Salladien met with Michael Prasetyo for almost two hours yesterday afternoon, and Prasetyo dropped out of sight almost immediately thereafter. So what do you people think?"

"The Indonesians are up to something." The speaker was a trim, dark-haired young woman. Her name tag read BURKE, and she wore a naval uniform with Lieutenant's insignia. "And in those waters there's always a chance the Chinese are involved as well, at least peripherally."

"I agree," said Weir. He tapped the report from Jakarta, lying in its folder on the table before him. "Exactly what they're up to—and who they're up to it with—I don't want to speculate. We could be looking at a breakaway group in the Indonesian defense department. And there's always a chance that the meeting and Prasetyo's subsequent movements could just be a drill, or even some kind of game. Or possibly just my own paranoia, but I don't think so. Not when first we have the observed meeting"—he tapped the report again—"and within hours, Prasetyo is on the move."

"Do we know what he's up to these days?" Lieutenant Burke asked. "Other than the usual, that is."

The third person in the office was a civilian so bland and forgettable in appearance that the effect could only be deliberate. He wore a security badge clipped to the pocket of his suit; his name, according to the badge (not that Weir believed it for a moment), was "H. Potter."

"We don't have any assets in place with Prasetyo," Potter said. "Sorry."

"Think we should alert the Yanks?" asked Lieutenant Burke. "They are supposed to be our friends, after all."

Weir shook his head. "Countries don't have friends. People have friends. All countries have is sets of self-interest. Besides," he added, "I don't see how passing a rumor off to your opposite number would aid us. We're more likely to come out of it looking like fools than like angels, and I doubt that the Yanks would thank us for it in any case."

"May I suggest, then," said Potter, "that you have the appropriate personnel standing by and in readiness, just in case something in our self-interest needs to happen later?"

"Exactly what level of response did you have in mind?" Weir asked. "As long as you're making suggestions."

"My recommendation?" Potter said. "MacGillivray."

Weir looked thoughtful. "Risky business, bringing the Mad Major into it. Remember what happened during that training exercise in Adelaide."

"He and his group met all of the mission objectives for that exercise," Lieutenant Burke pointed out. "With almost twelve hours to spare."

"Leaving behind an entire office block full of outraged citizens who didn't have the faintest idea what was going on," Weir said. "We made the global news with that one."

Potter said, "Still, as Lieutenant Burke reminds us, he is a fast worker. Speed may be of the essence here. How long do we have?"

"From the intercept, something under three days," Weir said.

"Do we know what kind of operation is being planned, if one is being planned at all?"

"We're talking about Prasetyo," Lieutenant Burke said. "Violent, capable, and deniable in Jakarta."

Weir looked thoughtful. "With Salladien involved, look for something that touches on our defense. He wasn't pleased after the Timor op."

"When he goes high order, we'll need to do the same," said Lieutenant Burke.

"Just so," Potter said. "And for that you need the Major. Quite violent and extremely capable. And—considering that mess in Adelaide—he's definitely deniable in Canberra."

6

Heavy rains had swept the river mouth on the island of Bangka all night and most of the following morning. The downpour had abated for the moment, but the air was still thick and humid, the water unsettled. Michael Prasetyo stood at the head of the wooden pier, smoking a cigarette and looking out at a scene of intense activity.

Where earlier a single floatplane had rocked gently on its pontoons, now there were two of them tied up to anchor buoys. The second plane, a new arrival, had an open motorboat alongside, with men shifting metal cases from the plane to the boat. On the other side of the pier, moored one outboard of the other, lay a trio of Chinese-made 80-footers, painted dead black.

Prasetyo's men had been working since dawn under the shelter of tarpaulins, welding metal brackets to the decks of the boats. Eighteen 55-gallon drums of marine diesel stood in rows on the pier, waiting to go into the brackets: extra fuel, to extend the boats' operating range.

Those fuel drums constituted a key part of Prasetyo's plan. So did the three sets of laser sighting goggles in their boxes, one set per boat, and the Forward Looking Infra-Red, with its rotating disk and the box housing a small cylinder of nitrogen for coolant, already mounted atop the cabin of one of the boats.

Prasetyo regarded the Forward Looking Infra-Red with satisfaction. He'd paid out a lot of money for it—and in American dollars, which he always resented—but with luck, the results from the FLIR would be worth the cost. The picture, displayed on a tiny TV monitor installed inside the vessel's cabin, would pick up targets even on a stormy night, without alerting the electronic countermeasures suite of a wary foe.

All that extra fuel had cost money, too. This wasn't a business that could be done on the cheap, not if you were going to do it right. Prasetyo had run the spreadsheets, back in Jakarta, when the prospect of this job first came his way. He knew how much he could expect to clear after selling off all of a US ship's equipment, plus any money and valuables among the crew's personal effects—*these Americans*, he thought; *even their common sailors have bankrolls that would feed a man for a year*—and paying all the bills for the operation. The numbers were very nice indeed.

If the American vessel should happen to have special weapons aboard, the profit margin would be even higher. Colonel Qadaffi had a standing offer of ten million for an ASROC with a Mk 1 nuclear depth bomb.

What a bidding war that would be, Prasetyo thought. *We'd have to buy a bank of our own just to keep the money in.*

On the other side of the ledger, having nukes on board would make the Americans more likely to resist an attack. Surprise would be needed to counteract that possibility; surprise and sudden over-whelming force.

He'd laid out money up front, with the promise of an extra cut of the profits at the end, in order to hire men who could meet his needs. They were exiting the floatplane now, the specialists whom his contacts—not the man in Jakarta, this time, but his other con-tacts—had arranged for him. Three sharpshooters, for the laser-scoped rocket launchers, and a high-ropes man, for the boarding itself.

All four of the men wore civilian clothing, but the set of their shoulders and the trim of their hair told a different story. Prasetyo's contacts had never said exactly where the specialists would come from, and Prasetyo had never asked. As he had more than half ex-pected, however, the newcomers appeared to be ethnic Chinese.

The first man out of the floatplane approached Prasetyo, duffel bag on shoulder, and didn't quite salute. The other three men waited a little distance away.

"Michael Prasetyo?" the man asked. His Indonesian was heavily accented.

Chinese indeed, Prasetyo thought. *Mainlanders.*

"Yes," he said.

The specialist gave a quick nod of acknowledgment. "You will tell us what we need to do."

"Go below; secure your gear. I'll have instructions for you later."

The four walked past. Prasetyo noted with some amusement that they were walking in step.

His amusement was short-lived, however. That kind of help sometimes had a higher price tag attached than originally negoti-ated, and the specialists were a weak link in any case, men of un-certain loyalty a long way from home. If they ran into trouble, they'd have every incentive to save themselves at his expense—or if they could not save themselves, to at least save their country's public face.

The solution to *that* problem, at least, was obvious, but he couldn't do away with the specialists until the raid was an accomplished fact. Afterward, though, was another story . . . he wondered idly how the specialists' ultimate bosses would react when the four men failed to return from their latest mission.

"*Carelessness in bad weather has put more than one sailor over the side.*" That would be the thing to say, he decided, smiling a little as he rehearsed the words to himself. "*And these . . . these were not even sailors, after all.*"

USS *Cushing*
73° 22' E/07° 16' S
2140 Local/1540 Zulu

Chris Warner looked around his father's cabin. It was a lot like all the other such cabins Chris had seen in his years as a Navy brat, except that this one was larger—comparatively; though in absolute terms it was still smaller than Chris's bedroom at home—and his father didn't have to share it with anybody else.

What kind of a stupid job is it, Chris wondered—and not for the first time, either—*where a man has to work for nearly twenty years just to get a single?*

All the contents of the cabin had been secured for sea: a desk, locked; a safe, also locked; everything else either closed or fastened or shut away. Even the little ship model of Stephen Decatur's *Enterprise* was held in place on top of the desk with bungee cords.

Chris decided that he could take a hint. He unpacked his bag and secured his own gear. Most of what he'd brought with him—the books, the jeans and tee shirts—wouldn't mind if *Cushing* ran into heavy seas, but the camera equipment was something else again.

He'd hoped to take some pictures of the abandoned coconut plantation on Diego Garcia, maybe enough to make into a photo essay later when he got back home, but that plan hadn't worked out. Nobody got onto the restricted half of Diego without a pass from the British, and the Brits only gave out passes on the weekends.

With any luck, he'd find another, better photo essay subject on the other side of the Strait of Malacca. Something about Indonesia and Borneo, maybe, where people were burning off the rain forests in order to clear new land for development. Meanwhile, he could get some pictures of tropical cloudscapes—dead boring, as far as subject matter went, but pretty to look at.

With his clothes and equipment put away, he pulled out part of one of the drawers under the bed, noted with a shudder that his father still had a taste for garish multicolored Hawaiian shirts, then lay down, hooked his feet under the drawer, and commenced doing sit-ups. The long airplane trip had left him feeling more like a jointed wooden dummy than a human being, and he needed to work the kinks out somehow if he was going to get any sleep. *Cushing* had a weights-and-exercise room somewhere in the after portion of the ship, but he didn't have time to go there tonight. He'd look for it tomorrow sometime, he promised himself; in the meantime, he'd make do.

USS *Cushing*
73° 22' E/07° 16' S
2150 Local/1550 Zulu

H. L. Morrison hadn't realized that she would be sharing a berthing compartment with the Captain's wife.

You should have figured that out already, she told herself in exasperation. *The only two females on the entire ship—there's no way Daddy and the Captain would let either one of you bunk alone.*

Mrs. Warner still looked as cool and calm as she had back in Guam, before the start of the long flight to Diego. "Hello again, Holly," she said. "It looks like we're going to be roommates for a while. I hope you don't mind."

H. L. shook her head. "No, I don't mind." She didn't, not really. After two years at VMI, she could keep up a polite and respectful façade almost indefinitely. *A useful skill,* she thought. *I wonder if I could get away with listing it on my résumé?*

It helped that Mrs. Warner was a lot nicer than some of the other officers' wives she'd met—nice enough that she felt okay about adding, "Could you call me 'H. L.,' please? I'm still trying to get Daddy used to the idea."

Mrs. Warner smiled. "I gather you decided that 'Holly' wasn't a good name for a VMI cadet."

" 'Holly *Lynne*,' " she said, making a face. "I really didn't need trouble like that."

"Then I'll be sure to call you 'H. L.' " Mrs. Warner said. "Especially where Master Chief Morrison can hear me." She looked around their shared berth in Forward O. "I've been a Navy wife for twenty-two years, and I still don't know how they live in these boxes."

H. L. had to agree. Her first impression of Forward Officers' Berthing came down to one word: green. The pipes were green. Air ducts and cable runs, lagged pipes and bare pipes, all painted the same shade of pea-green and running like snakes across the equally pea-green bulkheads and overhead. Even the linoleum underfoot was green.

Almost everything in the compartment that wasn't painted green—and some of the things that were—had a label stenciled on it in black paint. The pipes bore labels for what they carried—FW SUPPLY, POT WATER, CHILL WATER RETURN, AC SUPPLY—with stenciled arrows showing which direction they carried it in. An aluminum frame next to the cabin's outer door held a list of all the labeled items. The cabin's inner door had its own label: WR/WC, for Washroom/Water Closet.

The cabin also had four bunks, two on either side of the stateroom. Each bunk was neatly made, with a salmon-colored bedspread—*finally, something that isn't pea-green!*—stretched across the mattress and a gray wool blanket folded at the foot.

H. L. nodded toward the bottom right-hand bunk. "I'll take that one, if you don't mind." Not that she could see any real difference between it and any of the others. She wondered which of the junior officers the bunks really belonged to. "What happened to the men who usually sleep in here?"

"They're probably hot-racking it somewhere else."

H. L. frowned. "I hope not."

She'd heard her father talk about hot-racking, a method of sharing sleeping quarters on crowded ships when bunk space was at a premium. The men in the watch coming below would sleep in the same bunks that the watch going on deck had left empty. It was called "hot-racking" because the bunks never got a chance to cool down in between.

Mrs. Warner smiled again. "Don't worry about it too much. If I know sailors, they're all walking around right now with dreamy expressions on their faces, just from the thought that a real live girl could be in one of their beds at this very moment."

Brisbane, Australia
115° 51' E/31° 57' S
0156 Local/1556 Zulu

Nothing by phone, nothing by radio. So of course the bastard's either gone or asleep.

Lieutenant Kerrie Burke stood outside of an apartment complex in downtown Brisbane. According to his personnel folder, Major Donald MacGillivray currently lived in the downstairs front, where the shades were drawn and the windows dark.

Damn Weir for giving her this job, anyhow. The man had to have known that she and the Major had once been, however briefly, a couple. Knowing things like that about people—even his own people—was part of Weir's job. The relationship hadn't lasted, of course: proof positive, if Kerrie had needed it, that not even a steady supply of mindblowing sex was good enough to guarantee a happy-ever-after.

These days, MacGillivray's work kept him on an irregular schedule. If he wasn't here, she'd have to check on base.

And if Donnie-boy isn't here and he isn't on base, she thought in resignation, *then he's probably out raising hell somewhere in the city, and it'll take the entire Brisbane police force to locate him in time.*

Getting the civilian authorities involved will not *make Weir a happy man. And finding out that I'm the one who called them in won't make Donald happy either.*

Lieutenant Burke decided to cross that bridge when she came to it, and stepped up to the apartment door. She was dressed in mufti—chinos, in this case, with a cotton shirt and a light tailored jacket. A naval officer in summer whites would have been conspicuous, and this mission required deniability the whole way.

She knocked, heard no answer, and knocked again, harder. This time she felt the door give a little under her hand, and realized that it wasn't locked. Or even latched.

Damn, she thought, as memories of past episodes with Donald MacGillivray stirred and began making their way up to the surface. *What kind of trouble has he gotten himself into now?*

Lieutenant Burke pushed the door open, using the back of her hand to avoid leaving fingerprints. No point in making unnecessary work for the police, if she wound up having to contact them.

Inside the apartment all of the lights were out, but from what she could see by the light from the street lamps behind her, the place looked like it had been ransacked.

A struggle? Or just Donnie's normal housekeeping? Not enough light in here to tell.

She took one step inside, then another.

If the mission's turning to shit this early, maybe there really is *something to those reports out of Indonesia.*

She was fully into the room, looking to right and left—hoping that she wouldn't spot a body on the floor, but ready to deal with it if she did—when she felt something hard and cold pressed against her throat from behind.

At the same time, the door behind her swung closed, locking with a snick and cutting off the light from outside.

"Don't move," a familiar voice whispered in her ear. "Or you'll regret it in a hurry."

Lieutenant Burke let out her breath in an exasperated sigh. "So tell me, Major—do you want to know why I'm here, or are you planning a body disposal drill just for jollies?"

The knife edge moved away from her throat. Lieutenant Burke took a step forward and turned.

Her eyes were becoming accustomed to the dark, and a little light was leaking in around the shades from the lights outside the building. She faced a wiry man of medium height, dressed in a dark tee shirt and cammie trousers, with close-trimmed hair and a thick mustache.

"I spotted you in the parking lot," MacGillivray said. "And lurking about on the sidewalk across the street. I knew right then you hadn't come all the way here just to drop in and say hello. More's the pity."

"More's the pity," Kerrie agreed. "I have a job for you."

"It's Weir again, isn't it?" When she didn't deny it, he said, "What does the crafty old bugger want us for this time?"

"There's trouble brewing up in Malaysia," she said. "We're supposed to gather the clans and go on hot standby aboard HMAS *Tobruk*. Prasetyo is on the move."

"I told them three years ago to keep an eye on that boy," MacGillivray said. "When does the bus leave?"

"We have to be at the air base in three hours, for transport by chopper to *Tobruk*."

"Then we've still got time for a proper hello," the Major said. "If you take your clothes off right now and don't waste any more time talking."

In spite of herself, Lieutenant Burke smiled. "You're on," she said.

7

Gunnersmate (Guns) Seaman Ryan Stryker stood just inside the non-tight door, starboard side in the fore-and-aft passageway midships on the main deck. Before taps every night came the SAT/BAF muster, and GMGSN Stryker, who was junior in 3rd Division (Gunnery), had to hand out and collect the gear, so that the more senior men in the division could watch the movie or get some sleep.

All the members of *Cushing*'s Security Alert Team and Backup Alert Force would take out their weapons for the muster. Afterward, Stryker would take all the weapons back, count them, and return them to their racks. The serial numbers on the weapons weren't ever going to change, but Stryker had to look at each one, match up the numbers, and check off the weapon anyway.

Luckily for him, the small arms locker didn't hold a lot. A dozen M14 rifles, two with selector switches that turned them full-auto, plus two with winter triggers—trigger guards that folded away, so that the rifles could be used by men wearing mittens. These were for the Ship's Self Defense Force, a squad that could theoretically go ashore if need be. Five .45 caliber pistols; the military was switching over to 9mm weapons, but Uncle owned a shitload of M1911s, and it'd be a shame to waste them. Another five Model 870 riot guns, each one with a bandolier of red double-ought buckshot cartridges. A box of black wooden nightsticks with white holders and pistol belts to carry them—largely symbolic weapons, these, for the pier guards and the Messenger of the Watch.

The bulkheads in the weapons locker were painted pea-green, the deck was tiled in dark green linoleum, and the light hanging from the overhead was too small to be worthwhile. The workbench against the aft bulkhead had a rack of tools, an oil can, and a vise, for doing light repairs and adjustments on the weapons. An aluminum box of PMS (Planned Maintenance Subsystem) cards was pop-riveted to the bench. The cards described the Daily, Weekly, Monthly, Quarterly, Annual, and As Required checks for each of the weapons, using an esoteric system of numbers and letters—all part of the 3M, or Material Maintenance Management, system, commonly known in the fleet as "Mirrors, Magnetism, and Magic."

The passageway outside the weapons locker was barely big enough to hold the Security Alert Team and the Backup Alert Force, a total of ten men out of the ship's complement of 340. Whenever a Security Alert went down, Stryker had to get there in a hurry to unlock the small arms locker so the SAT and BAF could get their weapons. After that—since the locker was his Security Alert station—he'd remain behind and stand guard, while the SAT and the BAF took care of whatever the problem was.

At this evening's muster, ET2 Fred Larousse, one of *Cushing*'s twidgets—electronics technicians—and the senior man on the BAF, was holding forth on the subject of security alerts.

"So there we were," he said, "anchored out in Lanai Roads, Hawaii, and we're Visit Ship for the day."

"Lucky you," said Stryker. On weekends in port one of the

Navy vessels is designated as Visit Ship, so that tourists who want to see their tax dollars at work can go look at a ship. This means that the duty section has to act as tour guides and show people around and tell them interesting things about the vessel, but keep their language clean while they're doing it.

Larousse said, "Yeah. Lucky us. So anyway, there are these groups of tourists being herded around, and like it always happens, one of them gets lost and starts wandering around on her own."

" 'Her?' "

"Yeah, it's a her—nice looking, too. Short shorts and a halter top. Blonde. She's wandering around on her own, and pretty soon she comes up to one of those places no one is supposed to go, one with an alarm."

The various members of the SAT and BAF nodded. *Cushing* had spaces like that, too—and nukes behind them, valuable and deadly objects whose official presence could neither be confirmed nor denied.

"Anyhow," Larousse said, "this particular alarm is so sensitive that if you step on the deck outside too hard, it'll go. And she does, and it does, and here comes the Security Alert Team. Funny as hell, too . . . one of the SAT members was just stepping into the shower when the alarm went off. He grabbed his towel and ran, because of course a Security Alert is never a drill. And as luck would have it, his station was in that very passageway where the young lady in the halter top was wandering. So there he comes . . . and naturally, the first time he has to use his hands for anything he loses the towel, so the girl sees this guy running at her wearing shower shoes, a gas mask, and a pistol, and nothing else.

"She doesn't like this—"

"Big surprise," somebody on the BAF said. Somebody else said, "Shut up," and Larousse continued.

"Anyhow, she tries to get away. But pretty soon he's got her up against the bulkhead with the pistol pointed at her face, and he's waiting for the BAF to arrive and relieve him of his prisoner. He still doesn't have anything on besides the shower shoes and the gas mask, and somewhere in the excitement she's lost her halter top.

"At this point another civilian, an older gentleman, comes wandering by. He sees a half-naked lady with an all-naked sailor holding a gun on her. So he puts his hand on the sailor's shoulder, and says, 'There, there, son, you don't have to do that.' "

Stryker shook his head. "Whoa. Bad move."

"No kidding," said Larousse. "Because right then the Backup Alert Force shows up. And the team leader sees his man has a prisoner in custody in a sensitive area, and he sees a civilian touching his man. He plays nice, considering . . . he doesn't shoot the guy, just butt-strokes him across the passageway. At that point the young lady drops her purse. Out rolls this little silver pistol she's carrying for protection. And after *that*, things get interesting.

"Meanwhile, all the rest of the civilians are being herded back onto the fantail, where they're put under guard by a couple of sailors with submachine guns who are all excited because while a Security Alert is never a drill, this one is *really* not a drill. Everything eventually got sorted out, but let me tell you—that was one bunch of civilians who definitely got to see their tax dollars at work."

"Did they ever find out what the blonde thought she needed protection from?" Stryker asked.

Larousse shrugged. "If they did, they never told me. She did have nice tits, though."

Cape Samak, Malaysia
105° 48' E/01° 30' S
1745 Local/1045 Zulu

At the pirates' base camp, a steady rain drummed on the tin roof of the headquarters hut. In the dim light of the interior, Michael Prasetyo sat alone at the table and contemplated the glowing screen of his laptop computer. A half-finished cigarette smouldered beside him in an ashtray made out of an empty sardine can.

He'd run all the spreadsheets for the coming operation a dozen times already, had pored over the available schematics he'd downloaded, and had worked out the timetable days ago. But it was a habit with him to spend the last hours before departure going over his work. There was always the possibility that he might have missed something, or that a last-minute change might occur to him.

Careful preparation had always been the secret of his success, and this time careful preparation would be more important than ever. The target wasn't a merchant ship crewed by a handful of men, and it wasn't a pleasure yacht manned by rich amateurs. He wouldn't be able to rely on superior numbers for this enterprise, or on the shock value that unexpected violence always possessed for people whose wealth had previously insulated them from such things. On this occasion, only superior planning and execution would suffice.

It was still a gamble. Failure in this would not be a matter of simply pulling back and licking their wounds until the next opportunity came by. Failure would mean blood and death, possibly even his own.

But the cash up front had been good, just for agreeing to make the attempt—and *that* money was safely banked, whatever else might come. The profits of success would be even better, by several decimal places.

Prasetyo picked up his smouldering cigarette and drew on it reflectively. The tip glowed like a tiny red eye in the dimness of the hut as he looked over the table of men and assignments.

Forty men in the boarding party—forty-four, counting the specialists, who would participate only in the operation's opening stage—in three boats. He would have to strike hard and secure his objectives quickly, before *Cushing*'s sailors could rally and mount an effective resistance.

An interesting problem: If he hesitated or held back for fear of losing too many men, he would surely fail; but the chances of failure increased with each loss to his total strength. The trick was knowing when to strike and when to get out.

He'd learned that lesson during his years in America, when his family sent him to prep school and university and business school to acquire First World polish and an MBA. The classwork had been the least part of it. The connections he'd made were another matter, and the experience that he'd gained in supplying the material for assorted casual vices to the offspring of America's old money and its super-rich.

The rules of the game were second nature to him by now: Take what you came for—take what you could find—and be gone before the deal went sour, the house of cards collapsed, and the forces of law and order arrived on the scene to pick up the pieces.

It was too bad, Prasetyo thought, that the other members of his family hadn't learned the same lessons. Intoxicated by the prospect of turning their wealth into a fortune that could buy or sell whole governments, they had risked everything—only to lose it when the Asian economy collapsed. Prasetyo had expected to come back from America and take the place waiting for him in his family's enterprises; but when he finished his schooling and returned to Indonesia, the enterprises were a shambles and his place was gone.

In spite of himself, Prasetyo smiled. He'd done well during his American school years. He would have made a more than adequate cog in the family machine.

But he made an even better pirate.

8

By two hours after local midnight, everything was ready. The black boats—their decks loaded with 55-gallon drums of marine diesel and their superstructures abristle with new weapons and equipment—lay tied up at the pier, waiting for the pirate commander to give the word to depart. Except for Prasetyo himself, no one remained ashore. His own men and the quartet of specialists had embarked some minutes earlier.

Prasetyo wore a hooded poncho over his green tee shirt and cammie pants, but the heavy driving rain soaked him to the skin within minutes just the same. He ignored the wind and wet and continued his final circuit of the camp.

Like a thrifty householder, he thought, *checking the locks and turning out all the lights.*

And like the householder of his imagination, he had to make certain that the camp had been sanitized, cleared of everything that would allow investigators to discover that he and his men had been there. Not a scrap of identifying paper could remain, not a fragment of metal or stick of wood that might tell an intelligence analyst who the owners of this base had been, or where they might have gone.

Within a few days, if the operation went as planned, this site—and any other sites that might be associated, in the minds of the authorities, with Michael Prasetyo—would be swarming with troopers from the US Special Forces, big men in full camouflage with their senses of humor surgically removed.

The investigators would be very thorough, and he needed to be thorough in anticipation of their response. If any evidence remained to pin this job on him, then he could expect a visit from even more humorless men, dressed all in black this time. They would leave no survivors. If he could not be located, then he or someone close to him could expect a cruise missile or two on their home or place of business.

Before going onto the boats, his men had stirred buckets of water into the ashes of the fires where, earlier, documents had burned. Prasetyo knew better than to trust that the falling rain alone would suffice to break down what remained of the written material. Other, harder-to-destroy pieces of gear—radios no longer needed and the like—the pirates had disassembled and dropped into deep water. All that remained was for Prasetyo to detonate the explosives and incendiary devices his men had rigged earlier, and destroy the encampment's wooden buildings.

Even there, he had been careful. The explosives in the demolition charges he'd be using came from a source other than his usual. Tracing them would, he hoped, provide the American investigators with more blind alleys to explore at fruitless length. Other, less material, things would be harder to conceal. With just a little luck, however, they might shine so blindingly bright that Prasetyo himself could remain hidden in their shadows.

What became of the other parties in this affair—the men in Jakarta who had hired him, for example—didn't concern Prasetyo except as something that might lead the investigators back to him. But he'd built enough cut-outs into his operation to make following the trail from that direction tricky. He'd have plenty of warning before the hunt came too close.

Somebody might talk, of course. One of the crew, perhaps, although he knew them all, had worked with them all more than once—except for the specialists, whom he still did not entirely trust.

The rain was picking up, harder than usual for the season. The wind was rising, too. The tops of the trees swayed beneath the gusts. The surface of the sea was rough, even here in the sheltered bay, and the rain—pushed sideways by the wind—slanted down in heavy sheets.

Good, thought Prasetyo. *Rain harder. Bring on the typhoon and hide us from watchers in the sky.*

His inspection completed, Prasetyo hunched his shoulders and ran for the boats. Once aboard the craft closest to the dock, he waved an arm, and the engines on the outboard craft kicked up. Sailors on deck cast off the lines and the sleek black 80-footer slid away from its sisters and out toward the channel. The second boat cast off and followed.

Then the third of the 80-footers fired up and pulled away from the pier. The deep rumbling of the vessel's engines pulsed through Prasetyo's feet as the sailors on board it cast off. The wind caught the side of the craft and pushed it away from the pilings, and the pitching of the deck increased as the 80-footer turned into the waves.

Kino Tansil made his way across the heaving deck to where Prasetyo stood. "Everything is stowed away safely and secured for heavy seas."

"Good. Keep an eye on the specialists. They may not be used to rough weather, and we'll need them to be ready when the time comes."

The shore was only a dark mass behind them by now, all but

indistinguishable from the night sky. Prasetyo kept his left hand on the railing that ringed the deckhouse, for balance. With his other hand he fingered the plastic case of the remote detonator. A thin chrome-plated antenna extended from the case.

He flipped up the safety cap and flicked the switch.

Abruptly the darkness behind them exploded into a half-sphere of fire, a glowing red fireball shot through with black tendrils of smoke and clods of earth. A moment later, the sound reached him, hitting with a shock that drove out the air from his lungs.

As quickly as it had come, the fireball contracted, leaving only a red glow behind. A few seconds later, a bit of smoking wood fell on the deck. Prasetyo kicked the piece of wood over the side into the ocean, then tossed the detonator in after it.

USS _Cushing_
082° 10' E/01° 12' S
1800 Local/1300 Zulu

USS _Cushing_ **sailed eastward for the Strait of Malacca, scouting** ahead of the main body of the _Nimitz_ battle group. The island of Diego Garcia was only a memory behind them now, and the view in all directions was nothing but the open sea and the sky.

Cushing's Tigers and their sponsors had gathered for a cookout on the helicopter landing pad aft—the so-called "steel beach." CAPT Warner, getting ready to make his obligatory welcome-aboard and orientation speech, had no trouble telling the Tigers from their Naval sponsors. The civilians wore bright clothing in a range of styles from K-Mart cheap through L. L. Bean practical. _Cushing_'s officers and chiefs wore khaki, and her enlisted, blue chambray.

Chris, still draped with camera gear, was taking photos of the cookout preparations. Ever since early afternoon, the mess cranks and cooks had been setting up tables and charcoal grills, the latter made of 55-gallon drums split lengthwise and resting on sawbucks of angle iron, with heavy expanded metal gratings laid over the open sides. At another table, an MS3 was cutting up watermelons for dessert.

Master Chief Morrison's daughter stood a few feet away from the picnic tables. Captain Warner noted with some amusement that she was attracting a great deal of covert—but respectful—admiration on the part of *Cushing*'s sailors. *They'd better be respectful to the Master Chief's daughter*, Warner thought. *Anyone who isn't is going to have a lousy rest-of-his-enlistment.*

The wind whipped the flag at the mast straight out to port, and broke up the surface of the ocean into sun-sparkled wavelets. On the picnic tables, large machine nuts weighed down the stacks of napkins and paper plates to keep them from blowing away over the side. The smell of chicken barbecue began to waft over the deck, reminding Warner that he couldn't delay making his speech any longer.

He stepped over to the portable podium that had been set up for the occasion, tapped the microphone to make certain it was live, and began.

"I'd like to welcome all of our visitors aboard," he said. "A Navy ship, a warship, is like a living thing. It has a pulse—you can feel the engines. It breathes. You can hear it. The bulkheads—that's what we call walls—move beneath your hand, and the decks twist under your feet. One rule that sailors live by is 'one hand for yourself, one hand for the ship.' It's a good rule; make sure you follow it yourselves. Always know where you're stepping, and always have somewhere in mind to grab hold in case the ship moves underneath you.

"The weather decks—that is, the decks where the wind blows and the rain falls, topside—are off limits to Tigers after dark," he went on. He let his gaze rest for a moment on the Bailey twins, a pair of lively-looking youngsters who—if they hadn't already been planning nocturnal explorations—would certainly have come up with the idea before long. "That's for your own safety. If anyone falls overboard—well, the sea is big, you're small, and the sharks are hungry. I'd be upset if I lost one of you. I'd have to fill out a lot of forms, and I really hate doing paperwork.

"A couple of other notes. From time to time we'll be holding General Quarters drills, Fire drills, and other drills. If you hear the alarms for GQ, everyone will be hurrying to their stations. For you Tigers, your station is in Chiefs' Berthing, amidships. Once you get there, stay put until the drill is over or until someone comes by to tell you to move. The traffic pattern for going to your station is up and forward to starboard"—he gestured toward the right side of the ship—"and down and aft to port." He indicated the left side. "Reason for that is, a lot of people will be hurrying, and we don't need traffic jams. So to avoid footprints on your body, follow that pattern. You'll usually know when a drill is going to happen; it's listed in the Plan of the Day.

"There's another kind of event that may arise from time to time. That's a Security Alert. You'll know that one of those is going on because you'll hear the word passed over the 1MC, 'Security Alert, Security Alert, all hands stand fast.'" Once again Warner directed a stern glance at the younger Tigers. "What 'stand fast' means is 'freeze.' A Security Alert is never a drill. Anyone who isn't a member of the Security Alert Team or the Backup Alert Force *will* be shot if they're found moving, and again, I don't want to have to do the paperwork.

"That about covers the essentials—most of you have been with the Navy long enough to know this stuff already. Any questions you may have that your sponsor can't answer, I'll be happy to address. Now it's time to pipe chow."

Warner stepped away from the podium and allowed a boatswain's mate to take his place. The enlisted man put a call to his lips and blew a long tune of sharp notes interspersed with rattling trills: the signal for *Cushing*'s crew members and their Tigers to form up in line by the barbecue grills.

Lieutenant Commander Flandry made his way through the crowd and joined Warner beside the podium.

"How's it going, XO?" Warner asked.

"All secure," Flandry said. "We should get to the Strait a little before noon, day after tomorrow."

"Anything interesting in the Local Notice to Mariners?"

"A Chinese missile-firing exercise in the South China Sea. Should be finished a long time before we pass anywhere near. State Department travel advisory for Indonesia in general and Jakarta in particular. No specifics on that one. Weather-wise, there's a low pressure system building to the east. That one could affect us."

"Very well. What's on deck for tomorrow?"

"Since you promised a GQ drill, I think we should have one. Maybe add a Surface Gunnery drill while we're at it, and give the Tigers a thrill."

"Let me know after Eight O'clock Reports," Warner said.

"Yes sir," Flandry said, and moved off to take his own place in the chow line.

A couple of minutes later, Laura Warner emerged from the crowd. She had a partially eaten plate of barbecued chicken in one hand and a paper cup of fruit punch—indistinguishable from Boy Scout "bug juice"—in the other. The standard Navy red sauce on the chicken had stained her fingers, and little flecks of paper napkin stuck to the skin where she'd tried to wipe them clean. Warner found the overall effect sexy as hell, paper bits and all.

Down, boy. You're the Captain. Your strength is as the strength of ten because your heart is pure. Or something like that, anyway.

Laura smiled at him, and he wondered if she knew what he'd been thinking about this time. She usually did. "Hello, sailor," she said. "New in town? Looking for a good time?"

"I dunno," Warner replied. "I had a good time once. You think that girl is still around here somewhere?"

"You never can tell," Laura said. "If I see her, I'll tell her I ran into a *Cushing* sailor who might be interested." She glanced over at the line by the barbecue grills. "Now's your chance; it looks like everybody else has gone through at least once. Better grab some chicken before the youngsters start lining up for seconds."

"Good idea." He wished he could afford to take Laura off to his cabin to have a few minutes alone, but that would have to wait until Yokosuka at least. A strong feeling of "not in front of the children"—in this case, the entire crew of USS *Cushing*—severely limited his options. In the meantime, he felt almost as tongue-tied as a high-school kid on his first date with the girl's dad watching, reduced to making inane commentary about the food and the weather.

Soon Warner had his own cup of bug juice and plate of chicken to juggle. As the afternoon grew later the sun fell down the western sky, the bright disc turning from pale yellow to reddish orange as it passed behind the layers of clouds. Before long, four bells sounded—two taps, followed by two more—and the word was passed over the 1MC: "Now relieve the watch and the lookout. On deck, condition four, watch section two."

Warner checked his watch. The bells were right on time. "Time for me to get up to the Bridge," he said to Laura. "I'll see you at the movies later, okay?"

"It's a date. What's showing?"

"According to the Plan of the Day, it's *Kung Fu Fists of Death* on the ship's entertainment system at 2000, followed by a double feature of 'Deadly Shipmate' and 'Trial By Fire'."

She raised an eyebrow. "And what are those?"

"A safety film on the dangers of electricity, and a documentary about the fire aboard USS *Forrestal* back during Vietnam."

"I'll try to control my enthusiasm."

"Just be glad I told the corpsman he couldn't show 'The Return of Count Spirochete'."

Bridge, USS *Cushing*
082° 10' E/01° 12' S
1801 Local/1301 Zulu

Cushing's navigational Bridge had wide windows looking out over the Forecastle. On either side of the space, a door led out onto to the Bridgewings. There the lookouts stood, wearing sound-powered phones on the JL circuit. JL connected the Bridge, the lookouts, the Combat Information Center, and the Signal Bridge. Sometimes Main Control listened in as well—all the sound-powered circuits could be selected in Internal Communications Central—and sometimes the watch-standers in engineering would try to set up Moboard solutions for contacts and break signals ahead of the Bridge team.

When CAPT Warner entered the Bridge, he went first to the chart table on the port side, where the Quartermaster of the Watch was penciling in the latest satellite fix. At the sight of the Captain, the QMOW called out, "Captain's on the Bridge!" and noted the fact of Warner's arrival in his rough log. The Officer of the Deck approached the Captain and saluted.

"Good evening, sir."

"Good evening, Lieutenant. Any contacts?"

The OOD shook his head. "That's a negative."

"Intentions for the rest of your watch?"

"Maintain course and speed. No land expected on this watch."

"Very well. Keep a close eye on the weather."

Warner seated himself in his chair on the starboard side of the Bridge. The chair was covered with orange vinyl and mounted on a swiveling pylon, and no one except Warner was allowed to sit in it.

He picked up the clipboard labeled CO's TRAFFIC from its hook on the bulkhead to his right. The clipboard was full of yellow message flimsies. Warner flipped through the pages, initialing each of them in red ink after he'd read it. Most of the reports were routine. The State Department Advisory that the XO had mentioned covered several aspects of terrorism and insurrection in the region, including an act of piracy against a moored tanker, Liberian registry, which had been awaiting daylight for its passage through the Strait.

After a while, the duty yeoman arrived with a rough of tomorrow's Plan of the Day. Warner read it over. A GQ drill was scheduled for 0930. Under it, he penciled in "Repel Boarders drill," then initialed the top right corner and handed the sheet back to the yeoman.

After that, Warner read over and signed the Night Orders book prepared for him by the Navigator: "Steer courses and speeds as necessary to maintain track over ground, inform me of any course or speed deviations greater than five degrees or five knots to maintain track, inform me of any contact with a CPA of 10,000 yards or less, and in any case wake me at 0300." Then he left the Bridge and made his way down to the wardroom to watch the second half of *Kung Fu Fists of Death*.

Laura and Chris were already there. Chris looked bored; Laura's expression was that of an anthropologist observing the peculiar rituals of some isolated and newly discovered tribe. Warner drew himself a cup of coffee from the silver urn beside the wardroom pantry window, then took a seat next to Laura.

"How do you like the movie so far?" he asked.

She smiled. "It has a certain *je ne sais quoi*. When I figure out what it is, I'll be sure to let you know."

"Hey, Dad," said Chris, "where do you find all of these movies anyhow?"

"Fleet Motion Picture Exchange, Brooklyn, New York."

"Uh-huh. And do they pick them for plot, for acting, or for uplifting social commentary?"

"None of the above." On the ship's entertainment television, one of the Kung Fu Fighters was busily kicking another Kung Fu Fighter in the face, accompanied by sound effects that made Warner think of a baseball bat striking blubber. "Now be quiet. Here comes the good part."

"You mean you've seen this movie before?"

"I think it's been in the fleet since before I made Ensign."

Chris slouched back in his chair and shook his head. "Rest easy, America. Your Navy is on watch."

9

In the tropics the dawn comes fast, and this morning it came up deep red. A low mist hung over the water, tinted green with the light reflected off the forested islands that lay on either hand. Birds wheeled and soared overhead—gulls, terns, goonies, other species too many to count—their voices filling the blood-warm air.

Closer up, the morning was less pristine. The tropical humidity made everything feel damp and sticky. Sweat lay on the skin instead of evaporating, and garments clung to their wearers' bodies like wet sheets. The air smelled of wood smoke, with an underlying hint of dead fish. Wisps of oil trailed a sickly iridescence across the swells, and twists of garbage—plastic bottles, mostly, mixed with scraps of paper and colored cardboard—bobbed and swirled on the surface of the water.

Ensign Somers and Lieutenant Gilano had an excellent view of both the beauty and the squalor from *Cushing*'s port Bridgewing.

They'd been on watch since 0400, however, and their minds were occupied with other things.

"God's own supply of boats this morning," Gilano said. He took a bearing through the telescopic alidade. "Can you make out the opening range marker? . . . You know, I think I've finally figured it out."

"No kidding there's a lot of ships. Think any of them know the Rules of the Road?" Somers took a horizontal angle on the second range marker. "There . . . got it. Figured out what?"

"They know the Rules of the Road, all right: 'If it's painted gray, it'll stay out of your way.' . . . Figured out what I want to do if I ever quit working for Uncle."

The two officers went to the chart table just inside the door to the port Bridgewing, and laid in the line of bearing and the sextant arc. At the point where the two crossed, Gilano marked the spot with a dot. He drew a circle around the dot, and wrote "0523" beside it. When he extended the dead reckoning course, it lined up with the center of the channel.

Once the two junior officers were back outside on the Bridgewing, Somers returned to the unfinished conversation. "So what *are* you going to do?"

"I am going," Gilano said solemnly, "to take my Civilian Readjustment Allowance and open up a bordello."

"Sure you are. And I'm going to get a pegleg and an eyepatch and call myself Long John Silver."

"Don't forget your parrot," Gilano said. "And these days you'll want a speedboat and an AK-47 to go along with the rest of your gear."

"Think so?"

"Damn straight. Pick out a nice fat freighter with a high-tech cargo and a registry in some place like Cyprus or Liberia—come over the rail some night in the dark of the moon—and the next thing anybody hears, the freighter's tied up in China or the Philippines and the cargo's sold to God knows where. And you're back out in the Strait with more fuel and ammo, waiting for another ship to come along."

"Sounds like fun," said Somers. "Parrots and whorehouses, though . . . that reminds me of a joke. This lady goes into a pet store, and says, 'I want to buy a talking bird,' and the guy says, 'We only have one, and it used to live in a house of ill repute—' "

"I've heard that one," Gilano said. "Brand new house, brand new lady, same old Charlie. And piracy sounds like I'd have to stay at sea. No . . . for a good, comfortable retirement, I'll take a bordello every time. On Long Island, maybe. Convenient to New York and all the major airports."

"I thought they had zoning regulations about that sort of thing."

"This is my fantasy," Gilano said. "I'll put a bordello out on Long Island if I want to. Something Victorian, I think. Three stories, maybe four, with a cupola on top. Landscaped grounds—"

"A circular driveway." Somers fell into the spirit of the game. "With crushed-coral gravel."

"And bouncers," said Gilano. "You can't have a bordello without bouncers. A whole bunch of guys—ex-boxers, maybe—all of them wearing starched shirts and sleeve garters and waxed mustaches."

"And wingtip collars," Somers added. "But what about girls? You can't have a bordello without girls."

"I was just getting to the girls," Gilano said. He scanned the sea ahead with his binoculars. "Do you make the ferry?"

"Yeah. Good right bearing drift. Did the lookout report that?"

"Yeah. All this small junk out here, radar isn't going to catch half of it. The girls . . . they'd all have nice tits. And they'd wear laced corsets and fishnet stockings. Except for the madam, of course; she wears pince-nez glasses and a dress with a bustle. She greets you by name when you come in, and asks you if you're interested in the perversion *du jour*."

"All the comforts of home," said Somers. "Next thing you know, you'll be putting in red flocked wallpaper and Tiffany lamps."

"And a genuine Renoir nude over the bar." Gilano turned to the Quartermaster of the Watch. "Weather forecast up yet?"

"Yes sir," the QMOW replied. "On the board."

Gilano walked to the Raytheon Pathfinder just to port of centerline in the Pilothouse, and looked at the screen. He turned the range lines on, and set it to short.

"Let's get a twidget up here to tweak this sucker," he said. "I'm getting nothing but sea return inside of a quarter mile. I'd hate to go to piloting detail like that."

Main deck, USS *Cushing*
099" 20' 12" E/04° 04' 50" N
0600 Local/2400 Zulu

Chris Warner had been up on *Cushing's* **main deck since just** after dawn, taking photos of dolphins and floating garbage.

The garbage would make a good contrast with images of the sleek, graceful Pacific dolphins. A pair of the elegant creatures had been pacing the destroyer ever since sunrise. Chris was hoping now for a shot with dolphins, trash, and one or more ships, all in the same frame. For that, he needed cooperation from the dolphins—the ships and the garbage, he felt certain, would remain long after the dolphins got bored and went away.

The sound of running feet distracted him from his latest series of dolphin shots. He wondered for a moment if the footsteps heralded some kind of trouble, then dismissed the idea. Any trouble on shipboard would be planned in advance, listed in the POD, and come with its own announcement over the ever-present loudspeakers. That was the way his father worked.

Besides, these weren't rushed or panicky footsteps; they had a steady, even rhythm.

Exercise nut, Chris decided. *Coming this way.*

He turned his camera toward the source of the sound, thinking to get another picture for the series he thought of privately as his "how to stay sane on shipboard" photo essay.

"Hey!"

The voice was indignant and female. He lowered the camera.

Holly Lynne Morrison—he knew even before he saw her that it had to be H. L., because his mother was the only other female on board, and Laura Warner wasn't crazy enough to go running before breakfast on a destroyer in the middle of the Indian Ocean— Holly Lynne Morrison stood with her feet braced apart, glaring at him. She wore running shorts and a faded VMI tee shirt cropped to midriff level, and her fair skin glistened with a fine sheen of perspiration. A terrycloth sweat band kept her short blonde hair out of her eyes. Chris decided he was glad he'd gotten off at least one shot before she made her protest.

"Hey, yourself," he said. "For a minute I thought you were one of the sailors."

She remained unmollified. "Do I *look* like a sailor?"

"Well . . . no."

"And did I say you could take pictures of me?"

"That was an accident, sort of," he said. "I'm mostly interested in nature photography."

She looked out at the panorama of the ocean and the sky. The clouds that had blazed crimson at dawn were shading back to gray and white as the sun rose higher.

"Try pointing the camera back in that direction, then," she said. "Lots of nature out there."

"Go ahead, crush my pretensions."

"They could probably use it."

He shook his head. "Harsh."

"Poor baby."

H. L. didn't seem averse to sharing the deck with him, though.

She began to do a runner's cooling-down bends and stretches, instead of jogging on and leaving the conversation to languish.

"If scenery is what you're after," she finally said, between stretches, "there's a lot of it here to go around. But the clouds were prettier about half an hour ago."

"I'm not interested in pretty. I want my pictures to make a point."

"What kind of a point?"

"Trash," he said. "In the water. And everywhere else."

"You got up at dawn to photograph *trash*?"

He shrugged. "The light's better."

The mewing call of a gull reminded him that there were other things besides sea-trash waiting to be photographed. He turned away from H. L. Morrison and began snapping pictures of the wheeling sea birds. H. L., her cool-down exercises finished, came up to stand a couple of feet away from him and look out at the ocean. Her eyes were good. He heard her breath catch at the sudden appearance of a patch of frothing water on the side of a wave almost before he spotted it himself.

"What's that?" she demanded.

Chris was already snapping pictures as the foaming wave spilled out a golden phalanx of winged and streamlined creatures, soaring up into a long low glide above the water's surface. "Flying fish."

"They're beautiful."

"As far as our feathered friends are concerned," he said, "they're breakfast."

His camera clicked and whirred furiously. Oh, yes . . . these were pictures that he could use, shots of the elegant sea birds quitting their circles above the waves and descending on the golden fish that dared to skim above the waves instead of swimming below. The eternal predator/prey relationship, with humanity the biggest predator of all . . . he could do something with that.

So far, Kyle and Tyson Bailey were enjoying their cruise aboard USS *Cushing*. Sleeping in bunks was fun, and so was going up and down the metal stairs that everyone said were ladders—and that were almost steep and narrow enough to *be* ladders—and so was the way the ship was always moving, sometimes only a very little, like something breathing, and sometimes more. Kyle and Tyson also liked how the sailors talked once they forgot that civilians were listening; the twins had already expanded their vocabulary quite a bit. It was better than cable TV.

The meals on board the ship, except for the picnic, weren't as exciting as some of the other stuff. The food was a lot like the food Kyle and Tyson got in the school cafeteria at home—a bit better-tasting, maybe, but cafeteria food was cafeteria food just the same.

Getting to eat with the ship's officers was something different, though. This morning the Captain and his family were all there at the same time. Chris Warner was eating scrambled eggs and talking about photography while his mother drank black coffee and put marmalade on her toast. "The sky this morning was beautiful," she said to Captain Warner. "Are we going to have good weather all the way to Yokosuka?"

"Probably not—we're looking at a dirty spot up near the Strait." The Captain turned to his son Chris. "You'll have to photograph seagulls while you can."

"Not seagulls," Chris said. "Flying fish. A whole bunch of them, just this morning. If I hadn't had my camera . . ."

"Did you get any good shots?" his mother asked.

"One at least," he said. "And some interesting conversation. H. L. Morrison runs in the mornings."

Meanwhile, the XO was saying to the Captain, "That storm system's been intensifying. If it turns into a full scale typhoon, I don't know if we're going to be able to miss it completely."

Kyle and Tyson looked at each other with suppressed excitement. A real typhoon would be something to brag about when they got home.

The Captain said, "We'll skirt as much of the storm as possible, and issue Dramamine to the Tigers if we have to."

Kyle nudged his father and asked in a low whisper, "What's Dramamine?"

"Seasickness medicine," LTJG Bailey said.

"Does it taste very bad?"

"It's just a pill, and you swallow it fast. It doesn't taste nearly as bad as barfing," said Bailey. "I'd be happy if you took some."

Kyle and Tyson both nodded. "Do you take the medicine, Daddy?" Kyle asked.

"I sure do. Every day."

"I'll be sure to note that on your Fitness Report," Captain Warner said.

"Sir?"

"Diplomatic skills and forehandedness, I'll call it."

"Thank you, sir."

Chris Warner had apparently been listening to his father's conversation as well. He turned to the Captain and said, "Is there any chance I might be able to get a few pictures of that storm once we hit it?"

Mrs. Warner said at once, "No."

The Captain, however, laughed a little. "You might be able to get a shot or two of the early stages. But trust me, if we end up going through a full-fledged typhoon, we'll all have other things on our minds. Even you."

10

Cushing's **Plan of the Day called for a Fire drill at 1000.**

"They list it right out there with Reveille and Taps and Break-fast for the Crew," Chris Warner said to his mother. "Is that anal-retentive, or what?"

They were in the Wardroom, and Chris was getting ready to go back out on deck. Laura, for her part, was planning to retire to her berthing space with one of the paperback novels she'd brought along in her luggage—the kind of gaudily-colored sex-and-shopping novels that the Captain's Wife (or even the Respected Family Ther-apist) would never be caught reading in public.

"This isn't a school fire drill," she said, with as much patience as she could muster. It didn't help that she remembered making a similar flippant remark to Andrew back in the first weeks of their relationship, when the Navy had still been a new and alien country to her—and not one that she'd planned on living in, either. "On a ship, they can't just proceed out of the building in an orderly man-

ner and wait for the nice guys in the red trucks to show up and put
out the flames. They have to do it all themselves. That's what the
drill is for."

"Oh. Okay." Chris looked thoughtful. "I could get some good
pictures from that, I think."

"You can stay out of the way and stick to taking snapshots of
seagulls. These people are doing their jobs and they don't need a
photographer underfoot."

"All cloudscapes, all the time," he grumbled. "It's like video
easy-listening out there."

Chris departed the Wardroom, still looking disgruntled, and
Laura made her way to her bunk in Forward O. H. L. wasn't there,
which Laura—somewhat guiltily—found a bit of a relief; it meant
she could take her shoes off and stretch out with her feet up without
fear of destroying her public image. With a sigh of relief, she pulled
out the first novel from her hidden stash and did exactly that.

Promptly at 1000, her concentration was broken by a voice
coming over the 1MC: "This is a drill, this is a drill, Fire, Fire, Fire.
Fire in compartment 2-21-3-L."

After twenty years, and after listening to Andrew explain the
system to her almost as many times, she knew how to decode the
location of the supposed fire. The first 2 meant the second deck—
where the main deck was 1, the next deck down from the main deck
was 2, the next deck up from the main deck was 01 (and for reasons
she'd never figured out, wasn't called a deck, but a level), and so on.
The second number, 21, in this instance, was the frame number—
the frames were the steel ribs of the ship—and the third number
was the compartment. The compartments were numbered outward
from the ship's centerline, odd numbers to starboard and even to
port. The result located every compartment in the ship on a three-
dimensional grid, and threw in a shorthand description to boot: L,
the final letter in the whole sequence, stood for "Living," and meant

that the area in question was a passageway or a berthing space or something similar.

The voice came back over the 1MC: "Supply from Repair Two." Then came the alarm bell, first ringing rapidly, then a single stroke, followed by the voice again: "This is a drill, this is a drill, Fire, Fire, Fire. Fire in compartment 2-21-3-L."

Not being a member of the fire party, Laura stayed where she was. She hadn't found a note on the compartment door earlier saying "This door is hot," or one on the deck saying "The linoleum here is melting," so she knew that the constructive fire wasn't in this space. Her role as a civilian was to stay the heck out of the way while the damage control investigators made their way through the ship looking for signs of trouble.

She put her shoes back on and sat up on the edge of the bunk, rather than lounging stretched out—the Captain's Wife had some dignity to maintain, after all—and continued to read her novel. She'd finished another two chapters by the time the #2 Investigator reached the cabin. She heard footsteps outside the closed door first, and then a pause: the investigator would be going through the movements of checking for fire inside the compartment, holding the back of his hand to the door to test for the presence of heat on the other side.

After a few moments, the door opened and the #2 Investigator entered the compartment: a sailor wearing a lighted helmet like a miner's, and an Oxygen Breathing Apparatus. Since this was a drill, he had a dummy canister in the OBA, and carried the mask slung over his shoulder. There was a line tied to the D-ring on the back of his OBA. The other end of the line was in the hands of the #2 Investigator's tender, a few feet back. One tug on the line would mean "pay out more line," while two tugs meant "take up slack," and five or more rapid tugs meant "haul my burning ass out of here."

The investigator proceeded to scrutinize the deck, the bulkheads, and the pipes and ductwork. Finding no signs of fire or structural damage—in the form of notes saying things like "the paint here is blistering" or "this bulkhead is bulging towards you"—he said "Just checking, ma'am," to Laura, and departed.

USS *Cushing*
Off Kelang, Malaysia
100° 55' 18" E/02° 52' 19" N
1215 Local/0515 Zulu

A little after noon, H. L. Morrison went out onto the weather decks again. She didn't plan on more exercise, at least not for a few hours, but lunch for the Tigers had been meat loaf and mashed potatoes and green beans and dinner rolls and milk, and she did want to stretch her legs a bit after all that.

She'd changed out of her running shorts and cropped tee, switching to jeans and a loose cotton shirt topped off with a *Cushing* ball cap. The overall effect—she hoped—was stylish without being fussy. H. L. knew her own limitations. She was never going to have the kind of eye that allowed a person to set fashion, rather than follow it. Staying current, on the other hand, didn't require genius, only research.

The rose-tinged cloudscapes of the morning had faded since the last time she'd been out on deck. Instead, the sky was a pale, washed-out gray. The sparkling waves had mutated into long, greasy-looking swells, imparting a subtle difference to the motion of the ship under her feet. She'd heard her father and the other chiefs talking about bad weather somewhere in the ocean up ahead; she supposed the changes she was seeing marked the edge of it.

One thing hadn't changed, though. Chris Warner was still out on deck photographing seascapes, including the clouds. She hadn't seen him at breakfast or lunch, but that didn't mean anything by itself. Being the Captain's kid, he would have eaten in the officers' wardroom.

He must have heard her approaching, because he lowered his camera and turned around to face her instead of gazing out over the ocean.

"Hi," he said. He wasn't bad-looking, she had to admit. He wore his golden-brown hair quite a bit longer than she was used to seeing around the VMI campus—longer, in fact, than her own—but it was well-trimmed and not shaggy, and he had more muscle on him than she'd expected.

He probably needs the muscle to carry around all that camera gear, she thought. *If he hangs any more knapsacks and belt-packs and carrying-cases off of himself, he's going to topple over onto the deck.*

The mental image made her smile. "Hi there to you, too. Are you planning to spend the whole day taking pictures?"

He nodded. "Probably."

"What on earth *for?*"

"Not much else to do," he said. "Besides, it's how you get the good pictures. Take a whole raft of them, and then print them up and decide which ones to throw out."

"You're going to waste a lot of film that way."

"The film's only wasted if it doesn't work." He gave her a quick, lopsided grin. "When I do it, it works. Some of the time, anyhow."

She ignored the grin. If he didn't know how attractive it made him look, he was a whole lot stupider than she thought he was. "All this and you're modest, too."

"Hey, I didn't claim that every shot was a masterpiece. One or two keepers out of every couple of dozen doesn't exactly make me Ansel Adams." He paused. "At least, not yet."

"You want to make a career out of taking pictures of birds and trees and stuff?" She couldn't help staring at him. Ambition she understood—she had ambitions of her own, after all, that had pushed her into the still mostly male ranks of VMI cadets—but this was a variety she hadn't seen before.

"Why not? Do you plan to make a career out of doing calisthenics and five-mile runs while some troglodyte in a uniform bellows insults at you?"

"That's different!"

"I don't see how. As marketable experiences go, it's right down there."

"The *money* isn't the *point*."

"Exactly," he said.

She looked at him. At least he wasn't laughing—and she'd have been hard put not to laugh, herself, at somebody falling so neatly into the trap she'd dug for them.

So now he's nicer than I am, too. If he weren't so cute I really would have to hate him.

"All right," she said. "What is the point, then?"

"Communication," he said, after a moment or two. "Show people the right pictures, and they'll go along with you every time."

"Go along where?"

"Wherever you need them to go," he told her. "Make them understand that the oceans are all full of trash, maybe, and the rain forests are burning, and the climate of the whole world is going to hell in a handbasket. That's what I want to do—one of the things I want to do, anyhow. What about you?"

The sudden change of direction left H. L. blinking. " 'What about me,' what?"

"What do you want to do?"

"I don't—"

He cut her off with a quick downward gesture. "Everybody wants to do something." Another pause, a thoughtful one this time. She noticed that his eyes were not light brown, as she'd at first thought them, but hazel. "I'll bet that with you it's something political."

"You got me," she said—a bit resentfully, since she'd never thought of herself as transparent. "How did you figure it out?"

"Why else would you be going to VMI?" he said. "If all you wanted to do was become an officer, you'd have been better off joining ROTC or trying for one of the service academies."

"What, and pass up the chance to have group-bonding experiences with half the future businessmen and politicians in the Old Dominion?" She shook her head. "Making it through VMI won't convince most of our local mossbacks and knuckle-draggers that I've got what it takes, but it just might convince enough of them to make a difference."

"You're planning to go after the conservative vote?"

This irritated her. "I'm not allowed to for some reason?"

"Well, it's not what I'd call exactly typical. Most of the politically active women at UC Long Beach are a bit more, um, left of center than that."

"Long Beach isn't Virginia."

"No kidding. So you think you can beat the good old boys at their own game?"

"Who knows?" she said. "But it's the only game in town."

USS *Cushing*
Off Kelang, Malaysia
100° 55' 18" E/02° 52' 19" N
1300 Local/0600 Zulu

The Plan of the Day called for a skeet shoot off the fantail at 1300, and GMGSN Stryker was one of the gunner's mates in charge of setting up and running the operation. 1300 found him back by the rail, just above the prop wash, putting down tarps on the dark gray nonskid and laying out a couple of the Model 870 shotguns from the weapons locker, in company with GMG2 Stoddard. Up on the 01 level forward of the fantail, yet another of *Cushing*'s gunner's mates was busy setting up the skeet thrower. Money for the shells and the skeet birds came out of the crew's Welfare and Rec fund, which got its money from gedunk profits, soda machine sales, and bingo night—the buck-a-head fee for a chance to shoot got fed right back into the fund.

From the look of the sky—a high, flat haze instead of the usual intense tropical blue—Stryker could tell that *Cushing* was getting closer to heavy weather up ahead. They had a while to go yet before things got bad. For now, *Cushing*'s wake stretched out straight as a ruler behind them, unmarred by the "knuckles" that came when the sailor at the helm grew sleepy or inattentive. The Boatswain's Mate of the Watch probably had his best helmsman on right now. If the Captain took it into his head to shoot some skeet, and happened to spot knuckles in the wake, the Chief would hear all about it, and life for that watch section would purely suck for some time afterward.

So far, it didn't look like Captain Warner was in the mood to blow away clay pigeons. Some of the older Tigers had come up to join the fun, and were standing mixed in with the off-watch crew, in two lines going back port and starboard along the weather decks outside the superstructure. The XO was there, standing near the head of the line on the port side. He was talking with BM1 Dellamonica's father about the ship's guns. The older Dellamonica was a short, square-built man with curly gray hair. He had a pair of crossed cannons tattooed on his right bicep, which meant that he'd been a gunner's mate while he was in the service.

"Got the Gunnery E twice," the XO said.

Stryker, meanwhile, was busy loading up one of the Model 870s for the first shooter on the port side, putting in three rounds of #4 birdshot. Cushing also had 00 buckshot in her armory, but those shells weren't for clay pigeons. As soon as the shotguns were loaded, the first two guys in line handed over a dollar apiece to MM1 Clay for the ship's Welfare and Rec fund and came aft to shoot skeet.

BM1 Dellamonica's father was the first shooter on Stryker's side. "Been a while since I used a shotgun," he said. "Let's see if I remember anything."

He brought the shotgun up to his shoulder. Stryker called out "Pull!" and the gunner's mate up on the 01 level with the skeet thrower threw a clay pigeon back out over the stern. The older Dellamonica fired, and the bright orange frisbee-shape shattered into fragments in mid-trajectory. Stryker called out "Pull!" again, and the first shooter on the starboard side whaled away without success. Dellamonica, on his second shot, also missed, but connected again with the third and last.

"Two out of three," Stryker said. "Not bad."

The older man handed the shotgun back so that Stryker could reload it for the next man in line. "Should have done better."

He went back into the skin of the ship through the midships passageway, either to rejoin one of the lines or to go on about his business somewhere else, and the XO came up to take his place. Stryker loaded up the Model 870 with three more shells of #4 birdshot and handed the shotgun over to Lieutenant Commander Flandry for his turn.

The XO didn't have any better luck than the starboard shooter, and expended all three of his rounds without hitting anything. At least he, like the older Dellamonica, was able to put the birdshot somewhere in the rough vicinity of the targets. Stryker knew that a lot of the waiting sailors weren't even going to get that close. The real reason for having a pair of gunner's mates standing by on the fantail wasn't to load the Model 870s, but to make certain nobody shot at anything besides the sea and the sky.

Stryker had been at his job for about ten minutes when the Master Chief's daughter reached the head of the port line. She was wearing new blue jeans and a crisp white cotton shirt, like she belonged on the cover of a catalog, with a ball cap to keep the sun out of her eyes. Somebody watching the skeet shoot from up on the

01 level made a rude comment, which she ignored without so much as raising a blush. Stryker wasn't willing to bet, though, that Master Chief Morrison wouldn't hear about it later.

He handed her the Model 870. "You're sure you know how to use one of these, Miss Morrison?"

"I've played with them a bit," she said. She released the slide lock, racked a round into the chamber, and switched off the safety. "Whenever you're ready."

"Pull!" Stryker called out, and the gunner's mate on the 01 level threw out another bird.

The Master Chief's daughter shattered one of the pigeons with her first shot, another with her second, and another with her third, then handed him back the shotgun with a smile.

"Thanks for the chance to practice," she said. "I'd really hate to get rusty during summer break."

Stryker and GMG2 Stoddard watched her as she went back into the ship. Stoddard shook his head in amazement.

"Whoof. You sure don't see one like that every day."

"I wouldn't even think about it, if I were you," said ET2 Dixon, who'd just come up from the starboard line for his turn. "She's the Master Chief's baby girl. If he doesn't like the way you're looking at her, he's likely to rip you a whole new asshole."

"Stand by AS350Bs, inbound."

First one and then a second Aerospatiale Squirrel helicopter came down to settle on the deck of the Australian heavy lift ship HMAS *Tobruk*. Each of the Squirrels in turn disgorged about a half-dozen men in battle dress, carrying rucks and firearms. The senior man—MacGillivray, by his name tag—was a sandy-haired officer wearing the insignia of a Major in the Special Air Service Regiment; the other officer—Burke—was a female wearing a naval Lieutenant's bars.

"We need to speak with the Captain," the SASR Major shouted to the nearest crew member. "I've got orders—don't know if he's heard."

"Right this way," the sailor said. "I'll escort you to the Bridge."

The SASR Major turned to his men. "You lot stay here. Stand easy—if you can find someone who can get you some provender, so much the better."

"Sir," the senior Sergeant said.

"Right, then," the Major said; and to the sailor, "Lead on"—
and off they went, Major MacGillivray and Lieutenant Burke together, following the sailor up ladder after ladder to *Tobruk*'s Bridge.

The Captain was sitting in his chair on the bridge when they
got there. He'd arrived there just ahead of them—roused out of bed
when word came in of a late-night arrival. The Major saluted,
though the gesture was all but invisible on the darkened Bridge.
Only faint red glows came from some of the instrument panels.

"Good evening, sir," MacGillivray said. "Is there somewhere we
can speak alone? What I have is classified at quite a high level."

"Starboard wing do you?" the captain asked.

"Suits me fine."

"Let's go, then."

The Captain pushed himself up out of his chair. Trailed by the
SASR Major and the naval Lieutenant, he walked out onto *Tobruk*'s
starboard Bridgewing. Lieutenant Burke closed and dogged shut the
bridge door behind them.

"So what's this all about?" the Captain said.

"Marine HQ's put us on hot standby," the Major said. "I'm
authorized to requisition a helicopter from you for use when and if.
Have you gotten the orders?"

"No."

"Not to worry, I have a copy." The Major pulled out an envelope from inside his battledress smock and handed it to the
Captain.

"This is all highly irregular," the Captain said, after a moment's
quick glance by flashlight at the envelope's contents. "What's it
about, can you tell me?"

"They're getting nervous in Canberra, that's all," the Major reassured him. "Nothing's happened yet. We're just here in case it
does."

Engineering Berthing, USS *Cushing*
East of Papan Island, Indonesia
103° 30' 8" E/00° 55' 1" N
2100 Local/1400 Zulu

Fireman Raveneau—"Tommy J" to his friends, "Ratty" to casual acquaintances, and "Thomas James" to any officer who'd ever written him up for Captain's Mast—stood beside his rack in engineering berthing, getting ready for the night. Tommy J had a coffin-type locker, one where the rack itself formed the lid of the locker, second up in the stack of four bunks on this row. The crew members who slept in the two top racks had standup lockers nearby. There were six stacks of bunks altogether, separated from the outer common area by a thin metal partition.

Most nights Tommy J would have been on the other side of the partition, watching the ship's entertainment system for lack of anything more exciting to do, but tonight he had the four to eight watch in the engine room, and he thought it might go better if he had a few hours of sleep first. Chief Otto had been on his case ever since the start of the cruise; Raveneau suspected that the Chief was still pissed at him for coming aboard with uniform shoes that were made of Corfam synthetic instead of real leather, even though the Corfams were a lot cheaper, and easier to get clean.

"If there's ever a fire on board, Raveneau," Otto had said, "those shoes are going to melt your fucking *feet* to the fucking *deck*." And the Chief had gone on to write Tommy J up for having nonregulation footgear, as if he had any place to go and buy new leather shoes while *Cushing* was out at sea. The second time, the Chief had said, "Catalogs, Raveneau—you order shoes from fucking catalogs," and written him up all over again. That would have been fairer if Tommy J hadn't already lost all of his money from being busted back to Fireman Recruit at Captain's Mast. How was he supposed to buy anything, when it looked like he was going to be getting by on half a recruit's pay for the rest of his enlistment?

By this point in the cruise, the offending Corfams were scuffed from hard usage, and spotted all over with red deck paint—the official color name was "terra cotta," which as far as Tommy J could tell was just another word for red. He hung the shoes over the horns that were supposed to be for the guys in the top racks to use in climbing up. Then he stripped off his uniform shirt and trousers, folded them, and put them under his mattress. They were clean enough, in his opinion, for tomorrow—though his Leading Petty Officer and his Chief might not agree.

He rolled into his bunk and pulled a sheet around himself. Then he closed his eyes and let himself drift off to sleep, thinking pleasant thoughts about going on liberty in Yokosuka—he was actually going to have some money this time, thanks to winning the ship's unmooring pool. It had only been a dollar-a-square pool, not one of the big ones, but winning it still meant sixty more bucks in his pocket when *Cushing* hit port.

He came up out of his half-drowse an indefinite time later, to the sound of feet and voices in the outer portion of the compartment.

". . . I put a dollar on a Big Chicken Dinner."

That was Damage Controlman Testa, one of the other sailors who shared the berthing compartment. Raveneau wondered who he was talking about. A Big Chicken Dinner meant a BCD, or Bad Conduct Discharge, for somebody on board. Nobody ever used the real name, though, when they talked about it; even Raveneau knew better than to do that. The only thing worse than a BCD was a Duck Dinner—a Dishonorable Discharge—and you didn't call one of those by its real name, either.

"You and half of Engineering," said somebody else—Hull Technician Third Class Charley Ross, it sounded like. "What good's winning if you have to split the pool a dozen or so different ways?"

"So which one did you take? The full Duck?"

"Nah. I went for an admin discharge."

"Too easy," another voice cut in. It sounded to Raveneau like Machinist's Mate Second Class Charvon; he was a couple of years older than either Testa or Charley Ross, near the end of his second hitch and well on his way to becoming a lifer. "There's lots of different discharges, including some where you aren't allowed to wear your uniform home and you aren't allowed to fly the flag on the Fourth of July for the rest of your natural life."

"You're shitting us," said Testa.

"I wouldn't shit you, you're my favorite turd. Seriously, I knew a guy once who got himself a discharge like that. One of those white supremacists from Montana or Idaho or someplace . . . skinny little geek. Stupid, too. The color of his skin was the only thing he had going for him, and it didn't go real far."

"So what did he do?" Ross asked.

"Other than spending his life trying to create hate and discontent, and talking about blowing up the ship? He went UA"—Unauthorized Absence—"one time and went to England, because he'd heard that there weren't any black people there. As soon as he got to London and found out different, he turned himself in to the US Embassy, and the Embassy sent him back to the ship." Charvon laughed. "Not only did that guy get his sorry ass booted out of the Nav, but our XO saw to it that he got escorted to the main gate by the biggest, blackest boatswain's mate on board."

"Ratty's nothing like that bad," Testa said. "Just kind of all-around hopeless. A Convenience of the Government kind of a guy, or maybe a General Under Other Than Honorable. Unless he does something spectacular like steal the Admiral's car and drive it through the front window of a liquor store during a Presidential visit."

"That's been known to happen," said Charvon. "Anybody got money on an Honorable?"

"Not that I've heard of," Testa said. "You interested?"

"In throwing away good money? No, thanks."

Raveneau didn't listen any more. Instead, he pulled the pillow over his head and tried to get back into the comfortable, drowsy state from which the arrival of Testa and the others had awakened him.

He wasn't as successful as he would have liked to be. It didn't surprise him, really, that there was a Rat Boot pool going on his eventual discharge—sailors would bet on anything, and if somebody had asked him he might even have put in some money himself. But it did depress him that nobody at all was betting on an Honorable. Tommy J's ambition, to the extent that he had one, was to join the carpenters' union when he got out, and without an Honorable Discharge the union wouldn't take him.

Maybe if he threw away his Corfams and used the money from the unmooring pool to send off for a pair of real leather shoes . . . but if he did that, he wouldn't have any money to spend in Yokosuka. And Chief Otto was pissed with him about so many other things by now that it probably wouldn't do any good anyway.

Still fretting, he drifted off eventually to sleep.

Pirate Vessel
East of Papan Island, Indonesia
103° 30' 11" E/00° 55' 21" N
2150 Local/1450 Zulu

Four hours had passed since sunset—the sudden tropical sun-set, where the sun goes down hard and fast, straight into the sea, and all the light goes with it—and Michael Prasetyo's Chinese-built 80-footer had been sailing steadily eastward all that time. The pirate craft, dead black and running without lights, moved almost invisibly through the rainswept darkness.

Prasetyo himself stood beside the wheelhouse, the vessel's three diesel engines rumbling under his feet, and strained his eyes in an effort to penetrate the night ahead.

The Forward Looking Infra-Red showed a ghostly blue image on the screen above the wheel. Right now, all he could see were waves. But that didn't mean there wasn't anything out there. The radar painted a green screen, lighting up a number of contacts of all sizes. The Strait of Malacca is crowded with ships, the sea to the southeast is crowded with islands, and the entire plan hung upon finding a specific vessel in all of that visual clutter.

Prasetyo frowned. One of those radar contacts, beyond the visual range of the FLIR . . . "Where *is* the bastard?"

"Out there somewhere," said Tansil. "They were spotted making transit."

"Intercept," the man at the radar broke in. "This one here"—he tapped at the screen with his finger—"has the right course and speed."

"What kind of radar is it showing?" Prasetyo asked.

"That bearing has AN-SPS series," said the man at the radar. "One of them is him."

"I want the ones that are going on the standard track to Japan."

"There's only about a thousand of those," Tansil said.

"So keep looking until you get the right one," Prasetyo said. "It's what we came out here for."

The radar man was silent. Radar and FLIR continued their search. The rain picked up, and Prasetyo regarded with satisfaction the droplets beading up on the windows of the pilothouse.

The weather was worsening, just as he had expected. The storm would block any chance of air support from the American carrier, and would provide his operation with a cover that even spy satellites would be unable to penetrate. By the time the typhoon had passed, he would have his quarry captured and well hidden. Out on the open ocean, there would be nothing left for the searchers from the air.

12

The night was going well so far, Captain Warner reflected, in
spite of the bad weather outside. Wind-driven rain lashed against
Cushing's Bridge windows, making an irregular backbeat against the
steady throb of the engines. Warner sat in his chair on the starboard
side of the Bridge, listening to the low call and response of the watch
standers' voices over the JL circuit: Combat Information Center to
Bridge, Bridge to CIC, back and forth and back again.

"Bridge, Combat."

"Bridge aye."

"Update Skunk Mike November. New course zero three six,
speed twelve. Showing Raytheon Pathfinder."

Warner wasn't surprised. The Raytheon Pathfinder is the single
most common merchant radar in the world.

In the language of radar operators, a "skunk" means a surface
contact. A bogie is an aircraft, a ghost is a submarine. The one to
worry about is a vampire: a missile in the air. Each new contact,

starting at midnight, gets designated by a letter of the phonetic alphabet—starting with Alpha, then going on through Bravo all the way to Zulu. After Skunk Zulu comes Skunk Alpha Alpha. Since local midnight the night before, *Cushing* had gone through the alphabet nearly eighteen and a half times—which for a passage through Malacca, wasn't bad at all.

The Bridge JL talker wrote down the new information in grease pencil on the status board. Keeping a status board requires the ability to write legibly, backward, on the back side of a vertical sheet of Plexiglas. The information on the status board tells the Officer of the Deck and the others of the Bridge team what the rest of the world is doing, at least as far as local shipping is concerned.

"Bridge, Combat, new CPA Skunk Mike November five thousand yards to starboard."

"Bridge aye."

The brief exchange meant that Skunk Mike November had altered course, and that the Combat Information Center had picked up on the change. The status board keeper marked down the information with his grease pencil.

Warner glanced at his watch. It was about time . . . yes. Almost on the minute, the Boatswain's Mate of the Watch turned to the Messenger of the Watch and said, "Rotate."

The word was the cue for the various members of *Cushing*'s Bridge team to change places. SN Holland came in from the port Bridgewing, traded off his standard green rain gear to the Messenger of the Watch, and took over the Engine Order Telegraph; the crewman at the EOT took the wheel; BMSN Serra left the wheel to take over the status board. SN Kelly, formerly on the status board, put on his rain gear and prepared to stand starboard lookout.

"Like you see," he told Serra. "We have a pile of active contacts."

"Got it," said Serra, and put on the sound-powered phones.

Kelly went out onto the Bridgewing. There, Warner knew, the

rest of the dance would take place, with the former starboard lookout heading aft to relieve the stern lookout, who would move on to port lookout in turn.

Aboard *Cushing*, rotation on this watch came every half hour. It keeps a man sharper to do different things, and even with all the radar and electronics she carried, *Cushing* needed her flesh-and-blood watchers fresh and alert. Human eyeballs pick up things that electronics miss. Merchant ships can engage the autopilot, leave the ship's dog on watch, and let the crew hit their racks. Navy ships can't.

Warner checked the time again: 2200. He was pleased. The practiced efficiency of the changeover, even late at night and so far into a long passage through the Strait, said good things about the crew's training and morale.

Pirate Vessel
East of Papan Island, Indonesia
103° 30' 11" E/00° 55' 21" N
2200 Local/1500 Zulu

"That's not him," Prasetyo said. The FLIR showed the ghostly form of a container ship. "Next?"

"Two miles, heading 105, speed 15," the man on the radar said.

"Let me know."

Prasetyo felt the blood-warm rain on his face. His clothing was already soaked, hours since, but he didn't care. Up ahead, somewhere in the dark, were a whole pile of Tomahawk missiles, each worth a quarter of a million on the open market. If there were nukes, so much the better. The price for those weapons would be very high indeed.

But the ship . . . the ship will be mine.

The wind picked up, a sudden strong gust buffeting against him.

A wave higher than the others broke over the bow of the 80-footer, adding salt flavor on his lips as the spray hit.

The diesels sounded louder as the boat came left and picked up speed to pass behind the merchant ship and attempt visual identification on the next vessel. The ocean is large, even in restricted waters, and ships are small. Prasetyo had confidence, however. His intel was always very good.

Another ship-form appeared on the FLIR. This time, the blocky outline was unmistakably that of a *Spruance*-class destroyer. Prasetyo let out his breath in a quiet sigh.

"And there we are," he said. "That's our target. Drift forward along his starboard side. Match his course and speed."

Bridge, USS *Cushing*
East of Papan Island, Indonesia
103° 30′ 8″ E/00° 55′ 1″ N
2201 Local/ 1501 Zulu

On *Cushing*, Captain Warner leaned back in his chair, drained his coffee, stretched, and stood.

The storm outside had increased in intensity over the past few hours. Rain lashed against *Cushing*'s Bridge windows, and the wind howled around the corners of the Signal Bridge above. The dogs on the Bridge windows never did make them entirely watertight; rainwater kept seeping through to pool on the angle iron just beneath. Or it would have, if the ship's constant rocking and rolling had allowed water to stay in one place long enough to puddle.

Officer of the Deck Lieutenant Gilano had already rescued the copy of ATP-1B—the Allied tactical signal book—and had stowed it in its holder on the side of the chart table, rather than sticking it into the brace beside the 21MC where it would be handy if Sigs or CIC called something in. Ernie Gilano was a good shiphandler;

Warner could turn in for the night with a clear conscience in spite of the weather.

"Night orders, Captain," Gilano said, handing over the three-ring binder. Warner took it and walked over to the chart table. The red lights there were a little brighter.

The night orders were written with the Navy's standard neat block letters, and most of the entries were equally standard. In the narrative portion, Warner added one line: "Inform me of weather forecasts and of observed deteriorating weather conditions."

He signed the bottom of the page. "I'll be in my sea cabin," he told Lieutenant Gilano, then closed the night order book and handed it back. He took the non-tight door on the aft bulkhead, and started down the ladder.

Pirate Vessel
East of Papan Island, Indonesia
103° 30 ' 8" E/00° 55' 1" N
2202 Local/1502 Zulu

The wind kicked up spray, torn from the tops of what would have been whitecaps, had there been enough light to see them. Rain poured down, and the trio of small craft that had moved to surround the US destroyer were pitching and rolling amid the waves and swells.

Prasetyo picked up his hand-held radio. "Move in. Gunners, take your stations."

Two men came up the ladder from below, through the Pilot-house and out onto the wind-and water-swept deck. They carried launching tubes, modified with stedicam technology to compensate for the rough water.

Prasetyo nodded to the men. "Position?" he shouted above the wind.

"Position," one of the men shouted back in the distinctive

mainland Chinese accent of the mission specialists.

Then, into the handheld, Prasetyo said, "One, position. Report." He held the radio up against his ear to catch the responses.

"Two, position."

"Three, position."

In spite of the rain and the turbulent sea, Prasetyo felt a moment of profound satisfaction. His men had their marks, their aimpoints, their weapons. *Cushing*'s command and control spaces, all her antennas, the Pilothouse, the Bridge, the Signal Bridge, the skin of the ship outside CIC—marksmen had all of them targeted with Chinese-made shoulder-fired missiles. At this range, most of the missile damage would come from unexpended fuel rather than from the bursting charge.

"On my command," said Prasetyo. "Aim. Fire."

Tongues of flame, lurid in the blackness, shot out from the launching tubes. Prasetyo didn't wait to see where the missiles hit.

"Move in! Take her in!" he shouted into the Pilothouse. "Boarding party on deck!"

The helmsman cranked in left rudder and pushed ahead on the throttle. The boarding party—all heavily armed, muscular men—came up the ladder, holding tight against the boat's motion and the wind when they came out onto the deck.

"Grapnels away!"

A shotline fired up and out, a thin cord with hooks on its head, propelled by a shotgun blank. The line went over *Cushing*'s rail, but didn't fall back when the shot-man pulled on it. He grabbed hold and started up the side, toward the top of the ship's superstructure.

Cushing's sidelights were out now, destroyed by the missiles that had hit the Bridge. A fiery glow shone out from within the wrecked Pilothouse. More than that, Prasetyo couldn't see. Wind-whipped water makes men squint, and the night was dark.

The shot-man climbed out of sight. A moment later, the knotted cord that he had worn around his waist came tumbling downward to hang beside the vessel, its end marked by a Cyalume glow stick.

"There it is," Prasetyo said. "Go! And watch out for our friends. They're coming up the other side."

His men started climbing, hand over hand, along the smooth metal side of the destroyer. One by one they advanced into darkness, until only Prasetyo remained behind on deck.

He waved to the man at the wheel in the Pilothouse. Then he, too, took hold of the knotted cord and began to climb.

Bridge, USS *Cushing*
East of Papan Island, Indonesia
103° 30 ' 8 " E/0° 55' 1" N
2202 Local/1502 Zulu

With the Captain gone to his sea cabin for the night, Lieutenant Gilano was the senior officer present on the Bridge. The watch was going to be a long one, with a lot of ships and boats around, most of them small, and nothing by way of visibility.

Gilano picked up his one-liter coffee mug—a German beer stein, actually, souvenir of a wild night in Hamburg on a NATO exercise two tours back.

"Boats, could you have the messenger get me a cup of coffee?"

As he spoke, he stepped away from his position by the Bridge windows, intending to hand off the mug to the Boatswain's Mate of the Watch. A small decision, but a critical one—it meant that he wasn't standing beside the bridge windows, or by either Bridgewing, when the world exploded without warning into deafening noise and a flash of blinding light.

When the light and noise stopped Gilano was flat on the deck, covered with water and hurting all over. His mind, fumbling to make sense out of the unexpected, at first produced nothing but the memory-picture of a one-liter beer stein, ready to be filled.

Now you're really in trouble. You've got the twenty to twenty-four hundred, and you're still lying down. Late for watch . . . my head hurts. I knew I shouldn't go out drinking . . .

He tried to push himself to his feet, got up, and fell down again. His leg hurt, and the space around him was full of bright light. The Bridge—that was where he was.

You're not late for watch, stupid; you're already here.

Full understanding came back in a rush. He was on the Bridge, and *Cushing* had just taken a serious hit.

Who could have . . . it doesn't matter. What matters is they blew up the forward magazine.

The Captain is going to be really pissed.

Gilano opened his eyes all the way. He was still dazzled by the light. He'd only been confused for a couple of seconds, though it seemed like much longer. Something nearby was burning. He could smell it. Unexpended fuel, he realized, from the missiles that had hit forward on each Bridgewing. The Bridge windows themselves were all blown out by the concussion, and most of the men who had been with Gilano on the Bridge were down. He could see them in the firelight, and they weren't moving.

"Shit," he mumbled. Talking made his head hurt worse, but he did it anyway. He didn't want to slide back into the confusion inside his skull. "My FITREP is going to really suck."

The fire was all over the aft bulkhead. His leg wouldn't support his weight. He rolled forward, and heard something above the ringing in his ears. Maybe he was feeling it through the deck. Another impact.

"Oh, hell. We're under fire." *Talk your way through it . . . that's the trick.* "The Captain will want to know."

The bitch box was a long way away. Fifteen feet, which looked about forever far. But the SRBOC launcher was right here, and *Cushing* was under fire, and Gilano had a letter in his service jacket that allowed him to shoot off Super Rapid Blooming Offboard

Chaff—the metal fragments that confuse and distract targeting radar—without asking permission.

He dragged himself upright against the port side bulkhead, knees buckling, feeling rough metal tear at him, and pulled open the launch panel.

He hit the fire switch. Nothing happened.

"Broken," he said.

The Captain would really, really be pissed now. Gilano wondered if anything worse could happen. Then he spied a fire extinguisher, still strapped to the bulkhead, and in reach.

He yanked the extinguisher off of the bulkhead, pulled the safety pin, slapped the top to activate the cartridge, and shot a burst of Purple-K at the fire. The paint was peeling and blistering. Without the wind and rain whipping through the now-open Bridge, he wouldn't have been able to breathe.

The fire died. Not much to support it up here. Gilano exhausted the PKP, then fell forward again. He was tired, he hurt. He pushed forward with his hands, trying to get to the 21MC. He had to report the problem to the CO.

Then the pain overcame him, and he passed out for a second time.

13

Captain Andrew Warner was halfway down the ladder to the next level, between the peach-colored bulkheads that proclaimed this part of USS _Cushing_ to be senior officers' country, when he felt the railing shudder underneath his hands. The next thing he knew, he was sprawled facedown on the deck at the foot of the ladder.

The overhead lights had all gone out. The only illumination came from the red glow of the bulkhead-mounted battle lanterns. Something had happened to bring them on line—probably the same something that had caused the impact—and the air in the passageway suddenly smelled odd. His head hurt, his ears were ringing, and there was a sharp pain in his left wrist when he tried flexing it.

"Damn," Warner said inadequately.

He pushed himself first to his knees, then to his feet. His knees hurt too. He couldn't hear anything above the ringing in his ears.

The crimson-colored air was thick with haze—dust or smoke, he couldn't tell which. He turned, holding the handrail of the ladder, and made his way up back up toward the Bridge.

Even before he reached the non-tight door at the top, he could see the paint peeling off in bubbles from the metal surface. He reached out with the back of his hand to touch the door, but withdrew it hurriedly when he felt intense heat radiating outward into the ladder well.

Fire, he thought. *Can't go back that way.*

A fire on shipboard—with no help coming from anywhere outside, and no place to run to except the equally hazardous and unforgiving sea—was every sailor's nightmare, guarded against by dozens of regulations and prepared for by regular drills. Warner spared a second to wonder what had happened to set *Cushing* ablaze, and whether Laura and Chris were safe. Then he forced himself to put both questions aside.

Later, after everything was back under control, there would be time to count heads and sort out how the trouble had started. For now, the only hope of safety for everyone aboard lay in prompt action.

He turned away from the door and made his way back through the passageway to the ladder. He could feel that the ship was in a hard right turn; she was heeling to starboard. That could mean a loss of control—or it could mean that the helmsman needed to blow the fire away from himself. Hard to say, and no point in speculating.

Warner made it down the ladder in one swing and ran toward his sea cabin. The door opened, and he was in.

By the head of his rack stood three alarms: green for Chemical, yellow for Collision, and red for General Quarters. Warner pushed the safety bar on the red alarm and turned the lever to the right to sound General Quarters. Dimly, he heard the GQ alarm begin sounding in response. His hearing was coming back.

He turned to the 21MC, switched the dial to the Pilothouse, and pressed the key. "Bridge, Captain, report."

No answer.

He turned the dial to Signal Bridge. "Sigs, Captain, report."
More silence.

"Combat, Captain, report."

No answer.

Hell of a time for the SP circuits to go down, he thought. He turned
the dial to Main Control.

"Main, Captain, report."

This time, to his intense relief, a voice answered. "Going to
GQ, sir. DCC isn't on line yet."

Okay, it isn't the SP circuits.

"Main, believe we've taken some hits," Warner said. *Hits or
something . . . we'll find out what's really going on soon enough.* "Report
manned and ready, get me some investigators out. Find me in CIC."

"Aye aye, sir." Main clicked off.

Deck 2 Frame 45, USS *Cushing*
East of Papan Island, Indonesia
103° 30' 8" E/00° 55' 1" N
2202 Local/1502 Zulu

Master Chief Morrison had left Chiefs' Berthing at 2130, when
the ship first started doing some serious rocking and rolling. He
wanted to see if all his spaces were secured for sea, like they should
have been. If they weren't, and if things began shifting around inside
the ammo spaces . . . well, that could ruin everybody's day.

He took his keys and began a circuit of all the spaces and compartments under his authority, starting with the deep magazines aft
and working his way forward. He found all secure in the ready service lockers, where ammunition was kept for immediate use, and all
secure in the armory.

The SAT/BAF muster was going on as usual in the small arms
locker. GMGSN Stryker was there, looking like he had everything
under control. Morrison decided that he approved of Stryker; the

kid was a self-starter and didn't mind hard work. *If he finishes up the scratch-off study sheet for Gunner's Mate Third Class in time, I'm going to let him take the test soon's he's got time in service and time in rate.*

Taps sounded as Morrison neared missile control—no music, this not being the fucking Army, just an announcement over the 1MC: "Taps, Taps. Lights out. All hands turn in to your own bunks. The smoking lamp is out in all berthing spaces. Now Taps."

So far, everything looked copacetic. In just a couple of minutes Morrison would be finished with checking things out, and could head aft to get some sleep. He heard the rack monster calling his name already, even through the ship's pounding and pitching.

And then he heard something else—something real, this time, and not just a sailor's joke. Detonations, three of them, *wham wham wham*, heavy blows punching into the ship like fists.

Oh, fuck, he thought. *It's the forward deep mag.*

Then he realized that the noise had come not from the powder magazine—one of the few spaces he hadn't yet checked—but from *Cushing*'s superstructure. Moments later, the General Quarters alarm sounded, and within a few seconds the passageway was full of sailors heading to their assigned stations.

Deck 3 Frame 60, USS *Cushing*
East of Papan Island, Indonesia
103° 30' 8" E/00° 55' 1" N
2202 Local/1502 Zulu

Kyle and Tyson Bailey had settled down for the night in S Di-vision berthing—Kyle in his dinosaur-print pajamas and Tyson in the blue-and-white striped ones that he always wore when he was sleeping over someplace away from home, because they made him feel grown up. He was fifteen minutes younger than Kyle, and sometimes needed the extra help.

The ship was moving around a lot more than it had the first

few days. They'd felt the deck shifting and tilting under their feet while they were brushing their teeth and getting ready for bed, and their father had given them the Dramamine in case they were seasick.

"But we won't be seasick, will we?" Tyson said later to his brother, who was sleeping in the bunk just above his.

"Nope," said Kyle firmly. "We rode on the Tilt-a-Whirl at the carnival, remember, and we didn't get sick then. This isn't going to do it, either. And when we get home we can tell all the other kids that we were in a real storm at sea."

Tyson thought about that for a few minutes. The mental pictures it brought were pleasing ones—the story would make him the center of attention for as long as it lasted, at least if Kyle didn't push in and tell it first, and Kyle was in a different class from him this year. He drifted off to sleep with that thought still in his head, only to come awake again before he went all the way under.

He sat up. Noises—loud noises, like explosions or something—that was what he'd heard. He thought about the storm, and was suddenly afraid.

"Kyle?"

"Yeah?"

"You heard that?"

"Yeah."

"What do you think it was?" Tyson asked—but one of the older Tigers said, "Be quiet, kid, and listen," before Kyle could answer, then an alarm began to sound, the steady gong-note that even Tyson remembered as meaning General Quarters.

Almost in the next breath, everyone in S Division berthing started tumbling out of their bunks and going places very fast. Mr. Willis—the older Tiger who'd spoken to Tyson before—said, "Come along with me, you two; we'd better move it."

Kyle was already climbing down from the upper bunk. "It's a General Quarters drill," he said. "You heard him—come *on*."

Mr. Willis ushered the twins out the door. The deck felt cold under Tyson's bare feet, but he was afraid to stop and put on his shoes. Almost everyone else was out of the compartment by now, and he didn't want to get left behind.

The narrow passageway outside was full of sailors. They all seemed to know exactly where to go, and were in a rush to get there. Tyson was running, stumbling sometimes on the deck as the ship moved under him.

He almost tripped over Kyle as the motion of the ship threw him forward unexpectedly. His brother grabbed him before he could fall all the way down, and they hurried on together.

"Do you think this is really just a drill?" Tyson asked.

"Dunno," said his brother. "Those noises—"

"Yeah. I wonder where Dad is?"

"He has to be someplace else," Kyle said. "Remember? And he'll expect us to be where we're supposed to be, so he can find us when it's all over. So stop sniffling and come on."

"I was *not* sniffling."

"You were, too."

"Shut up," said Mr. Willis, coming to a stop outside a door labeled CHIEFS' BERTHING in stenciled block letters. "Here we are."

Captain's Cabin, USS *Cushing*
East of Papan Island, Indonesia
103° 30' 8 " E/00° 55' 1" N
2202 Local/1502 Zulu

Chris Warner had rolled up in his sheet and gone to sleep a little after Taps. He wondered how his father managed, year after year, in an environment where without moving your feet you could see the sun come up out of the sea and see it go down into the sea, with nothing in between except the sky and the ship, always the same.

Sure, Chris liked solitude as much as the next man. The forests of the Pacific Northwest, in places where he might as well have been the first person to walk since Lewis and Clark were tenderfeet, provided him with one of his favorite refuges. He'd done his first professional photo essay about that experience, documenting a backpacking trip taken over spring break in his junior year. He'd enjoyed making the sale almost as much as he'd enjoyed the trip itself. For the first time he'd been able to think that maybe, just maybe, he could make a living doing something that he really wanted to do, instead of taking orders and punching a time clock for the rest of his life.

But the wilderness was always changing, while the ocean was not ("timeless," his father had called it once; Chris privately considered "monotonous" to be a better term)—and not only was the sea always the same, these days there were too damned many people on it. During *Cushing*'s passage through the Strait, you could have walked from one side to the other on the decks of all the ships. Even in the middle of the Indian Ocean, he'd spotted a grass-and-barnacle-encrusted truck tire floating on the waves.

At the moment, Chris hovered somewhere between waking and sleep, lulled by the humming of the ship around him, its mechanical sounds and creaks. The motion of the vessel was greater on this side of the Strait than it had been back in the Indian Ocean—though nothing, his father had claimed, like the rolling of the old pre-World War II tin-can destroyers, where the sailors were given "hard-lying" pay because the ride was so bad that any sleep beyond an exhausted stupor was impossible.

This morning's Plan of the Day had spoken of heavy weather ahead, requiring all spaces to be secured for high seas, and had urged the Tigers to report to sickbay for Dramamine. So far, Chris hadn't felt the need.

Something in a locker was going softly *clang, clang,* with each roll, a steady and almost reassuring noise. Then, abruptly, the ship's sound and motion changed. Chris was jerked awake by three loud, heavy noises, like hammer blows. He wondered muzzily if someone with a sledge hammer was hitting the other side of the bulkhead.

The lights were still out in the compartment, but he heard someone's voice shouting "What the *fuck* was that?"

Then a loud *wong-wong* sound started going and didn't stop. He recognized it as an alarm, and a second after that, he identified the alarm as General Quarters.

That one wasn't announced in the Plan of the Day, he thought, *and who runs a drill in the middle of the night?* Then he heard people moving about outside the cabin—moving fast, without much talking or cursing. The conclusion was inescapable. *The world has suddenly turned to shit.*

What do I . . . right. Chiefs' Quarters. Second deck, centerline, midships. And sit tight.

He began pulling on his shirt and pants and lacing up a pair of shoes. He was halfway through tying the second shoelace when he noticed he'd forgotten to put on his socks.

The hell with the socks.

He grabbed his copy of *The Critique of Pure Reason* to read in case he was at his GQ station for a while—maybe the world was falling apart, and maybe it wasn't, but at least he could look calm while it was happening—and left the cabin, his camera swinging from its strap around his neck. He plunged into the stream of hurrying, purposeful sailors, going up and forward to starboard, down and aft to port, just as if it were a drill.

Exercise Room, USS *Cushing*
East of Papan Island, Indonesia
103° 30' 8 " E/00° 55' 1" N
2202 Local/1502 Zulu

XO Ted Flandry was doing his nightly thirty minutes on the stationary bicycle when the alarm went for General Quarters.

Flandry believed in keeping fit. He'd never had any problem keeping himself well below the Navy's maximum allowed weight, even on shore tours with required attendance at well-provisioned diplomatic bunfights. At sea, with plenty of time on his hands and nowhere to go when he was off-duty except the Wardroom, his rack, or the exercise room, staying trim was even easier.

He preferred to use the exercise room late at night whenever possible, even though the lack of regular company at that hour limited him to machines like the bicycle that didn't require a spotter for the sake of safety. On a night like tonight, all the weights were secured for heavy seas anyhow—but the stationary bicycles, already fastened down securely, were still available.

At the moment the alarm sounded, he was well into his regular half hour on the bike, and up to that point he'd been generally pleased with both himself and the world. His tour aboard *Cushing* had gone smoothly, just as Admiral Mayland had predicted—"Warner's a capable officer," he'd said to Flandry, back at the start of this tour, "so you won't have to spend all your time as XO making some asshole look good." Now Flandry had only a few weeks left before he would be attending PCO school, and on the way to a command of his own.

The sound and feel of three heavy, percussive impacts striking the ship, followed by the persistent gong of the GQ alarm, changed all that. His first thought was that the heavy weather had caused some kind of mechanical problem with the ship. An instant later, he realized that the sounds had been not a natural result of the storm, but the product of hostile intent: *Cushing* was under attack.

Flandry's GQ station was on the Bridge, and the fastest way to get there was through the midships passageway. He started out in a hurry, but didn't get far before he discovered the passageway to be full of smoke—there was a fire someplace close up ahead.

He turned back. There was a scuttle aft of his current position;

going through it would bring him out onto *Cushing*'s weather decks just forward of the after gun mount. He should be able to get to the Bridge from there—if anything functional remained of the Bridge after what was looking more and more like an act of war.

14

With the ship beginning to roll in the increasingly heavy seas, H. L. Morrison had been more than willing to turn in early for the night. She didn't think she was likely to become seasick—she'd been pretty much immune to any other variety of motion sickness, even as a kid—but she'd just as soon miss watching seasickness happen to everybody else. With luck—*luck and good management*, she amended—USS *Cushing* would travel through the edge of the bad weather while she and all the other Tigers were tucked snug in their bunks.

She stripped out of the jeans and shirt she'd worn during the day and put on the loose boxer-style shorts and oversized tee shirt she'd brought along for nightwear. She'd chosen the outfit for comfort, since it was cool and loose in hot weather; but it had the added advantage of looking at least minimally decent if for some reason she had to wear it in public. Then she went into the Washroom/Water Closet to take off her makeup and brush her teeth. Scrubbed and brushed, she went back into the main compartment of Forward Officers' Berthing, and found that Mrs. Warner had arrived to join her.

Mrs. Warner was still wearing the tailored slacks and contrasting blouse that she'd worn during the day. While she'd slipped off her shoes in order to put her feet up on the bunk, she hadn't yet bothered to take off her socks.

"I see you decided to turn in early, too," she said to H. L. "A wise idea, I think. It's going to be a bit of a wild night."

"That's what everybody says. Do you know how long the storm is supposed to last?" H. L. still felt a bit awkward about trying to make conversation with the Captain's Wife, but it would have been even more awkward to bunk with her for the entire Tiger Cruise and not say anything.

Mrs. Warner shook her head. "Not really. Predicting the weather isn't my—"

She stopped. A split-second later, the sound that had stopped her came again, and a third time.

H. L. had read about noises that made people's blood run cold. She'd never expected to feel the sensation herself. She wasn't sure what the sounds meant—they might have been explosions, but she couldn't tell if they'd come from inside the ship or from somewhere outside, in the storm—but she already knew that they meant trouble.

So did Mrs. Warner, apparently. The Captain's Wife stood up and shoved her feet back into her shoes. "Better get ready," she said. "Any minute now, they're going to sound General Quarters."

In fact, the steady gong-beat of the alarm began even before she had finished speaking. H. L. snatched up her running shoes—no time now to put them on, even without socks; she'd have to wait until she was at the Tigers' GQ station in Chief's Berthing—and followed Mrs. Warner out.

Pirate Vessel
East of Papan Island, Indonesia
103° 30' 8" E/00° 55' 1" N
2210 Local/1510 Zulu

Prasetyo had known that boarding the destroyer would be dif-
ficult. The wind and rain had grown stronger even while his three
boats maneuvered into position and the specialists worked the missiles and the lines. Now the deck of the 80–footer was a crazily
tilting platform under his feet, and the line that led up *Cushing*'s
side was slick with spray and whipped back and forth by the wind.

It would be a bad climb, but he had planned the assault this way
for a purpose, so that he would have the time he needed. While the
storm raged, the Americans could neither find their missing ship
nor send out help. *Cushing* would have to fight alone.

The sheer cliff of the destroyer's side loomed up over him for
an interminable distance as he began his ascent. The ship swayed
constantly, and the line he was climbing swayed with it. He swung,
pendulum-like, first away from the skin of the ship and then toward
it, and timed his climbing to match the rolls.

Before he was halfway up he heard a gonging sound coming
from the ship. *Cushing* was going to General Quarters.

At last he came to the top, where the line was tied off to a
stanchion. He put his hand on the rail, and one of his men on the
far side took hold of him and helped him over. *Cushing*'s deck was
steadier than that of the 80-footer had been, but still he had to brace
himself against the constant movement.

"What do we have so far?" he asked. He had to shout to make
himself heard over the rain and the wind.

"We've got secondary conn."

"Take me there. Patrols out. Secure the ship. I want everyone
aboard under my control. Who's got the charts?"

"Here." Kino Tansil's voice, coming to him over the noise of the storm.

"Right. We need to get off the shipping channels, and down into the islands. The storm will give us cover. Kino, take the wheel before we start to drift, and get going. Our first course is 127. And someone, make a sweep of the Bridge. Make sure that no one's alive in there and that all the radios are dead. If you see an antenna, pull it down. Now, places, everyone."

By this time he'd come to secondary conn, aft of the Signal Bridge, forward of the helo hangar. Two of his men lifted the metal covers off the wheel and binnacle combination, where the magnetic compass and gyro repeater stood before a miniature trick wheel.

"Rudder is right," Tansil reported. "Helm is answering the wheel."

"Very well," Prasetyo said. He had a waterproof chart unfolded, a course drawn on it with grease pencil, and a red-lensed flashlight turned on it. "We have some miles to go, and it won't take the Americans long to learn that we're here."

Second deck, portside, USS *Cushing*
Off Kundur Island, Indonesia
103° 35' 6" E/00° 19' 54" N
2224 Local/1524 Zulu

When GQ went, LTJG Bailey rolled out of his rack in After O and slid into his khaki trousers. He pulled on his socks and shoes, but didn't bother with a shirt. Instead he grabbed a green foul-weather jacket with "Lambchop" stenciled in black across the back. His GQ station was at the gun director, and that would put him out on the weather decks, high up.

The alarm was still sounding when he'd finished dressing. He wasn't the last one out of After O. *I'll bet the twins are enjoying this,* he thought, wondering what the alarm was about. *It's all just a big fun ride to them.* He hit the starboard midships weatherdeck door, snaking past the light locker, then headed up.

The night was black, the air—between the spray and the rain— more water than anything else. The shocks from waves hitting the side vibrated through his feet.

Up, holding on to both ladder rails, moving by touch through the familiar route, he arrived at the director. Forward, at after conn, he could see figures moving, shining red-lensed flashlights. They moved oddly. They weren't in US uniforms. Then a shout came back to him, and it wasn't in English.

"Oh, fuck me," Bailey whispered. When he was in the Army he'd done time in Somalia. He recognized an AK slung across one of the men's backs.

The rest of the gun director team was showing up. The talker was setting up his phones and getting comms checks.

"No reply from Bridge, Combat, or Sigs," the talker said. "No answer from Missile Control." He had to shout to be heard above the storm. The wires overhead were singing in the wind.

"Who do you have?"

"Nobody."

"Keep trying. When someone comes on, tell them to go to intruder alert and stand by to repel boarders."

The GMG3 who should have been on sights arrived.

"Take a fire axe," Bailey ordered. "Go forward and stand behind the mast. If anyone comes aft who isn't in uniform, you hit him upside the head. I'm going to go to my safe, pick up my .45, and return. Stand by, don't leave this post."

"Aye aye, sir."

The lambchop, as *Cushing*'s Disbursing Officer, kept a weapon in the safe with the payday money. Ships being what they are, it was the same money from payday to payday: the men were paid in cash, those who didn't have allotments to family or to a bank. The cash money went to the post office to be turned into money orders to be sent home or to a girlfriend or to people who advertised in *Easy Rider* magazine, and the rest got spent in the gedunk. In either case, the dollar bills and fives and tens and twenties made their way back to the Disbursing Officer's safe in time for the next payday.

But there was a .45 pistol in there too, along with the several hundred thousand dollars in cash, as if anyone would turn Jesse James on shipboard. The traditional joke is that the pistol was for the Disbo in case he turned up short at an audit, to shoot his way out "and save the last round for yourself."

Bailey went down the weather ladder. Habit's hard to break— he went down and aft to port. The weird howling and the shocks of the wind and water were his only company. Second deck, admin area, portside passageway, there were the Supply offices. As he crossed the threshold, the lights went down from red to black, and the battle lanterns clicked on.

One battle lantern, white lensed, was fixed to the bulkhead and aimed at the combo dial on the disbursing safe. The disbursing safe was a huge, nineteenth-century looking affair, black crackle paint, massively thick walls. It sat in the middle of a place where lots of men had access to cutting torches and knew how to use them.

Government combination locks are notoriously sensitive. A fraction off on any number, and they won't open. Dialing in a four digit sequence on a pitching, rolling ship, by the light of a battle lantern (and the lantern was cunningly placed so that the act of trying to dial put the shadow of his hand on the numbers) in order to face armed intruders, while trembling with an adrenaline reaction, is tough. It took Bailey three tries.

The safe swung open. He pulled open the drawer that held the weapon. He took the single magazine, five cartridges, slid it in, and jacked a round into the chamber.

He carefully noted the time of opening on the log sheet inside— habits are very hard to break—and shut the door. He spun the wheel three times to clear it, tested the locking bar, and turned to go.

He stepped out of the door to the Disbursing Office, turned to go aft, and suddenly felt a hot, burning sensation in his right chest. It took him a moment to figure out what had happened.

Damn, he thought. *I've been shot. I hate it when that happens.*

He tried to turn, because the guy had to be behind him, but two more punches in his back knocked him forward to the deck, and it was too hard to move.

The intruder walked past him, on his way to the messdecks and Repair Five, and didn't pause. Bailey was still alive and conscious, but he couldn't find the strength to move to bring his weapon to bear, let alone to aim or fire on the moving man.

Shortly after that, the pain stopped, and the light went away, and breathing was too much trouble too, so he stopped.

15

Repair Five, USS *Cushing*
Off Kundur Island, Indonesia
103° 35' 6" E/00° 19' 54" N
2231 Local/1531 Zulu

When the GQ alarm sounded, Hull Technician 3rd Class Charley Ross headed for his station at Repair Five.

Ross was a welder assigned to A-gang, and Repair Five was a locker—a space with a door and nothing much else. The locker at Repair Five contained the tools needed to put a ship back to rights after taking damage: the canvas bags containing the clamps, rubber pads, and wedges of the Plugging and Patching team; the helmets, safety lines, and OBAs—Oxygen Breathing Apparatus—of the investigators; the first-aid kit of the Corpsman assigned to the repair locker; the shoring battens, the clipboards, the flashlights, the sound-powered phones, the eductors, the electric sub pumps; all the gear, in short, that a ship might need in order to keep out water, put out fires, and keep on fighting.

Repair Five was situated low down, amidships. Big Plexiglas sheets swung out from the bulkhead to show the layout of the entire ship, with its vital systems, so that the Damage Control Talker could mark damage in grease pencil as other repair lockers reported it, or as Repair Five's own investigators brought back word. All of *Cushing*'s repair lockers reported to Damage Control Central, and DCC reported to Main Control and the Bridge on the 2JZ circuit.

The locker at Repair Five was located just aft of the mess decks, which made it, in Charley Ross's opinion, a pretty good GQ station. The mess decks are wide and open—at least by comparison with almost every other space and passageway on shipboard. The crew's dining tables are bolted to the deck, but the space itself goes almost all the way across the beam of the ship. There's plenty of room to get around. And during drills, the damage control investigators could go investigate the soda machine on the mess decks and bring back drinks for the men who waited behind at the repair locker.

Ross didn't think that this was a drill. He'd been asleep in his rack when the noise and vibration of three sudden explosions rocked the ship, followed by the sound of the GQ alarm. The combination of explosions and alarm brought him wide awake and hurrying to his station a lot quicker than usual.

The same no-shit-this-is-the-real-thing urgency seemed to possess the rest of the team in Repair Five as well. Everything was going faster and smoother than Ross had seen it go before. Repair Five was already manned up and the investigators were putting on their OBAs, turning the timers to 60 then back to 30 and getting ready to go out, when a civilian came dashing through the mess decks carrying a machine pistol.

That guy sure isn't one of our Tigers, was all that Ross had time to think, before Joe Pelletier—the #1 Investigator, who under more normal circumstances would be checking for damage aft and down from Repair Five—yelled out "Intruder!" and pulled a low-pressure nozzle from the bulkhead.

Ross never knew what Joe planned to do with the nozzle. Use it as a club, maybe; a low-pressure nozzle is six feet of metal pipe with a brass fog nozzle on the end, and a man with fear and excitement pumping adrenaline into his system could swing it with deadly effect. Pelletier never got a chance to try it, though. The intruder brought up his weapon and shot him down.

The sound ripped through the mess decks and back to the repair locker. The talker stepped back into the locker and reported "DCC, Five, sound of small arms forward."

The intruder continued walking steadily aft, firing in bursts— three rounds, two rounds, five rounds—at each man in the repair party as they moved or came into his line of sight.

Then the sound of firing stopped for an instant—*the fucker's reloading*, Ross thought, *gotta reload to get some more of us*—and the First Class in charge of the locker, HT1 Terrell, shouted out, "Fire party, charge one, solid stream, go!"

The hose team was behind the turn of a ladder well, where the fireplug stood, and out of the line of fire. When the #1 Plugman turned the handwheel, the hose stiffened up in long loops on the deck. The #1 Nozzleman pulled back on the bail of the hose, all the way back, putting a solid stream of water down the passage, coming out at better than 250 gallons a minute in a stream an inch and a half wide. The nozzleman pointed the stream of water out through the door to the mess decks, where the intruder was slamming a new magazine into his machine pistol, and knocked him back and down. The machine pistol flew off in one direction, the man in another.

"Hose team, advance," Terrell shouted. "Charge #2!"

The #1 Nozzleman kept his stream on the intruder, keeping him down, pushing him across the deck to the forward bulkhead of the mess decks. The crew members who had already fallen, a half-dozen of them, rolled bloodily in the salt water flooding from the hose. The rest of #1 hose team followed the nozzleman, keeping the hose under control.

They were halfway across the mess decks when a second intruder entered from the forward starboard door and sprayed the hose team with automatic fire. Hose team #1 went down and their hose went loose—slamming up and down and from side to side, rocketing around, a wild hose.

Damn, thought Ross. He was the #2 Nozzleman, and in another couple of heartbeats he was going to have to step up to the doorway and into the line of fire.

At least #1's lost hose was still out there in the way of the intruders, flailing and thrashing about like a live thing.

The new intruder pulled a grenade from his belt, armed it, and tossed it into the doorway. A second later Ross heard the *whoosh* of a grenade explosion—like the sound of someone lighting a gas stove, only a lot louder—and a thin white smoke cloud appeared. The wild hose dropped to the deck, punctured by a multitude of debris fragments, its pressure gone.

The second intruder walked aft through the door. Blood trickled from his ears as a result of the grenade's concussive effect, but he paid it no attention. HT3 Charley Ross, lying half stunned and bloody in the puddle of sea water where the grenade had thrown him, saw the man go past.

The first intruder rose to his feet. He was bruised, but not hurt. He found his weapon and followed his companion. A second later the sound of firing—a burst of two, a burst of three—started up again. Not until it had stopped did Charley Ross dare to pull himself upright and go stumbling away from Repair Five.

Frame 70, USS *Cushing*
Off Kundur Island, Indonesia
103° 35' 6" E/00° 19' 54" N
2231 Local/1531 Zulu

With the gong-note of General Quarters—and the percussive thud of running feet—filling his ears, Master Chief Morrison headed for his GQ station in Missile Control. The press of hurrying bodies in the passageways thinned out rapidly as the other sailors found their own stations. He was just forward of frame 70 when he heard a burst of loud popping noises coming from the next level up.

Small arms fire, he thought. *Intruders.*

Scarcely had he formed the thought when a body tumbled down the ladder onto the deck: ET2 Harness, the roving patrol. Harness had been shot a number of times—there was no doubt in Morrison's mind that the man was dead—but he still had his .45 and two magazines on his belt.

Whoever killed him, Morrison thought, *is going to be showing up here any minute.*

Morrison abandoned the idea of continuing onward to Missile Control. If *Cushing* already had intruders on board, the problem wasn't one that could be solved by having someone throw missiles at it. He ran his hands down Harness's body, his hands suddenly slick with hot liquid, feeling for the man's pistol belt. The belt was rough beneath his hands. He braced his feet against the bulkhead and pushed to get to the holster. He unsnapped the flap and drew the weapon. Then he scrabbled to the other side to search for magazines in their pouch. Moving fast, he faded back to put two corners between himself and the ladder well. If anyone wanted to get to the Special Weapons spaces, they'd have to come through him.

From that vantage point, if anyone came his way he'd see them turning the corner before they got a good look in his direction. He had time now to lock and load, take the safety off, get into an ambush position . . . intensely aware, all the while, that he wasn't at his GQ station.

Anybody asks why, I'll explain the whole thing at my court-martial.

Second deck, portside, USS *Cushing*
Off Kundur Island, Indonesia
103° 35' 6" E/00° 19' 54" N
2234 Local/1534 Zulu

Captain Warner left his cabin and headed for CIC. The door to *Cushing*'s Combat Information Center was a quick-acting watertight door set directly aft of the Captain's Sea Cabin. Like the Bridge door, it proved blistered and hot to the touch. Warner put his foot against the door's lever and pushed it all the way down with his shoe sole, dogging the door down hard.

A ladder led downward past CIC to the main deck. Warner pulled the pins on the hatch support, lowered the hatch to close off the ladder well to the deck below, and cranked down on the dogs. Then he returned to his cabin and tried the bitch box a second time.

"Main, Captain," he said. "Believe we have a fire in Combat and on the Bridge. What's your status?"

"Not yet manned. Repair Five reported armed intruders, then lost comms."

"Fuck," Warner said, off mike, then pressed his key. "You have the conn. Away the SAT and BAF."

"Away the SAT and BAF, aye. Course to steer?"

Warner thought back to the chart. "090, and come dead in the water."

"Zero niner zero, DIW, aye."

"See if you can get a messenger up to Radio Central. Put out a distress call, all freqs, in the clear, max power. Reach me on the 2JZ."

"2JZ aye."

Warner sat back on his rack. A storm blowing in, no comms, and fire and explosions on board . . . this was more excitement than he'd strictly bargained for on the cruise home.

Dimly, he could hear the 1MC, probably from IC Central, calling "Security alert, security alert."

Security alert. Probable intruders. He turned to the little safe set into the right hand side of his desk and spun the dial. In the back of the safe, wrapped in an old tee shirt, was the CO's personal weapon: a standard US government model 1911A .45 semiautomatic.

Civilians on board. Relying on him, and here he was, dragging out a pistol. Rest easy, America . . . and this was all the protection he'd been able to give them.

"I'm sorry," he said. He inserted the magazine and pulled back the slide.

The alert would make going to GQ just that little bit tougher. But he had confidence in his crew. They'd be looking to him for guidance. He'd have to provide it. The Tigers . . . the Tigers would be all right. Laura was with them, and Laura would cope.

Gliding through everything, like a swan on calm water . . . he'd think about Laura again later, when he had more time.

Warner opened the drawer below his rack and pulled out a pair of sound-powered phones, a head and chest set. He plugged the phones into a socket, dialed the 2JZ circuit, and listened to the talkers' chatter. He closed his eyes, and took in the reports, building a picture of what was happening on his ship, like a chess master playing a blindfolded game against a dozen opponents.

The situation was bad, he knew . . . just how bad, depended as much on whether word got out to the carrier task force as it did on *Cushing*'s own response. Worst case, the word didn't get out at all, and *Cushing* had to fight alone against fire and intruders in the midst of a howling storm.

If word did get back to the rest of the task group, though, things might not be so bad. Davy Mayland might be ambitious and egotistical—not to mention bad-tempered—but he could be counted

on to back up a fellow-sailor when the going got rough, and that
qualified him as one of the good guys.

Warner remembered the first time he'd had to count on Mayland for backup in a tight situation. Warner had been a Lieutenant
on *Wally Wood* when it went into the yards at San Diego for exten-
sive repairs and refitting. The San Diego yardbirds—civilian shipyard employees; also sandcrabs, because they were sidewalking
beach creatures—rendered *Wally Wood*'s main gun completely and
totally All Fucked Up when they decided to strip the gun mount
for cleaning by heating up one of the jammed pins in the breech
block with a blowtorch. Which worked just fine, until the time came
to put the mount back together, and the breech block was no longer
usable because the temper of the metal had been destroyed by the
heat.

That had been barely a month before a major deployment, and
the four-striper in charger of DESRON 1 had said to then-
Lieutenant Commander Mayland, "Tell *Wallace Wood* they've got
two weeks to fix it and I don't care how." Mayland had passed the
hot potato on to Warner, as the commissioned officer most directly
concerned with *Wally Wood*'s guns, along with the unwelcome intelligence that *Wallace Wood* no longer had sufficient money in her
OPTAR—the operational part of the ship's budget—to pay for a
new breech block.

"So what am I supposed to do?" Lieutenant Warner had in-
quired of Lieutenant Commander Mayland. "Spin straw out of gold
and pay for it that way?"

"Whatever it takes," Mayland had replied. "My ass is on the
line here, too."

"Whatever it takes, aye," Warner had said.

Looked at that way, the answer turned out to be fairly simple.
Money was money—it all came from the same place, it all went to
the same place, it all stayed in the Navy. So acquiring a new breech

block was merely a matter of finding a ship that was out at sea and sending in a NAVSUP Form 1250 with that ship's OPTAR number on it, along with all the codes for rush delivery—it wouldn't do for the other ship to pull back in and find a piece of gear that they'd never ordered waiting for them on the pier.

"You're *flying* it in?" Mayland demanded after Warner told him about the plan. "Why not send up flares, too, and put an announcement in the Plan of the Day?"

"Don't worry. Nobody's going to think twice about it—we're talking about a hi-pri piece of gear. Besides, if we're going to work this maneuver everything has to happen fast."

" 'We?' "

"That's the other part of the plan. In case of trouble."

"Tell me more about this 'we' part, Lieutenant."

"It's like I told you," Warner said. "We're sending a sailor down to the airport to meet the flight the part's coming in on. There shouldn't be any trouble—he's got all the paperwork he needs to pick it up, and anyway he's the best liar on the ship—"

"Second best," Mayland said.

"Yeah," said Warner, "but I can't do the airport bit. I have to be waiting in a phone booth back at the shipyard, so that if my guy does get into trouble, I can pretend to be the weapons boss on the ship he's pretending to be a gunner's mate on. That's where you come in."

"You want to involve me in this mess? Lieutenant, I've already lost count of the number of federal crimes you're planning to commit."

"Six . . . no, seven. I need you to stand by in another phone booth in case I have to tell somebody that if they don't believe *me*, they can call the COMPACFLT Duty Officer for confirmation."

"You need me to do *what*?"

Davy Mayland had all but turned red and squawked, so acute was his outrage. He'd come through in the end, though, manning his phone and standing by to lie like a trooper. As it happened, the entire evolution had gone smoothly—more smoothly, in fact, than many that were twice as honest—and the difficult repair job had ended up reflecting well on Mayland and Warner both.

He owes me, Warner thought now, as he listened to the reports coming in over the sound-powered phones. *If he gets the word, he'll come through.*

Forward Sonar Equipment Room, USS *Cushing*
103° 35' 6" E/00° 19' 54" N
2234 Local/1534 Zulu

Electronics Technician 2nd Class Dixon sat in the pedestal chair at his GQ station in the Forward Sonar Equipment Room, where he was standing by to repair damage to the transducers and electronics. Dixon was worried—it wasn't like the Captain to schedule a drill for the middle of the night during a storm with a bunch of dependents on board—and to make things worse he hadn't heard from anyone in Sonar Control since he'd arrived at his station. Then the Security Alert sounded, and he started switching his phones from Control to 2JZ, listening to the chatter for a couple of seconds, then switching back, in the hope of discovering just what the fuck was going on.

What he found out didn't make him feel any happier: "We have a fire in Combat and on the Bridge." . . . "Repair Five reported armed intruders, then lost comms." . . . "Put out a distress call, all freqs, in the clear, max power."

ET2 Dixon thought about that last bit for a minute. Fire in CIC and on the Bridge, combined with armed intruders, might well mean that Radio Central had also gotten hit. If such were the case, the Captain's distress call might never get sent, and everyone aboard USS *Cushing*—*including Dad*, ET2 Dixon thought; *I should never have invited him to come along on this cruise*—everyone was shit out of luck.

Or maybe not quite. The SQS-26 sonar normally makes a multi-tone signal when it's actively pinging, and no sound at all in passive listening mode. Most ASW—Anti-Submarine Warfare—ships remain in passive mode all the time, since in active mode a sub can hear a ship coming from roughly twice as far away as the ship can detect the sub in turn.

But still, the sonar is able to send meaningful sound, and in two ways. One is by CW clicks—you can do Morse that way, if you happen to know Morse. The other way is with hydrophones, which allow you to talk and have your voice hugely amplified underwater, so that other sonar operators can hear you.

One of the amusing things you can do with hydrophones and a submarine is turn on the 'phones, then switch on an electric shaver a couple of feet away from the mike and move it slowly closer. To a sub, the resulting noise sounds just like an incoming torpedo. For the ASW vessel, watching the speed and turning maneuvers the sub makes in response is a world of fun.

What Dixon had just heard over the SP phones, however, was distinctly not fun. He picked up the handset for the hydrophone, and started talking.

"This is USS *Cushing*, DD985. Position—" Dixon checked *Cushing*'s position on the dead reckoning tracer; the DRT's reading would be close to their actual position—maybe not an exact fix, but close "—position, 103 degrees 35 minutes 6 seconds east by 00 degrees 19 minutes 54 seconds north. We have armed intruders aboard. Request assistance."

Then he repeated the message. He decided that broadcasting a request for assistance once every five minutes would just about do the job.

He looked at his watch and settled back, feet braced against the bulkhead. It was going to be a long night, and offhand, he'd say that the odds of getting a fresh cup of coffee were very low. But he was going to do his duty.

"Any vessel, this is USS *Cushing*, position 103 degrees 35 minutes 6 seconds east by 00 degrees 19 minutes 54 seconds north. We have armed intruders aboard. Request assistance."

16

HMAS *Sheean* lay in the mud on the bottom of the Singapore Strait. *Sheean*, a *Collins*-class submarine of Her Majesty's Australian Navy, had been lurking in the same location for nearly three months, monitoring traffic through the Strait and gathering intelligence on local activity. Now, at nearly the end of the midwatch, the sonar tech on duty looked up from the clipboard where he was tallying ships' propellers by number, and said, "Mr. Crusoe, I think you should hear this."

The duty officer carried his coffee cup with him over to the sonar bench. "What is it?"

"This, sir."

The sonar tech rewound the large tape, the secondary, a few seconds, and set it to play. What came out was a voice message, garbled but clear enough.

"... USS *Cushing*, position 103 degrees 35 minutes 6 seconds east by 00 degrees 19 minutes 54 seconds north . . . armed intruders aboard . . . assistance."

"What else do you have?" Crusoe asked the sonar tech.

"Machinery signature consistent with a United States *Spruance*-class DD, sir."

"Damn. Well, I'll go wake the Skipper. Keep on listening."

Third deck, USS *Cushing*
Off Kundur Island, Indonesia
103° 35' 6" E/00° 19' 54" N
2245 Local/1545 Zulu

"Security Alert."

GMGSN Stryker rolled away from his GQ station at Gun Mount 52, aft, and hurried forward to the small arms locker. His goal was to unlock the locker to supply the SAT and BAF with their weapons. The rain was whipping down heavily now on the weather decks. The talker had been unable to establish comms with the Gun Director or the Bridge, though he could talk with Mount 51 forward and most of the other weapons spaces fore and aft.

Stryker continued forward, only to stop and press into the non-tight door at *Cushing*'s gedunk. Up ahead, he heard men talking, and they weren't talking English. Then he heard a burst of automatic fire. That was bad—armed intruders, blocking the way that he needed to go. The small arms locker was up in that direction, and the SAT would be there soon, looking for pistols.

Stryker knew what to do. He knew where the corridor light switch was located. Right now it was switched into the regular night-time red position, so that no one going down the main deck midships passage would have his night vision destroyed. But the light switch could also be put in the full dark position—and with the lights out, the inside of a passageway at night is pretty darned black.

He hit the switch and ducked low, pulling his Buck folding knife from his belt as he did so, and began crawling forward in the dark. He counted knee knockers as he passed through door frames, still heading for the small arms locker.

Maritime Headquarters, Sydney
151° 10' E/33° 56' S
0245 Local/1545 Zulu

Two o'clock in the morning, Commander Weir always said, is a lousy time for anything to happen on a duty night. So it was, inevitably, 0245 when the phone call came in. Weir in turn had to phone Mr. H. Potter from civilian intelligence and get him moving.

"There's been a development," Weir said, "and the powers that be said that you ought to be informed. Sorry, can't say anything more by phone. I've probably said too much already."

After that came some waiting, until Potter arrived, shaking rain from his hat. The weather outside was turning nasty, the sign of a big storm system in the offing.

"Well," said Potter, "what have we got that's worth calling a man out in this weather?"

"Message from our sub *Sheean*," Weir said. "On a sneak-and-peek off Jakarta. Popped up the aerial and sent us a sonogram. It checks, consistent with known units and capabilities. Thought you'd like to evaluate it."

He replayed the recorded transmission. Once again, the words came: ". . . USS *Cushing*, position 103 degrees 35 minutes 6 seconds east by 00 degrees 19 minutes 54 seconds north . . . armed intruders aboard . . . assistance."

"And you say the other noise was consistent with the ship they say they were?"

"That's right," said Weir. "Lots of surface noise—they have a big storm going on up there—but after enhancement, it's pretty clear."

"What's their game?"

"Who, the Yanks?"

"No, the Indonesians. Any possibility that this is a spoof?"

"Always a possibility."

"Then there's nothing official we can do," Potter said. "Since we aren't officially there to hear. But inform the American OTC—who is it?"

"Mayland," Weir said. "USS *Nimitz*."

"Right. Get to him, back channel. And activate Major Mac-Gillivray aboard *Tobruk*."

"Too right," Weir said. "He's got a contingency order. If Special Weapons are on board, they are not to fall into unfriendly hands. All levels of violence are acceptable to carry out his mission."

"You mean—"

"It wouldn't do to say anything, if you might be asked to testify . . . but Donnie understands."

Second deck, portside, USS *Cushing*
Off Kundur Island, Indonesia
103° 5' 6" E/00° 19' 54" N
2250 Local/1550 Zulu

Chris's mother was already sitting at the table in Chiefs' Quarters when he got there, a cup of coffee in her hand, looking serene and unmussed. Chris wasn't reassured; his mother only looked that calm for hurricanes and car wrecks and acts of war. H. L. Morrison was there, too, dressed in loose shorts and an oversized tee shirt—probably her sleeping gear—with her feet shoved, sockless, into a pair of running shoes. She looked either scared or excited—Chris couldn't tell which from her expression, but he had his suspicions.

Wonderful, he thought. *The Master Chief's kid is an action junkie. Just what we needed.*

The ship heeled to starboard. Over the 1MC came the word, "Security Alert!" Whoever was talking sounded excited, in defiance of all Naval tradition.

"What do you suppose is going on?" one of the older Tigers asked.

"It's trouble," H. L. replied. "General Quarters, a security alert, all in the middle of the night; we've got to be ready to—"

The ripping sound of a machine pistol firing on full automatic cut through the air from outside the compartment.

"—secure the doors and prepare to hold this space."

A smell of smoke drifted in from the overhead vents.

H. L. was on her way to the door when it opened from the outside. Two men stood there, not sailors, not at all. They were dressed in motley cammies, they looked Oriental, and they carried small weapons with large magazines.

"Back inside, get down, all of you," one of them said in decent enough English.

In case he wasn't understood, he fired a quick burst into the overhead, causing some arcing and sparking from the lights.

The other man spoke into a handheld radio. The language he used wasn't one that Chris understood, or even recognized, but it didn't take a genius to figure out what he had to be saying.

Hey, boss. Looks like we've got some hostages.

Captain's sea cabin, USS *Cushing*
Off Kundur Island, Indonesia
103° 5' 6" E/00° 19' 54" N
2250 Local/1550 Zulu

Captain Warner sat at the desk in his sea cabin, the SP phone headset in place.

He closed his eyes and tilted back his head, visualizing the lay-out of the ship. "Main, Captain," he said over the 2JZ, "Is DCC manned yet?"

"No reports," Main replied. "Based on what we have, Captain, the midships area, from the electronic warfare deck down to the DC deck, appears to be in the hands of armed intruders."

"Very well," Warner said, for all that he didn't think it was very well at all. "Keep me informed. I'll be maintaining my current lo-cation for as long as possible. I'll inform you if I move."

That was no joke. The doors that led away to the Bridge and CIC were both hot to the touch, showing the possibility of fire to either side of him. The hatch leading down to the next deck likely took him past armed intruders. But the sound-powered phone lines would at least allow him to stay in touch and keep going.

"Interrogative, can you get an investigator to the Pilothouse, moving outside the skin of the ship, and get a report? See if he can find any local charts. Take them back down to Main."

"We'll send someone," Main replied.

"Keep me posted. Don't waste lives going up against intruders until you have weapons. Any chance of getting to the Armory?"

"We're working on it, Captain."

"Very well."

A few moments later, another thought struck him.

"Main, Captain, can you cut power to all lighting circuits above the DC deck? I suspect the crew knows its way around in the dark better than the intruders do."

"Aye aye, Captain. We can do that from Electrical Central."

"Make it so."

"Yes, sir."

The ship took a sudden heavy roll as the phone clicked off. Warner pulled the bar that kept him from rolling out of bed from its place in the drawer under his bunk, and set it into the holder on the side of his bunk. Then he lay down, still wearing the phones.

He listened, switching from 1JV to 2JZ to JL, and back. The picture he was building up in his mind wasn't pretty.

The whole midships portion of his command from the lowest complete deck up was in enemy hands, and he still had no idea who the enemy even was. Or what they were after—

"The nukes," Warner whispered, and suddenly knew why the intruders had come aboard. "Somebody's after my nukes."

Well, he thought unhappily, *that* insight certainly clarified the motives and probable actions of the intruders. They would have to take the ship and take it whole, then steer it to a location where cranes existed to take the weapons off.

Hard on the heels of the first realization came a second one: The Tigers were in the part of the ship that was occupied. That meant that they were, or soon would be, hostages.

All of them. Even though none had volunteered to be casualties in the terrorism wars. At least the sailors had stuck their right hands in the air and taken the oath with their eyes open. But the Tigers . . . Laura and Chris . . . and the people in San Francisco who could never sleep easy again if international terrorists had the big ones.

Weighed against the prospect of nuclear weapons getting into those eager, and all too willing, hands, the hostages—even Chris; even Laura—were insignificant. As was *Cushing* itself, and everyone aboard.

After Steering, USS *Cushing*
Between Durai and Bangbesar Islands, Indonesia
103° 55' 8" E/00° 30' 1" N
2300 Local/1600 Zulu

Tommy J. Raveneau didn't get really worried until the fluores-cent lights went out in After Steering.

He'd been asleep in his rack when the General Quarters alarm went off, and he'd gone to his GQ station along with the rest of the crew. The whole time he was pulling on his clothes and hurrying out of engineering berthing and joining the purposeful stream of crew members moving through the ship's passages, he'd still figured that the whole thing was some kind of unannounced drill.

Or maybe, he'd thought as he descended the final ladder into *Cushing*'s after steering compartment, *all the excitement is a demonstration laid on to impress the civilians on board.*

A stupid idea, if that was really what was going on; but as far as Raveneau could tell, the Navy had a lot of stupid ideas.

After Steering lay far back and down in the very stern of the vessel. It was a cramped, irregularly shaped compartment whose sides were the inner side of the skin of the ship, all sheet metal and rivets and structural frames, painted terra cotta because the space belonged to the Engineering department. There was no solid deck, either, only an open metal grating above the bilges. The air stank of machinery and rotting sludge, and vibrated with the noise of the ship's screws.

This was the compartment where the commands for steering the ship were carried out. The ship's tiller was here, with the rudder itself only a few feet away in the water outside. Heavy electric cables ran down into After Steering from above, connecting the tiller's hydraulic mechanism to the controls on *Cushing*'s Bridge. Between the cables, on the forward bulkhead, stood a gyro repeater, the rudder angle indicator, and a small bronze ship's wheel—the "trick wheel" that enabled the men in after steering to control the ship, if necessary, without electrical signals from the bridge.

Tommy J wasn't supposed to be the only guy in the space when the ship went to General Quarters. Watson and Davis, a couple of boatswain's mates, were supposed to share it with him, but they hadn't shown up. Tommy J felt virtuous about this for a couple of minutes. Usually he was the last person to get there, not the first.

Then—since he was already at his GQ station and couldn't go anywhere else—he pulled out a well-thumbed copy of *Penthouse* from its storage space in a box that should have held gas masks, braced his back against one of the frames, and settled down to revisit the pictures in the feature spread. He'd just opened the centerfold when the fluorescent lights in the overhead went out and the battery-operated crimson battle lanterns kicked in.

"Shit," he said.

All the lights going like that pretty much ruled out any chance of this being a drill. Maybe the problem was something that damage control could handle—but as the minutes crawled by in the shadowy red-lit darkness, Tommy J became more and more convinced that it wasn't.

Worse, it was starting to look like Watson and Davis weren't ever going to show up, which was a prospect that Tommy J didn't care for much at all. He knew perfectly well that he wasn't assigned to this particular station because it was an important one. He was down here because After Steering, as GQ stations went, was like deep left field in grade-school softball—a place where nothing much ever happened, where the kids in charge stashed people they didn't want to put anywhere else. That didn't mean he could skip showing up here, and he hadn't, and he didn't think Watson and Davis would have either.

"Either they make it, or they don't," he said aloud. The compartment was so noisy that if he hadn't felt the words vibrating in his throat, he might as well have stayed silent. Saying the words, though, helped him to think. "And if they've got a good reason for not being here, then that's okay, unless they're hurt or something, but I can't do anything about that. And if they *don't* have a good reason, then the Chief will rip them both a new asshole, but that's not my problem either, because I'm down here where I'm supposed to be."

Tommy J considered the situation for a bit longer, then

shrugged and put on the headset for the sound-powered phones. If he listened for long enough, he thought, eventually someone was bound to tell him what was going on—and what it was that he needed to do.

17

GMGSN Stryker lay in the shadow of a ladder on the second
deck. He wasn't armed—not exactly. The only weapons that he carried were his Buck knife and a key ring with the keys to all of
Cushing's weapons lockers and armories. Lots of potential firepower
there.

If anything happened to him, no one would be getting into
those lockers at all. Wihout someone getting into them—without
him, Ryan Stryker, staying alive and getting from second deck to
someplace more useful—no one on shipboard would have weapons
except the enemy.

Whoever the enemy was. He still didn't know who the intruders
were or where they'd come from. Charley Ross had been in Repair
Five when they'd hit there; Stryker had bumped into him—liter-
ally—as Ross was staggering away from the mess decks, and had
conscripted the hull technician into his private squad of one.

Now Ross lay in the shadows a few feet away from Stryker, telling his story over again.

"The whole thing was fucking fucked up," Ross said. His teeth were chattering. "I don't know who those fuckers are, but they sure as fuck aren't fucking around."

"What did they do?"

"They killed Joey Pelletier, and after that they shot anybody who was moving."

"How many of them? What kind of weapons?"

"Fucking *machine* guns, man . . . I saw two guys. I don't know where they came from, or who they are. They came through, and I got the fuck out."

"Yeah, yeah." Stryker was trying to figure the situation out for himself. How many intruders, with how many magazines? How many bullets? Not that it really mattered. One man could carry enough rounds to shoot everyone on board. Two men could carry enough rounds to shoot everyone twice.

The lights in the corridor flickered and went out, and Ross yelped, "What the fuck?"

"Our chance to move," Stryker said.

The battle lanterns clicked in with their red glow. Somebody had just done for the whole ship what he had done earlier with the lights for a single corridor. At least he wasn't the only person still thinking and doing things.

The thought cheered Stryker up quite a bit. "Do you know where the nearest bad guy is?"

"Over by the goat locker—why?"

"Can we go back to Repair Five and grab a portable welding rig? Once we get our hands on one weapon, finding a second one's going to be a whole lot easier."

"Yeah," Ross said. "I can do that."

"I'm coming with you."

Bridge, USS *Cushing*
Off Sumatra, Indonesia
103° 57' 06" E/00° 19' 48" N
2401 Local/1701 Zulu

Lieutenant Ernie Gilano wondered why his shoulder hurt so much. Then—for a brief moment, when the only other thing he knew besides the pain was the feeling of water striking against his skin and his open mouth—he wondered why he was in a swimming pool. Then he came fully awake, and wondered what to do next.

He seemed to be lying face down, though without a clear memory of how he had come to be in that position, and his body didn't seem to want to get up. Something was probably broken in his left leg. He hurt all over and felt awful, and a set of racking coughs didn't help.

Slowly he oriented himself. He was on *Cushing*'s Bridge. The ship was rocking and rolling, and rain was lashing in through broken windows. That was where the water had come from to strike against his face.

Broken windows . . . there had been an attack. As his mind cleared, he had vague memories of heavy footsteps tramping onto the bridge, and the loud popping noise of a pistol firing twice, and voices speaking back and forth in a language he didn't know. Intruders . . . and intruders aboard meant the ship ought to be at General Quarters.

Gilano's GQ station was at Forward Missile. He pushed himself starboard in a painful crawl. Forward Missile was down from the Bridge, and you go up and forward to starboard, down and aft to port. To go down he'd have to go up and over first.

The non-tight door back to the interior passage was jammed, and he didn't have the strength to stand and put his full weight into opening it. He continued crawling.

As he crawled, he brushed his hand against the cables and pipes that ran along the after bulkhead—counting them, trying to keep himself on track—until he came to the rifle locker. Weapons were kept there for use in anti-shark drill and anti-mine drill, and because a warship should have the means to counter all manner of threats.

The Bridge weapons locker aboard USS *Cushing* contained two M14 rifles, a line-throwing attachment, and some ammo magazines. The Greenleaf and Sergeant lock—a heavy, high security armored shackle padlock—answered to a key on the Officer of the Deck's key ring, passed along from watch to watch and currently hanging from Gilano's belt.

He groped for the key in the dark, found it, and pushed himself up again onto his hands and knees. Leaning heavily against the bulkhead for support, he slid in the key and felt the solid *chunk* of the lock opening. He unlaced the shackle and swung the locker open, then took out the nearer, closer to centerline, rifle, along with a magazine from the tray beneath the buttstocks inside the locker. A feel across the top of the magazine told him these were live rounds, rather than the crimps that the line-thrower needed.

Gilano inserted the magazine into the rifle, pulled out another loaded magazine from the tray, and stuffed it into the slit pocket of his khaki working jacket. He jacked a round into the chamber, pulling back the bolt and letting it fly forward—all done while lying on his back, because the moves were less painful that way—then rolled to the door to the starboard Bridgewing and pushed himself out.

The ladder up to the Signal Bridge was not more than five feet away. He headed—crawled—in that direction, pushing with his feet, breathing between each push. One time he found himself waking up again, and supposed that he must have fainted. Loss of blood? Maybe—he knew he was hurt. Or maybe not blood loss after all, since he'd come back. It must have been the pain.

He was at the ladder now, and leaning against its risers, looking up. The clean rain here knocked the burnt smell of the Pilothouse interior away from him.

The salt taste in the rain was either spray from the pitching, or blood. Nothing to do about it either way, so he wiped his mouth against his sleeve—more salt, and a burnt taste—dragged the rifle to him, and switched off the safety. Then he rolled onto the Bridge ladder and pushed with his legs, allowing his hands to rise along the treads, then curl and hold on while he drew up his legs.

It was a long way up. The top of the ladder wasn't in sight. But the sounds of the storm drowned out the sound of his movements, the clang of the rifle barrel against the railing. He thought about his wounds, and figured that he wouldn't make it. But at last he was lying on a deck again, its surface all rough with nonskid, and knew that he was on the Signal Bridge, with his GQ station not too far away.

Frame 70, USS *Cushing*
Off Sumatra, Indonesia
103° 57' 12" E/00° 19' 35" N
2405 Local/1705 Zulu

Automatic in hand, Master Chief Morrison waited around the corner from a thwartship passageway, looking for someone who wasn't wearing Navy Blue to come by. He was fairly sure that somebody would.

He sat under a ladderback, supporting his forearms on his knees, braced and ready. The flood of crew members heading to their GQ stations had long since ebbed. No one came around the corner. Everyone who was going to make it to their station was there by now, and no one had a station on the portside second deck passageway.

"Hey, Master Chief, what are you doing?"

Morrison heard the voice—familiar, and talking in English—

before the speaker came into view. All the same he tensed, and didn't relax until he saw that the newcomer was HT3 Vance.

Vance was an investigator from Repair 2; he had an oxygen breathing apparatus slung around his neck, with the OBA's cartridge screwed into the chest plate but the starter candle not pulled. Another sailor followed along behind him, holding his safety line.

"There's intruders," Morrison said.

"Shit. How many? Where?"

"Don't know, but they were on the main deck starboard side about the time GQ went. Armed with automatic weapons. I'm holding this area. Go back and report."

"Right, Master Chief."

Vance and the guy holding his safety line faded back forward. The door they'd come through was dogged down behind them.

Morrison stayed where he was, waiting.

Bridge, HMAS *Tobruk*
112° E/19° S
0005 Local/1705 Zulu

"**The Yanks appear to have lost a ship,**" Major Donald MacGillivray said to *Tobruk*'s Captain. "Canberra wants us to go and make sure the right people find it."

The Captain looked at Major MacGillivray and Lieutenant Burke. *SASR and Naval Intelligence*, he thought. *Somebody out there is looking at bad trouble.*

"Not exactly your usual sort of Search and Rescue," he commented aloud.

The Major nodded. "You've got that right."

"Can we have a look at the chart table?" Lieutenant Burke asked. "We need to work out a place or two."

"Be my guest," the Captain said. "I suppose you can't be any more specific about what's going on."

"No," said the Major. "Sorry. I could explain everything, but then I'd have to put your head in my safe."

"I understand."

The Captain switched on the red light above the chart table. The Major looked at the chart and shook his head.

"This won't do," he said. "Where we're looking at isn't here."

"Mark our posit," Lieutenant Burke said. She traced the dead reckoning line with her finger, then took a pair of dividers to measure the current latitude and longitude.

Tobruk's Captain spoke to the Quartermaster of the Watch. "Could you bring me a small-scale chart of the region?"

"Aye aye," said the Quartermaster, and faded into the blackness.

A moment later, the QMOW was back. "Want me to get this aligned, Captain?"

"No, we can handle that."

The Captain laid the new chart out on the table, and Lieutenant Burke put a mark on the chart at their current location. The Major pointed to a location up near the Strait of Malacca.

"Right," he said. "I want to get up here."

"Can't do that," the Captain said at once. "It's beyond the operational range of any helo we carry."

"It's in range if it's a one-way trip," the Major said.

The Captain looked resigned. "Then I don't suppose I have any choice. Will you be wanting a pilot too?"

"Thank you, Captain, no. I brought my own."

"Thoughtful of you," said the Captain. Then he raised his voice and called out, "Messenger!"

The Messenger of the Watch appeared at his elbow. The crewman's face was lurid and ghostly in the reflected crimson light.

"Take the Lieutenant over to air ops for a briefing," the Captain ordered.

"Aye aye, Captain," the messenger said. "Ma'am, follow me please."

"And now, Major, can I offer you anything else?" the Captain said.

"No, just the thing I asked for, as soon as possible."

"You'll have it. That serious, is it?"

"The lads at Maritime Headquarters think so," the Major said. "And it's their job to worry."

18

Captain Andrew Warner heard a knock at the door of his sea cabin, and tensed. Knocking was the act of somebody familiar with the ship, and with its complex rituals of rank and privacy, but an enemy could hide behind those rituals just as well. He moved to the corner where he'd be out of sight from the opening door, and braced his .45 in a two-handed grip.

The door knob turned. The non-tight door swung open, revealing, to Warner's considerable relief, a figure wearing the chest plate and mask of an Oxygen Breathing Apparatus beneath the red helmet of an investigator. The investigator's lifeline trailed on the deck behind him—connecting him, Warner knew, to his tender, following along some twenty feet or so back.

Warner lowered the .45 and stepped forward to meet the new arrival. "What's up?"

"Investigator, Repair Two," the man said. "Conditions in the space?"

His words were muffled by the mask, and Warner heard the timer on the OBA clicking. The light on the man's helmet shone against the bulkheads as he turned his head from side to side.

"Conditions in this space are normal," said Warner. "Any intruders below here?"

"Yes, sir," said the investigator. "But there's a clear path down to Repair Two. Want to get out of here?"

"Sure thing. Probable fire in CIC and in the Pilothouse."

"Already reported CIC. I'll get up to the Pilothouse in a second." The investigator backed out of the sea cabin, his tender maintaining interval behind him, and made his way up the ladder. Warner left his cabin and followed.

Outside, the ladder well was lit by portable battle lanterns. A four-man hose team was getting set up to put a stream of high-pressure spray onto the watertight door to CIC. At the same time, a low pressure fog nozzle came up the ladder well from below and provided cooling water to protect the team.

Until the team cleared the ladder well, however, there was no way down to Repair Two, regardless of what the investigator had said. Instead, Warner followed the investigator up to the Bridge.

He waited at the after end of the passageway while the investigator put the back of his hand first near the door, then near the knob, and nodded to his tender. In case things turned out badly, the backup would be able to report the last thing that the investigator had found.

"Door's cool," the investigator said. "Opening Pilothouse door."

He put his shoulder against the door and it swung open. On the Bridge, everything was dark, and wind and rain swirled in through the broken windows.

"Moving forward into Pilothouse," the investigator said. He flipped on the battle lantern he carried in his left hand. Behind him, the tender paid out more of the lifeline attached to the center back of the man's OBA rig.

"Numerous casualties," the investigator called out. "Let's get a stretcher party up here to move 'em to forward aid. Backing out."

"Backing out aye," the tender repeated, and began to take up line.

Warner moved forward, edging past the investigator. "I'll be on the Bridge," he told the man as he went by, "or on my way to Repair Two."

"On the Bridge aye," the investigator said. "I'll let 'em know below."

Main Engineering, USS *Cushing*
Entering Lingga Archipelago, Indonesia
104° 10' E/00° 04' 30" N
0055 Local/1755 Zulu

Down in the ship's bowels, in *Cushing*'s **main engineering com-**partment, the air was sharp with the smells of ozone and hot metal. An electric welding rod shone blue-white against the dull crimson glow of the battle lanterns. Finally the white light went out, and Hull Technician 1st Class Byrne lifted his mask.

"Got it," he said. "That's the last one."

"Right," said the Engineering Officer of the Watch—Lieutenant Commander Raymond, *Cushing*'s Chief Engineer, a solid, heavyset African-American. Like everybody else in the hole, he was sweating profusely in the heat thrown off by the operation of the ship's power plant. "Report to the Skipper, hatches welded shut."

"Captain, Main," the 2JZ talker said. "All hatches welded shut."

"All right then," said Raymond. "The engineering spaces are isolated. Get me a count on the people down here, and the status of all machinery."

"As long as we don't hit a reef," Fireman Pete Santini muttered under his breath. With the hatches welded shut, Main Control had the potential to become a metal coffin for the men who worked there.

Another crew member—Machinist's Mate 1st Class Clay—said to Santini, "Hey, if we hit a reef, we aren't getting out of here anyway."

Machinist's Mate Chief Bob Otto frowned at the two sailors. "Enough of that, guys. Everybody—get your gas masks out, and get 'em fitted. I want to see everyone wearin' 'em. Suck a vacuum on 'em. If the bad guys have gas and figure out where our ventilators are, you're gonna have about one second to get the masks into place."

The crew members down in Engineering all had USN Mk VII gas masks in pouches hanging from their belts on the right-hand side. They'd picked them up from the gas mask lockers when the General Quarters alarm sounded. Now, with only a little grumbling, they put the gas masks on.

"All secure," Chief Otto said to LCDR Raymond. The Chief hung on to one of the overhead pipes as he spoke. The ship's motion was growing stronger, even this deep inside the vessel, where the rolling and pitching could only hint at what must be going on outside.

"Captain says, bare steerageway," the 2JZ talker called out.

"Bare steerageway, aye," LCDR Raymond replied, and nodded at the Chief. "You heard the man, make turns for five knots."

"Turns for five knots." Chief Otto passed along the order, then said to LCDR Raymond, "Let me know how she's minding the helm."

"I'll let you know as soon as I figure it out," Raymond said, most of his attention already back on the gyro repeater and the rudder angle indicator. "In these seas, we might need a bit more than five knots to maintain steerageway."

He kept on watching the gyro and the rudder. "Cranked over

hard right, still drifting left. Increase speed to make turns for ten knots."

"Captain, Main, making turns for ten knots," the 2JZ talker said over the sound-power phones. Then he stopped.

"Chief," he said, "there's someone else on the line. Want me to put this on the amplified circuit?"

Chief Otto and LCDR Raymond looked at one another briefly. Raymond nodded.

"Do it," Chief Otto said.

The talker switched the box to "amplified." A new voice came into the *Cushing*'s engineering spaces, audible above the sounds of machinery and the muffled tumult of the storm outside.

". . . of *Cushing*," the voice said, "I am in control of this ship. You shall follow my orders, and all will be safe."

Santini stared at the box. "What the *fuck*?"

"Shut the fucking fuck up," Clay advised him. "And listen."

"I have hostages—the civilians on board—" the voice continued. "I have no interest in creating an international incident of a greater magnitude than that which already exists. You were sailing in the exclusive waters of Indonesia, and as a result you have been captured. Now, follow my orders."

"Commander?" Chief Otto said.

"We take our orders from the Captain," Raymond said. "If he's captured or killed, then we take them from the XO. And if *he's* captured or killed, we go to the next senior officer. Who happens to be me. And since an order to surrender is never a legal order while the means of resistance exist, I say that we're going to ignore the motherfucker."

"Ignore motherfucker, aye," the Chief said. "Okay, you guys, get back to work."

Silence fell. After a while Clay said, under his breath, "Hey, Chief, what *do* we do about the Tigers?"

"Offhand," said Otto, "I'd say that right now it sucks to be them."

Bridge, USS *Cushing*
Entering Lingga Archipelago, Indonesia
104° 10' E/00° 04' 30" N
0055 Local/1755 Zulu

Captain Warner stepped forward onto the Bridge. He wanted to see for himself how things stood, what damage his ship had sustained, what could still be salvaged.

He unhooked the battle lantern from the bulkhead beside the Pilothouse door and switched it on. The lens was red, and added a bloody sheen to the smoke-blackened, twisted metal and broken glass of the Pilothouse.

The investigator hadn't been kidding. The Bridge watch team had been wasted. Bodies and parts of bodies covered the deck and a bit of the after bulkhead. The deck was full of trip hazards, too soft to be metal, too mobile to be attached to anything. The air stank of fire, blood, and bowel.

Warner looked around. The starboard wing door was open and slamming back and forth with each roll. With every pitch, sea spray came slamming through the broken windows forward. He could taste the salt water on his lips. At least, he could hope that the salt was seawater, and not blood from the casualties; sea water in these latitudes was warm, not cold.

On the port side of the Bridge, a door on a control panel was also swinging open and closed in time with the rolling of the ship: the SRBOC control. Someone had managed to fire it off. Had they seen the trouble inbound? Not much time to react, but still a good job, even if it hadn't worked.

More motion caught his eye. On the starboard bulkhead, just

aft of the open wing door, the door of the rifle locker was swinging back and forth. Warner walked over to it and pulled the door all the way open. The padlock lay on the deck beside the locker. Inside, one of the two M14 rifles normally stored there was missing.

Someone was alive and moving, and now was armed. Warner pulled back from the door. No telling where that someone was, or what he was planning. Nothing he could do, either, for the men on deck. The corpsman would be up soon to see if anyone was alive, and meanwhile Warner had a whole ship to fight.

He turned to the bitch box, dialed it to Main, and pushed the key. Sound-powered circuits are built tough; maybe the bitch box had survived the hit. "Main, Bridge."

To his relief, a tinny voice answered him over the circuit. "Main, aye."

"This is the Captain. Give me a status check."

"We have comms with you, with all propulsion spaces, with Repair Two. No comms with DCC or anything aft of frame 70 and above the DC Deck. Repair Two reports that Master Chief Morrison is holding at frame 70 portside."

"Very well. Any word from SAT or BAF?"

"That's a negative."

Warner looked around the Bridge again. The bitch box might be working, but the NAVSAT receiver was blown to hell. He wondered where on the face of the ocean *Cushing* might be. The sea was a bit darker than the sky, he thought, but no light showed from anywhere around. The seas were mountainous, and the rain lashed down without stopping.

"What's our speed?" he asked Main.

"Making turns for ten knots."

The depth finder was gone too, and CIC was out.

"What's our heading?"

"Zero-Eight-Six. Rudder orders are coming from Secondary Conn."

"Very well."

Warner flashed his light around the deck. Only one of the casualties was wearing khaki that he could see; the rest all wore blue chambray working uniforms. So—one officer survived, was armed, and was now at secondary conn? He moved right, to the rifle locker, and took out the remaining weapon and a magazine. He inserted the mag, jacked a round into the chamber, and went to sit in his command chair.

"Captain's on the Bridge," he said—but so quietly that even had there been a living quartermaster to keep the log, he would have been hard-pressed to hear the words.

HMAS *Tobruk*
112° E/19° S
0005 Local/1705 Zulu

On board HMAS *Tobruk*, a Sea King Mk 50A helicopter lifted from the deck, wavered in the wind, and turned away into the storm. A moment later, it was gone.

With a gale blowing and a heavy rain slashing on the deck, the sailors on the amphib hadn't been thrilled to go to Flight Quarters, not even a little. Only idiots and madmen would be flying in weather like this, which meant that somewhere out there in the storm was trouble bad enough that only idiots and madmen—and some people claimed that the SASR qualified as both—could handle it.

"What was that all about?" the air boss asked the Captain.

The Captain shrugged. "Either we'll read all about it in the papers, or else we'll never know. I've heard about MacGillivray's lot—the bad boys of Sabre Squadron, if half the stories are true—but I've never seen them at work." He sighed. "Well, write up the report to expend the bird. I don't think we'll be seeing it again."

19

The air in After Steering was dark and still, the blowers shut down. The compartment was hot, and sweat dripped from Tommy J. Raveneau's forehead. Not just from the heat, either—he'd heard the voice of the intruder making his announcement, and understood now why he was the only one who'd made it to After Steering when GQ sounded.

To his relief, another speaker eventually came on over the 1JV circuit, the words crackling in the earphones.

"After Steering, this is Commander Raymond." Raveneau knew LCDR Raymond's voice. He'd heard it often enough, usually expressing displeasure with Tommy J's performance on the job.

"After Steering, aye."

"Raveneau, I want you to get up there and blind-dog the hatch. Don't let anyone in unless I give permission."

"Blind-dog the hatch, aye."

Raveneau, on the end of his twenty-foot SP Phone cord,

climbed the vertical ladder to the hatch. He pulled a dogging wrench from its holder and stuck it through the spokes in the dogging mechanism. The hatch was already dogged down hard, but now no one was going to be able to open it from the other side. The thing was jammed.

"Main, After Steering, hatch blind-dogged."

"Now listen up, Raveneau. If you lose comms with Main Control, I want you to two-block the tiller hard right and leave it there until I personally tell you different."

"Say what two-block?"

"Put the rudder over as far as you can, and leave it."

"After Steering, aye," said Raveneau, then climbed back down the ladder and settled in for another long wait.

Chiefs' Quarters, USS *Cushing*
Approaching Lingga Island, Indonesia
104° 10' 54" E/00° 01' 18" S
0108 Local/1808 Zulu

In Chiefs' Quarters—the "goat locker," as ship's slang had it— the crimson light of the battle lanterns cast murky shadows onto the huddle of civilians and the armed pirate who was guarding them. The man with the submachine gun looked tense and edgy, and the skin of his face glistened with a fine sheen of sweat.

He's new at the hostage game, Laura thought. *One wrong move out of anybody, and he's going to lose it.*

She curled her fingers around her half-empty coffee mug and willed herself not to grip it too tightly. There were eleven other Tigers under guard here in the goat locker, and all of them would be looking to her for reassurance. She was the Captain's Wife, after all. According to the customs of shipboard life, that made her senior among *Cushing*'s embarked dependents.

She'd always hated that kind of rank-by-association. She had professional credentials of her own that she'd worked damned hard to get, and she despised the thought of trading on somebody else's. Right now, however, she was stuck with the job. Andrew would be counting on her to keep things calm with the Tigers while he did . . . while he did whatever it was he was currently doing, somewhere else on the ship.

So far, thank God, nobody had tried to do anything that might cause trouble. The two youngest Tigers—Kyle and Tyson Bailey, the eight-year-old twins she'd had to keep an eye on all the way from Honolulu—had started crying when the intruders showed up, but not loudly. They were both too scared for that, and their sobs trailed off into sniffles before very long. The others, so far, were enduring the fear and confusion, and the increased motion of the ship, in unhappy silence.

Master Chief Morrison's daughter hadn't said anything since the man with the submachine gun took control of the goat locker. The set of her jaw, however, had a line to it that Laura didn't like. She suspected that it wouldn't take much to push H. L. over the edge into doing something rash. A girl stubborn and aggressive enough to take on the hostile climate of VMI wasn't likely to be good at sitting quiet and waiting.

Laura caught H. L.'s eye and held it for a few seconds—*that's a good girl, pay attention to me and don't start trouble*—and didn't look away until she was fairly sure that the younger woman had gotten the message. Then she let her gaze move on to Chris, half-sitting and half-slouching on the vinyl banquette seat on the other side of the space. He'd had his camera with him when he came into the goat locker. Some time in the past few minutes he must have hidden it.

He had one of his course books open on his lap, but if he was affecting an air of unconcern it wasn't working very well. When he looked over at their guard, his carefully neutral expression changed to a kind of thoughtful dislike, as if the armed man were an oil slick he wanted to photograph as effectively as possible.

The red light and deep shadows cast by the battle lanterns brought out the underlying structures of his face. *He looks like his father*, Laura thought suddenly; and in the next breath, *I hope he isn't planning to do anything stupid.*

The moment passed, and Chris went back to reading his book. Laura relaxed, but only a little.

Repair 5, USS *Cushing*
Off Singkep Island, Indonesia
104° 10' 50" E/00° 12' 20" S
0135 Local/1835 Zulu

Stryker and Ross wormed their way through the darkened pas-sageways until they came to Repair 5's gear locker. Looking at the aftermath of the firefight—the crumpled bodies, the deck awash in blood and salt water—Stryker had to admit that the scene was worse than he'd expected. These were guys that he knew, guys he'd been eating chow with for two years.

HT3 Ross looked pale and sweaty in the red light of the battle lanterns. "Oh, man," he said. "This really sucks."

"Amen to that," said Stryker. "Where's the welding machine?"

"Right here."

Stryker breathed a sigh of relief. "Okay. Let's get as close to the goat locker as we can without getting seen."

"Without getting fucking shot, you mean."

"That's right. Let's go."

The welding machine was a heavy metal box. Neither Ross nor Stryker could pick it up and carry it back alone; the effort needed both of them working together. They paused at every hatch combing, waiting and watching for motion—but all that was moving was the ship.

Stryker had forgotten, for a little while, about the storm outside. Now that he had a few minutes of relative quiet, the weather was making its presence known again. *Cushing* was taking rolls so large that just standing up was a problem, and the welding rig kept trying to break free of their grip.

When they finally reached the ladder to the passage outside Chiefs' Quarters, the hatch hadn't been closed and dogged. Somebody had gone through there, and if they'd left the hatch open like that, then they weren't part of *Cushing*'s crew. Stryker pointed at the ladder to the passageway above.

"Up there," he said to Ross, "is our guy. What I want you to do is put a welding rod onto the machine, and hit an arc against something up there."

"Man, no way. I don't have a mask. That's like asking for flash burns. Chief'd fucking kill me."

"Can you do it with your eyes closed?" Stryker asked. "I *want* flash burns—on the bad guys."

"That idea's fucked."

"Try anyway, okay? The Chief can kill you later."

"I don't know why I'm listening to you," HT3 Ross grumbled. "You're just a seaman and I'm a Third Class."

"You're listening to me because I'm right. Now—can you do it?"

"Yeah, yeah." Ross squeezed the handle on the lead, inserted a rod into the holder, and switched on the machine. "Okay, here we go."

"Right," Stryker said to the hull tech. "Stick your hand up. One flash, tell me when it's over, and I'll go do my part of this thing."

"Man, you are fucking *brave*."

"Just do it."

Ross stuck his hand up into the passageway above, and tapped around with the rod. "Ain't working. It's all paint and tile. I need to touch metal. . . ."

"Try the knife-edge."

"Yeah, right. Close your eyes." Ross hit the tip of the welding rod against the "knife-edge"—the top edge of the hatch combing, the metal part that made contact with the gasket on the hatch to create a watertight seal.

The smell of welding filled the air, sharp and acrid. Even through his closed lids, with his hand over his eyes, Stryker could make out the bright white light.

Then came a sudden continuous stream of fire—a submachine gun, by the sound. The firing stopped just as suddenly. *Expended his magazine*, Stryker thought.

He opened his eyes, and shouldered his way past Ross and on up the ladder. His effort was rewarded. At the top, in the corridor amid red light, he saw a single man, his weapon dangling from one hand, the other hand and forearm pressed against his eyes.

Stryker sprinted toward him, slamming into him with enough force to put him down onto the deck, slashing with his knife. When the man stopped moving, he took the man's weapon, then called out, "Ross, it's okay, come get 'em."

HT3 Ross showed up a moment later.

"Fuck me," he said. "It fucking worked."

Chiefs' Berthing, USS *Cushing*
104° 10' 50" E/00° 12' 20" N
0135 Local/1835 Zulu

Laura Warner fought against the urge to look at her watch. She didn't know how much time had passed since the General Quarters alarm had sounded. Tension had a way of making the time stretch out unnaturally long at some moments and rush past at others—but checking her watch would make her look worried. She couldn't afford that right now. Emotional states were catching, and too many people in the goat locker—Chris, H. L., the guard—already teetered on the edge of losing control.

But I'm *fine*, she thought. *How does that line go, the one they used to put onto lapel buttons: "Someday I shall burst my bud of calm and blossom forth into hysteria"? Right now that sounds like a wonderful idea.*

When all this is over, I'm going to make Andrew buy me a drink.

Maybe two or three drinks. And then I—

The door to the goat locker swung open. Two figures in Navy work uniforms tumbled into the compartment, pushing a limp body between and ahead of them.

The guard inside raised his machine pistol and fired, the noise enormous in the small enclosed space. At the same time, the two *Cushing* sailors—one of them, anyhow—fired back. The guard, hit squarely in the midsection, slumped over and folded onto the deck; the sailor who had shot him also fell. The body of the unconscious man had shielded the sailor from most of the guard's bullets, but at least one round had struck him in the leg.

There was a lot of blood splattered about, decorating the walls and floor of the goat locker like the work of some mad artist. Laura found herself noting its presence with an odd detachment—a variety of hysterical reaction, she supposed, but a useful one under the circumstances. Most of the blood appeared to belong to the guard and to the other intruder; they were both dead now, or close enough to it that nothing in the goat locker was going to help them.

One of the Bailey twins was crying again, not that Laura blamed him. She'd have started crying herself if she'd thought it would do any good.

Instead she stood up, slowly and carefully so as not to startle anybody, and made her way over to the first aid box mounted on the bulkhead. If there were pressure dressings in there—yes, there were—"Let me help you," she said to the wounded *Cushing* sailor. "That leg needs taking care of before it gets any worse."

"Yes, ma'am," he said. The name stenciled on his chambray work shirt was STRYKER, and after a quick inspection she put his age at no more than twenty.

He drew a sharp breath when she began working to put a bandage on his injured leg, but didn't cry out. Instead he raised his voice enough to speak to the other sailor who'd come into the room with him.

"Charley, pick up the fu—" he glanced over at H. L. Morrison and caught himself in mid-word "—the machine gun. Then get a portable battle lantern and start breaking all the permanently mounted ones. I want this space dark."

"Right. You're the man; you want dark, you got it."

"Who's that man?" Kyle Bailey asked in a hushed voice.

"He's a Gunner's Mate, son," Chief Willis's father answered him.

"What's a Gunner's Mate?"

"A deck ape with a hunting license."

Kyle looked bewildered. "Oh."

The sailor called Charley picked up one of the goat locker's metal ashtrays and began using it to smash the battle lanterns. Stryker looked around at all the others in the compartment—*assessing them*, Laura thought, still working over his injured leg—before his gaze settled on H. L. Morrison.

"I know you," he said. "You're the Master Chief's kid."

H. L. gave a quick, sharp nod. "That's right."

"Then you probably know where the weapons locker is."

"Yes," H. L. said. "Daddy showed me."

Stryker reached down to his belt and detached a set of keys. "Here. Get to the locker and open it up and get weapons out to everyone—the SAT and BAF won't have anything until you do. There's a Security Alert on, so be careful."

Laura nodded at Charley, who'd almost finished smashing the battle lanterns. The compartment was a lot darker now. "Shouldn't *he* be doing all that?"

"I'm going to need him here, ma'am," Stryker said. "Miss Morrison—"

He tossed the keys to H. L., who caught them neatly and headed for the door through which Stryker and Charley had come barreling in.

"Not that way," Stryker said. "It's crawling with bad guys. There's a scuttle in the overhead aft, in berthing—you'd better go that way instead."

"Right," said H. L. "I'm off."

Chris laid aside his course book—marking the page first, a bit of conscious drama Laura hadn't expected to see from him—and stood up. "I'm coming with you."

"Chris—" Laura began, at the same time as H. L. put her shoulders back and said, "Who invited *you* on this party, Nature Boy?"

"Better cover that way," he said. "If we run into trouble, we can always claim we were off somewhere fooling around when the alarm went off."

"Don't you wish," she said. "Come on, then. We're wasting time."

The two of them were gone before Laura could recover her voice enough to speak.

And what could I say, after all? she thought. *That Chris is too young to take risks like that? Laughable, under the circumstances . . . this boy Stryker is probably younger than he is.*

And Stryker was once more giving orders. "Everybody down," he said to the Tigers. "Behind cover if you can find it. I'm going to sit against the bulkhead opposite the door. Charley, you take the bulkhead near the door. When the door opens, turn on the portable battle lantern and shine it on whoever's coming in. If the guy isn't in uniform, I'm going to shoot the son of a bitch."

20

The ship pitched and rolled as Chris and H. L. made their way back through the darkened interior of the Chiefs' Berthing compartment. The constant motion, combined with the poor visibility, made their progress awkward and stumbling.

I'll take technical rock-climbing over this any day, Chris thought. *At least the rocks stay put while you're climbing them.*

But the scuttle was there as Stryker had promised—a small, easily opened hatch, set into the center of the larger hatch that led up to the main deck. Chris climbed the ladder to the overhead and grabbed hold of the handwheel that would open the scuttle. He hung there, bracing his knees and feet against the ladder to offset the motion of the ship, and put all the strength of his arms and shoulders into turning the handwheel.

"Can you get it okay?" H. L. asked from behind and below him. "Do you need help?"

He twisted the handwheel, then twisted it again. "I can get it, all right? And there's only room for one person at a time up here anyway."

"Well, hurry up. Any minute now somebody's going to notice that the guy who was supposed to be guarding us isn't answering up when they try and talk to him."

"Yeah, yeah . . . here it goes!"

He gave the handwheel another twist, and at last the dogs loosened, the wheel spun, and the dogs retracted. The scuttle popped up a bit, just as a wave broke over the deck and a flood of warm seawater poured in through the opening.

Chris gasped and spluttered under the sudden torrent. "Damn . . . !"

"Push it all the way open," H. L. said. "Let's get out of here while we still have the chance."

"Right."

Chris pushed upward on the scuttle, causing it to open fully and lock in the upright position. He grabbed hold of the metal rim of the opening and pulled himself up. He balanced for a moment on his hands—the same as doing it in the gym, really, except for a few nagging details like the driving rain and the constant movement of the ship and the fact that somewhere behind them were a lot of very unfriendly guys with guns—then pushed himself the rest of the way out.

The deck was a bedlam of wind and pounding rain: wind that seemed to push and grab at him like a live thing, and a heavy, down-slashing rain that soaked all of his clothing in less than a second. He couldn't see the waves, it was too dark, but from the way the ship was tossing about the seas had to be bigger than any he'd ever encountered. His face and hands smarted under the lash of salt water whipped into spray by the force of the storm.

A moment later, H. L. emerged from the open scuttle to join him on the deck. She released the catch, and the scuttle slammed shut of its own weight. H. L. spun the wheel to dog it down again.

"Which way now?" Chris asked, but the wind took his words and they were lost in the noise of the storm.

H. L. took his hand and pulled, leading him aft into the shelter of *Cushing*'s slab-sided superstructure. She cupped her mouth and shouted, her lips barely an inch away from his head, "We have to get to the armory!"

Chris cupped his own ears, the better to hear what she said next, and shouted back, "I know. Where is it?"

"Down low. The third deck. This way."

She headed aft again, keeping one hand on the railing welded to the side of the deckhouse. Chris followed. In the darkness he couldn't so much see her as feel her presence. They went aft and around a corner, into the lee of a bulkhead, and then they stopped.

Or H. L. stopped and Chris ran into her, which amounted to the same thing. H. L had her hand on the lever of a quick-acting water-tight door. It opened, and the two of them went in. She closed the door and dogged it shut.

They were in a light locker aft. The black curtains designed to keep light from showing topside kept the inside of the locker even darker than the outside had been. The space smelled of salt and paint and the rubberized canvas of the curtains, but at least without the pounding of rain and the waves they could more or less hear themselves talk.

Chris said, somewhat breathlessly, "So far so good."

"We're not finished yet. We have to get weapons to the crew— if I can remember the way to the armory from here—and do it without getting caught."

"No kidding," Chris said. An unpleasant thought struck him. "We'll want to be careful around our guys, too. The first thing any sailor's going to notice about us is the civilian clothes. Once we start carrying around guns and stuff, we'll look enough like the other guys that some people might shoot first and double-check our bodies later."

"Doesn't matter; we have to do it anyway."

"I know, I know. We might want to be extra careful who we run up to and throw our arms around, is all."

"Careful it is, then," H. L. said. "Let me take a look at what's on the far side of this space."

H. L. dropped to hands and knees on the deck and wormed her way around the curtains. With her face nearly at deck level she peeked out at the interior passageway beyond.

"Looks clear," she reported. "Forward to the ladder, then down. My turn to go first, I think."

"Right behind you," Chris said.

The passageway outside the light locker was lit by the red lights of battle lanterns. H. L. hurried ahead of Chris, who couldn't help noticing the way her wet clothing molded to her body. He found himself rehearsing their cover story to himself as they ran.

We're just a couple of kids who were up here when the lights went out. We don't know what's going on; we just want to get back to where we're supposed to be and stay out of trouble with the Captain.

They reached the ladder without anyone spotting or stopping them—*just as well*, Chris thought; *that story is a really stupid one and I'd hate to have to try using it*—and H. L. grabbed the handhold and swung on down to the next level. A moment later she called back, "Clear!" and Chris came down the ladder after her.

When they were standing together on the lower level, H. L. said, "We know that the intruders are forward from here. That means we'll have to go aft and down before we go forward again."

"Can we get through there?"

"Only one way to find out."

"Then let's do it."

Frame 70, USS *Cushing*
Off Singkep Island, Indonesia
104° 05' E/00° 20' S
0155 Local/1855 Zulu

Master Chief Morrison waited in his ambush position for the intruders to appear. A part of his mind noted that—along with all of *Cushing*'s other problems—the weather was getting worse. The ship's pitching and rolling seemed to have increased, and waves were breaking against the skin of the ship to Morrison's right. Each wave hit the metal with a thud that he could feel through his rump where he was sitting on the deck, and with each wave the ship slipped a bit sideways.

A shadow moved under the battle lantern's light in the thwartship passageway. Someone was coming.

Morrison sighted over the top of the .45. The post of the forward sight fit in the notch of the rear sight. Just balance the target on top, and squeeze, and everything would work. He checked the thumb safety. Off. He cradled the weapon in both hands.

The shadow got nearer. A man stepped out of the passage. He was dressed in civilian clothes—dark jeans and a cammie tee shirt, both dirty and wet—and holding a submachine gun. Not a sailor, then, and not one of the Tigers. Morrison shot him in the head. The report of the .45 made an enormous noise in the confined space.

The man dropped. His weapon clattered to the deck as he fell. Somebody poked the muzzle of another submachine gun around the corner and started firing blindly forward. The spray of bullets punched holes in the thin metal of the interior non-tight bulkheads.

Morrison held his position while the bullets pinged around him. The shooter was firing blind, hoping to provide cover, which meant that yet a third somebody was going to come leaping through the gap at any moment.

One, two—here he comes now.

Morrison shot this man, too, center of body mass. The intruder sat down heavily on the deck as the hydrostatic shock knocked him off his feet. Then he fell backward and lay there without moving.

That still left at least one man, Morrison knew—the guy who'd been providing the covering fire. The submachine gun drew back around the corner. Its magazine had to be exhausted, and the shooter would need at least a few seconds to reload.

No time like right now—

Morrison rolled to his right and pulled his feet under him, then jumped up and sprinted for the corner. He got there, rounded it, and came face to face with the third man.

The owner of the submachine gun was in the process of loading his weapon. He'd paused to put back the empty magazine into the pouch from which he'd taken the fresh one. Morrison shot him before he could finish.

Except for the dead men, the passageway looked clear. Morrison dragged the three bodies out of sight aft, away from the corner, and took their weapons for himself. Then he resumed his earlier location, waiting in ambush with his .45 back in the two-hand grip. Three rounds expended, three hostiles down.

Secondary Conn, USS *Cushing*
Off Singkep Island, Indonesia
104° 05' E/00° 22' S
0204 Local/1904 Zulu

Michael Prasetyo stood at *Cushing*'s Secondary Conn. He had to brace himself in order to stay upright; the storm that had masked his initial assault, and that now protected him against search and retaliation from the air, also caused the deck to shift and tilt crazily under his feet. The howling of the wind made it difficult to hear the reports of his men, calling in with word of spaces secured, of resistance met and overcome.

They had found civilians in one of the berthing compartments, a development Prasetyo had not hesitated to exploit. His announcement over the 1JV circuit had been a warning, a psychological ploy intended to weaken the resistance of *Cushing*'s remaining defenders. He didn't want to do the civilians any actual injury—yet. The threat of violence could be extended almost indefinitely; the real thing, however, had a more limited shelf life.

One of Prasetyo's men came to Secondary Conn to make a report. "Sir," the man said, his words nearly drowned out by the racket of the storm, "there is a weapon loose on board."

Prasetyo raised an eyebrow. "How did that come to happen?"

"The team on the main deck forward shot an armed man, but when they checked his body, the weapon and magazines were missing from his belt."

"This is a warship," Prasetyo said patiently. "It is full of military men. Of *course* there are armed men on board."

He raised his handheld radio. The racket was incredible. The wind made the wires in the rigging scream like voices in pain, and he had to shout to be heard. "Magazine teams, report."

"Team One—small arms locker, secure,"

"Team Two—armory, secure."

"Stand by, One and Two," he said. "We have at least one weapon unaccounted for."

"Standing by," said Team One; and Team Two echoed, "Standing by."

"All teams," Prasetyo said. "Report. Radio Four—report."

Nobody answered.

"Radio Four is with the hostages," the messenger said. "Maybe he's having trouble."

Prasetyo hoped not. He still wanted to make use of the hostages.

"Where exactly did Radio Four say that he'd found them?"

"Midships, second deck berthing."

"Radio Seven is near there." Prasetyo raised the radio again. "Radio Seven, go to the midships second deck berthing space. See what the problem is with Radio Four."

"On my way."

Prasetyo pointed to the helmsman, though in the darkness of Secondary Conn no one could see the gesture. "Maintain course and speed. Guide on our lead vessel. We'll be on this leg for another hour; I should be back before then. I'm going to make a tour below decks."

21

Rear Admiral Mayland was asleep in his bunk when the alarm
on the sound-powered phone by his head whooped. He picked the
phone up without opening his eyes or turning on his bunk light,
and said, "Mayland."

"Admiral," said the voice at the other end. "Radio. Eyes only
traffic, Flash precedence."

"Very well. Send it up."

Mayland switched on the light—in the red setting so his night
vision wouldn't be killed—and swung his legs over the side of his
bunk. A moment later, with a whoosh of compressed air, the bunny
tube from Radio dropped out into its holder. It contained a "holy
joe"—a manila envelope fastened with a looped-string closure,
pierced at intervals to reveal the presence of whatever was inside.
An orange Top Secret cover sheet showed through the holes.

Mayland undid the closure, then pulled out the sheet of paper
inside and examined it. The headers told him that the message was

sensitive information, TS NOFORN WINTEL—top secret, not to be shown to foreign nationals, a possible source of information about sensitive intelligence methods—and that it came from the United States Naval Attaché to Australia.

He's awake late, Mayland thought. *I wonder what's up?*

The message was short, but long enough to answer that question even as it raised a host of others:

1. (TS WINTEL) INTEL SUGGESTS USS CUSHING [DD 985] UNDER PIRATE ATTACK.
2. (TS NOFORN WINTEL) AUSTRALIAN RESPONSE UNCERTAIN BUT LIKELY.
3. (TS) REQUEST ADVISE RAN YOUR INTENTIONS.
BT

"Fuck," Mayland said. CO of *Cushing* was Andrew Warner, and as far as Mayland was concerned, that was both good and bad. Good because Warner was a fine shiphandler and not likely to lose his nerve in a crisis; bad because whatever sins Warner decided to commit against international law and national sovereignty in the name of protecting his ship, Admiral Mayland was going to be the senior officer tasked with explaining them. And Andy Warner had a habit of getting creative.

Mayland pulled on his khaki trousers and buzzed the Bridge. "This is the Admiral. Have my aide meet me in TFCC."

"Bridge aye," came the response.

Mayland was still buttoning his shirt as he strode—not running, that would be undignified, but walking as rapidly as possible under the circumstances—the thirty-five feet from his compartment to Tactical Flag Combat Control. TFCC was a kind of super-CIC, where information from all the ship's sensors and comms was funneled so that the Admiral could fight the battle group.

A moment later Mayland's Flag Aide arrived. Lieutenant

Thatcher Remey was an Academy grad, third-generation Navy with family money on his mother's side. He must have been awakened from a sound sleep as well, but it didn't show much. He looked slightly less crisply pressed than usual, that was all.

"Admiral?" he asked.

Mayland shoved the flimsy across the plotting table in the center of the space. "What do you make of this?"

"They're getting froggy in Canberra," Remey said. He pulled the MOVREP board from the bulkhead and flipped through it. "Damn," he said. "Maybe not. *Cushing* missed her MOVREP about thirty minutes ago."

"Why wasn't I informed?" Mayland demanded. He could feel his face start to get hot. This situation was turning out to hold even more potential for disaster than the Gun Mount 51 fiasco—Mayland didn't even like thinking about that one—or the long-ago poker game in San Diego when Warner had won Mayland's entire paycheck by proving that drawing to a flush did in fact beat a pat straight. "There's a storm over there, they're in restricted waters, and now we hear that there's a pirate attack. What other little surprises haven't you kept on top of?"

Remey already had the OPGEN KILO annex Foxtrot open on another table. "Stats on *Cushing*, sir," he said. "Suggest we contact them by BG Secure."

"Do it."

Remey pulled the HICOMS satellite crypto handset from its cradle, keyed the mike, and waited for the double-beep of the crypto synching. He glanced over at the call sign board, then said, "*Cushing*, this is Task Group. Radio check, over."

He paused, mike off, waiting for a response. A minute passed. He repeated the radio check. Again no response. A third time, then "*Cushing*, this is task group, nothing heard, out."

"Flash precedence traffic, to *Cushing*," Mayland said. "Interrogative MOVREP, respond."

"Yes sir," Remey said. He was already writing on a red-bordered message blank. A moment later, he was finished, and handing it through the door from TFCC to Flag Comms.

"I want the Air Boss and the Captain up here," Mayland said. "Call it a drill for right now, but I am not going to sit in front of Congress and tell them how I fucked up when they should be voting on my next star. Understood?"

"Sir," Remey said. "We could see if satellite intel is available. Or ask the Aussies for amplification."

"I am not going to go asking those kangaroo-fucking goat-ropers for diddly," Mayland said. "It's bad enough that they're in on this at all. Now see if you can do something right tonight, why don't you?"

"Sir," Remey said. Then, on the 21MC to the Bridge, "Admiral requests the presence of the CO and Air Boss in TFCC." A double click from the Bridge meant message understood.

"Get me the latest weather," Mayland said. "And a satellite photo wouldn't be bad. Radar too. And draft me a message to one of the cruisers, make best speed to wherever *Cushing* was supposed to be at MOVREP time. Maybe we can pull something out of this fuckup."

Chiefs' Quarters, USS *Cushing*
Off Singkep Island, Indonesia
104° 05' E/00° 35' S
0240 Local/1940 Zulu

Down in the goat locker, with the battle lanterns all smashed and gone out, the hot air stank of sweat and blood. GMGSN Stryker had been sitting on the deck for what seemed like hours, feeling the wound in his leg throb with a steady rhythm and listening to Charley Ross in the dark behind him, swearing and fiddling with the portable lantern while a couple of the younger Tigers sniffled and whimpered in the background.

Stryker worried about the Tigers—especially the crying ones, LTJG Bailey's twin boys. So far they'd all done okay, but it was the Captain's Wife who was holding the whole bunch of them together. If anything happened to her, they'd panic for sure.

A couple of the Tigers had already been seasick—not the twins, who'd probably taken their Dramamine at bedtime, but a couple of the older men—adding the acrid stink of fresh vomit to the stew. The weather outside the ship seemed to be getting worse; Stryker could feel the deck heaving up beneath him then slamming back down as *Cushing* pitched through the waves. His leg hurt every time it happened, but there wasn't anything he could do about the pain except try not to think about it too much.

The door opened. Charley Ross flashed on his battle lantern. By its light Stryker saw an armed man dressed in civilian clothes. Or maybe not civilian clothes, but certainly not a US Navy uniform either.

Stryker shot him twice.

"Pull him inside!" he shouted as the man fell. "Come on, Charley, move it! Some of you people, bear a hand—get that guy in here, and get his weapon!"

At that moment, someone on the forward side of the open door pushed a submachine gun around the corner. Stryker saw the weapon coming in, and threw himself down face forward as the submachine gun opened fire. The battle lantern fell, its beam of light strobing crazily as the lantern slid and skidded about the deck.

Someone was screaming—probably a wounded or frightened Tiger—and Stryker felt something hard, hot, and metal pressed against the back of his neck. A heavy foot pressed down on his right wrist, immobilizing his weapon hand.

"Good evening," said a voice that didn't belong to any crew

member Stryker knew. "You are my prisoner. That means you have to do what I tell you." A pause, while the pistol at the back of Stryker's neck pressed harder against the skin. The man spoke sharply in a language Stryker didn't understand. Then Stryker heard men moving about behind him, and the metallic chink of someone checking the magazine in a weapon. "*Will* you do what I tell you?" the first man asked.

Stryker thought about rattling off his name, rank, and serial number. But there weren't any serial numbers anymore—the number on his ID card was his Social Security number, which didn't have quite the same ring to it—and besides, John Wayne was dead. Stryker decided it was time to start telling lies.

"Yeah," he mumbled. "I'll do what you say."

"That's good."

Stryker felt his weapon wrenched from his hand, and then he was pulled to his feet. The sudden increase of pain in his wounded leg made his head spin. He saw by the light of the portable battle lantern that Charley Ross was down and not moving. The nearest stranger carried two weapons, one in his hand and the other slung across his back. Blood swirled and eddied every which way on the deck as the ship pitched and rolled.

The speaker went on, "Now tell me. What are all these civilians doing here?" He paused, then addressed the civilians: "I will need you to help identify your Captain." He held up a color printout of Captain Warner's photo, downloaded from the *Cushing*'s Web page. "How long you live depends on how useful you are."

22

If I'd checked my diaphragm for leaks twenty-odd years ago, Laura Warner thought, *I wouldn't be in this fix right now. I'd be serving wine and cheese to my graduate assistants in a nice little apartment in a nice little college town, not sitting here in a room full of blood watching an armed pirate hold a pistol to the head of a twenty-year-old boy.*

She winced with sympathetic pain as the intruder forced the wounded Stryker to his feet. The new arrival, she felt certain, was either the leader of the pirate force assaulting the ship, or somebody of importance in their hierarchy. All the signals of status and authority pointed to that conclusion: he carried a handgun, rather than a rifle or a submachine gun; he spoke perfect English; and most telling of all, he had referred to Stryker not as *a* prisoner, but as *his* prisoner.

The pirate leader addressed Stryker again, in the same American English as before: "I ask you again. What are all these civilians doing here?"

Laura didn't want to see Stryker—who had to be in consider-able pain already—caught in the narrow gap between self-preservation and the duty to remain silent. She coughed once to draw the leader's attention and said, "We're what they call Tigers—dependents on board for the voyage home."

"Ah," the man said. He didn't take the pistol away from Stry-ker's neck, but his gaze shifted to where Laura was sitting. Even in the dim red light of the portable battle lantern, she could see that his eyes were alert and coolly intelligent. He was not a man, she thought, who would be easy to fool. "How many of you are there?"

"Ten," she lied. Chris and H. L. deserved as much head start as she could give them, and there was no easy way—she hoped—for him to check the veracity of her statement.

"Please be exact. If my men find nine or eleven, I will kill you. How many?"

"Ten," she repeated. She nodded toward where Charley Ross lay sprawled on the deck in a puddle of bloody water, and said, "That man is hurt. May I see if I can help him?"

"Go ahead," he said. "If you start trouble, I'll kill you."

She got up carefully, making no sudden moves, and began work-ing on Ross. He was unconscious. She was far from sure that her ministrations were going to be of any help, but she persisted. Mean-while, the pirate leader turned his attention back to Stryker.

"Where is the Captain of this ship?"

"I don't know," said Stryker.

The pirate leader gave a hiss of irritation. "You put yourself in unnecessary danger. Where is Captain Warner?"

Laura paused in her first aid and said, "He's probably telling the truth when he says he doesn't know."

"You, then. Tell me where to find the Captain."

"I'm afraid I can't."

" 'Can't' is not a good word to use," he said. "Remember where you are, and answer me again."

She shook her head. "It's the truth. I was alone when the alarm sounded, and I came straight here. I thought at first that it was a drill."

"It is not. And if this man cannot give me the whereabouts of the Captain, he can at least direct me to the hatches leading into the Engineering spaces."

Laura could see from the expression on Stryker's face that he was about to refuse—or worse, to try something reckless and probably suicidal. She caught the young man's eyes and willed him to be silent. Then she said, "You might as well show him the hatches. He's going to find them anyway if he looks long enough."

"Very sensible of you," the pirate leader said. "Mr. Stryker, I urge you to take her advice."

USS *Nimitz*
85° 01' E/00° 12' S
0050 Local/1950 Zulu

Rear Admiral Mayland was growing more and more frustrated. No country—not even the United States, as exemplified by the might of an entire carrier battle group—can fly warplanes through another country's airspace without permission. The locals in most places call an incursion like that an "international incident," and Congress doesn't like it when Admirals have international incidents in their service folders.

"What do you mean," Mayland snarled at his aide, "I can't get clearance from Indonesia to mount an air search for my ship?"

"No one who can give authorization is available," Lieutenant Remey said. "I've asked the Country Team at the embassy. They're not terribly available either."

Mayland gritted his teeth. "That's obstructionism, pure and simple. The weather's rotten and getting worse. I need eyes over there, dammit."

With a hiss and a clank, a new message popped up in the bunny tube. Mayland grabbed the container and yanked open the envelope inside.

FROM: AMEMB JAKARTA
TO: COMCARGRU SIX
SUBJ: AIR CLEARANCE
REF (A) COMCARGRU 21101951Z00
1.(TS) IRT REF A PER DENIED.

"What in the hell are they thinking of over there?" Mayland demanded. He wadded up the message and threw it into a burn bag. "Send a message to the Country Team—get me the permissions I need or . . . no, just get me the permissions."

"Sir," Remey said. Unobtrusively, he fished the crumpled-up message out of the burn bag so that he could copy the reference number from it for his response.

"And prepare a CO's SITREP for me. I want this documented with me doing everything I can but being shot down by those stripy-pants fairies."

"Sir," Remey said again, and pulled another message blank out of the bin.

Bridge, USS *Cushing*
Off Singkep Island, Indonesia
104° 02' E/00° 35' S
0250 Local/1950 Zulu

The wind howled across the shattered Bridge, and the driving rain stung Captain Warner's cheeks. The sky was black outside. Ahead, perhaps two thousand yards, he could see the sternlight of another vessel. Low in the water—probably under a hundred feet in length. With a sinking feeling he realized that he was looking at the intruders' mother ship.

He had sound powered phones on his ears. Over the SP lines he heard the voices of the destroyer's sailors at their battle stations. Their clipped reports of movement and gunfire let him track the intruders from space to space, spreading throughout the ship. Anger stirred in him, starting at the base of his stomach and moving outward; not hot red anger but the cold, dark, dangerous kind.

The rain was the hardest he could recall. And somewhere in the growing silent area of the ship, where sailors no longer reported from their stations, somewhere in there were Laura and Chris.

Laura. It had been raining hard on the night when he'd first met her, after a rock concert in L.A. Everybody knows that it never rains in California—except when it sluices down so hard that you can't even read your watch. When the concert broke up, he was standing out in the downpour next to a pretty girl who had straight blonde hair long enough to sit on.

He was a young Ensign with a beard and an attitude—back when both were common in the fleet—and she, well, she was good-looking. His ship was at Naval Weapons Station Long Beach, loading out for deployment. He got a cab for both of them, and told the cab to take her home first. They got to talking on the ride. When the cab stopped, he handed the driver a bill and told him to wait. The conversation continued up the steps to her door, and from there into her apartment. He leaned out of the open window and waved the cab away.

He'd stayed there with her until the very last minute; up to the point when he had to leave if he wanted to make it back to his ship before Quarters. Just before he left, he remembered to ask for her phone number so he could call her again sometime. He'd ended up calling her every night, and marrying her before his ship left port.

The noise of the stretcher team arriving to take away the casualties brought Warner back to the present. He wondered now if the last sight he'd had of Laura—her profile at dinner in the Wardroom—would turn out to be the last time he'd see her in this life.

Second Deck, USS *Cushing*
Off Singkep Island, Indonesia
104° 02' E/00° 35' S
0250 Local/1950 Zulu

Chris Warner and H. L. Morrison were lurking in the shadows of a fore-and-aft passageway, in the after end of *Cushing*'s second deck. Chris wished he had a knowledge of the destroyer's internal layout more exact than a dim memory of a generalized standard plan; it would have made things a lot less confusing right about now. H. L. hadn't admitted yet to any confusion, but Chris doubted that she had much more familiarity with the setup than he did.

"So here we are," H. L. said. "No guns, no lights—"

"We're not there yet," Chris said. "And things could be worse."

As he spoke a burst of automatic weapons fire sounded up forward, a noise like popcorn popping ferociously. H. L. said, "By 'worse' you mean like with gunfire or something?"

"Yeah. I think we need to go the other way anyhow."

They headed aft, keeping to the shadows and avoiding the circles of reddish light cast by the battle lanterns, moving carefully on the rolling deck. Chris had grown somewhat more accustomed to the constant movement of the ship underfoot and around him, but unexpected changes—and there were a lot of them, at least for someone as basically inexperienced as he was—still had the ability to make him lurch and stumble.

Even with his sketchy knowledge of *Cushing*'s interior, he knew that they'd have to find a ladder downward if they wanted to cross under the fighting in progress and go forward to the ship's armory. Eventually, they came to the farthest aft portion of the second deck, where weight racks and exercise bicycles welded to the deck formed the foul-weather and nighttime exercise room for the crew.

Chris felt H. L.'s warning hand on his arm. He glanced in her direction and saw her nod—fingers over her mouth for silence—toward the far side of the exercise room, where a pair of shadowy forms moved about in the dimming glow of the battle lanterns. One of the shadowy figures raised a radio to his lips and spoke in a language Chris didn't recognize.

No luck this way, Chris thought.

He and H. L. faded back forward as quietly as they could, trying to put some space between them and the intruders. Their retreat took them past the gedunk, source of junk food and sundries for the destroyer's crew. Chris hesitated briefly, then kicked in the Plexiglas square below the sales window. The sound was lost in the noise of the storm. He squirmed through the opening.

"The only question," he said to H. L., as she followed his example, "is how much violence you're willing to accept."

"Who said that? One of your professors?"

"Nope, my father. I have an idea."

It didn't take Chris long to find the ice cream machine that stirred up soft-serve treats for the crew during the gedunk's hours of operation. He pulled the plug out of the socket in the bulkhead, then set his foot and his back into pulling the other end of the power cord straight from the machine. He wound up with some ten feet of cord, with a plug at one end and bare wire at the other.

"What do you think you're doing, anyway?" H. L. asked.

"I'm going to see if this trick works like it's supposed to," he said. He was busy stripping the cord down even further as he spoke, so that the wires were laid bare for several feet.

H. L. watched him at work for a moment, then began casting about the small space of the gedunk looking for Chris didn't know what—until she lit upon the intersquadron baseball trophy, an 18-inch-high wonder of kitsch in metal, marble, and plastic, displayed in a place of honor on a shelf against the back wall. The trophy was wired down onto the shelf, but by the time Chris was finished with the power cord, she'd managed to pull it free.

"Blunt instrument," she explained, hefting it two-handed. "How's the science experiment coming?"

"This part's done. Time to set up part two."

He squirmed back out of the gedunk the same way he'd come in, with H. L. following close behind, and prowled aft in search of a ship's service power socket. When he found one, he looped the cord around his body and jumped up—not a particularly high jump; headroom aboard ship was at a premium—to grab one of the pipes that ran along the overhead. He pulled himself up far enough to slide the cable over the pipe, leaving the stripped wires to hang down and sway back and forth with the motion of the ship.

That done, he lowered himself to the deck, then led the other end of the cord over to the power socket and plugged it in.

"Are you sure you want to do that?" H. L. said. "You could fry one of us as easily as one of them."

"I'm sure," Chris said. He raised his voice and shouted, in English, "Hey, Joe—I think I spotted something down here!"

Then he grabbed H. L. by the arm and pulled her with him out of sight. Shortly afterward, they were rewarded by the sound of the intruders from the weight room moving cautiously forward. A few moments later came a sharp snap, a flash of blue light, and a thud.

One down, thought Chris.

Before he could formulate a thought about what to do next, H. L. was moving forward and past him. He heard a surprised exclamation in the same unfamiliar language as before, cut short by a noise like somebody dropping a ripe watermelon onto a concrete sidewalk.

Score another one for the home team, he thought, wincing slightly. He moved forward and unplugged the cord, then joined H. L. in scooping up the firearms dropped by the intruders. He didn't look any closer at the bodies than he had to; the dim light of the battle lanterns helped with that.

"Do you know how to work one of these things?" he asked, regarding the weapons uneasily.

"There are certain similarities to any weapon in the class," H. L. said. "But exactly? No."

"And here I thought you were planning to be the darling of the guns 'n' ammo crowd."

"Shut up, tree-hugger, and let me look at them." She played with the mechanisms of the submachine guns for a moment, then handed one of them to Chris. "I'm pretty sure that one of these is set on 'safe' and one of them is set on 'fire.' We'll find out which one is which when we pull the triggers. Now forward and to the armory, okay? I *know* how to work those weapons."

23

Rear Admiral Mayland's aide groped about in the drawers of the plotting table, trying to find a Moboard on which to work out the search for USS _Cushing_. Instead, Lieutenant Remey's questing fingers encountered thin cardboard and slick, rattling cellophane: some scope dope's stash of Bugles and Fiddle-Faddle.

The greasy, sweet gedunk was exactly what he needed right now, Remey decided. He opened the cardboard box and shook it to make sure any roaches had left, then fished out a handful of popcorn and started munching.

As he ate, he scribbled down the names of the US ships within one day's steaming of _Cushing_'s probable location, within two days' steaming, and within three days' steaming. After three days, though, they might as well wrap up the search and go to a different game plan, because a ship missing for three days was a whole order of magnitude worse. By that time God and the world would be on station, and either Remey or Mayland—probably both—would have been relieved for cause.

The gedunk drawer held another surprise: a warm can of Nehi Grape soda. *Nehi Grape and Bugles*, Remey thought, popping the top of the can and taking a long swallow. *The breakfast of champions*. He went back to his list of ships.

The closest available vessel was USS *Vincennes*, one of the *Ticonderoga*-class cruisers. *Vincennes* was known in the fleet as "Robocruiser," from the strength of its armaments and weaponry, and from its general bad attitude.

Hell, he thought. *Dispatch it anyway. Let everyone know that we mean business.*

He worked out the time/space/distance with a straightedge and the log scales on the bottom of the Moboard. *Vincennes* was already east of the Strait, at least, so they wouldn't have to do tricky nighttime maneuvering in a restricted waterway.

Remey reached into the drawer again. *A man should know better*, he thought, *than to leave Fiddle-Faddle out where anyone can find it. There's probably a ship's directive about it not being allowed in Ops spaces anyway*.

He plunged his hand into the cardboard box, grabbed a second handful of sticky caramel-butter popcorn, and munched it thoughtfully. Then he washed it down with another slug of warm soda.

Nehi Grape. At least it isn't as bad as Aspen. There were still cases of the legendary apple-flavored soda making their way through the Fleet, long after they'd vanished unmourned from civilian supermarkets. Every once in a while you ran into a can of the stuff.

Remey picked up a pad of message blanks from the plotting table and took a government-issue Skilcraft pen from his pocket. Then he set himself to composing a series of different messages to *Vincennes*, all Top Secret, all Not for Foreign Distribution, all Z precedence, all using the same endpoint lat and long. One simply requested that *Vincennes* go to that point; another one directed it to go there; and yet another one directed it to go there as soon as possible. The final message directed *Vincennes* to that position at flank speed.

All the sets of orders had their own dangers. A request might be ignored. The response to a simple order might be too slow. An order to go someplace as soon as possible might produce greater speed, but even "as soon as possible" might still be too late. And an order to go at maximum speed—given that the weather was dirty and getting dirtier—might cause the loss of a ship.

Of *another* ship.

If *Cushing* was truly lost.

The whole situation could still, embarrassingly, evaporate to nothing in the end. Maybe someone on the destroyer had just had a brainfart, and they'd forgotten all about sending their MOVEREP. Or maybe, with the bad weather, they'd had to take down their transmitters for repair. Maybe . . . but neither of those possibilities would explain the Australian interest, or the obstruction coming from Jakarta.

Remey neatly printed the varying message drafts, using the standard alphabet that crossed sevens, slashed zeroes, and put flags and tags on ones and the letter S, so that the radiomen could type them up correctly. Then he took all the sets of orders, attached them to a clipboard, and went looking for Admiral Mayland. Deciding which one of the four messages should get sent was well above Remey's pay grade, a fact for which he was profoundly thankful.

Remey found the Admiral on the Bridge. "Nearest available unit is a Tico," he told Mayland. "Twelve to fourteen hours out from *Cushing*'s presumed location."

He handed the alternate drafts to the Admiral. Mayland looked them over and selected set number three, the ASAP version. He lined out the letters BT, for "Break Transmission," at the bottom of the draft and added a paragraph 2: TS NOFORN US SHIP IN TROU-

BLE. POSSIBLE HOSTILITIES. STAY SHARP. Then he penned in a new BT, signed the release blank, and handed the draft back to Remey.

"Keep me posted," he said, and turned back to watching the Bridge window. The glass was beginning to show rain streaks, reflected in the red glow from the status boards.

Remey walked over to the bunny tube, selected a capsule, and shot the draft down to Radio Central. Then he returned to the plotting table, where half a can of Nehi Grape was calling his name.

Chiefs' Quarters, USS *Cushing*
Off Singkep Island, Indonesia
104° 02' E/00° 35' S
0250 Local/1950 Zulu

In the red-lit dimness of *Cushing*'s **Chiefs' Quarters, Michael** Prasetyo stood between his two armed men and contemplated shooting the American sailor, or possibly one of the civilians, out of hand. Doing so would undoubtedly make an impression on the rest of them, and Prasetyo was beginning to suspect that Stryker was as likely to lie to him as to tell the truth. Stryker might give Prasetyo and his men the exact location of the hatches leading to *Cushing*'s engineering spaces; or he might lead everybody down a false trail, wasting valuable time and leaving them vulnerable to ambush and assault along the way. Despite Prasetyo's downloaded schematics, every ship was different, even within a class, and the interior a maze—if a familiar one—even to those who lived and worked aboard.

But if Stryker alive was of only limited utility, Stryker dead could tell him nothing at all. Shooting one of the civilians, then, might be better. One of the younger ones, maybe, or the woman.

Prasetyo gave the woman a closer look. Not young, but well-kept and well-groomed, with the kind of self-possession he'd come to associate with American professional and business women. She was probably attached to somebody senior in the ship's crew, from the way she'd assumed she had the right to speak for all the others, and the way they had let her do it.

"Decisions, decisions," he said aloud. He shifted the aim of his pistol fractionally, from Stryker to the woman. "Perhaps I should shoot you, then, to convince the others that I mean what I say."

Her calm, he thought, was admirable. He knew from experience how black and enormous the mouth of a pistol barrel looked from the target's point of view. Her eyes widened considerably and her face became, for a moment, very still, but her overall demeanor never wavered.

"It might work," she said. Her voice was steady, too, as if she were discussing nothing of greater importance than a minor business opportunity. "An overt act of personal violence might demoralize the ship's crew and make your own job that little bit easier. On the other hand. . . ."

She let the sentence trail off—inviting him, he was sure, to ask the next question. Half amused and half irritated, he said, "On the other hand, what?"

"On the other hand, there's always the chance you might make them so angry that they'll never surrender." She gave a faint, apologetic shrug. "It's so hard to judge these things in advance. *I* certainly wouldn't want to try."

He laughed in spite of himself, though the pistol in his hand never wavered. "That, at least, is a shocking lie. You already know what your own answer would be."

"True enough," she admitted. "Leaving aside the gamble you'd be taking with the crew's temper—you never know when you might need live hostages for bargaining chips."

Before he could frame his next reply, the door to Chiefs' Berthing swung open and Kino Tansil burst into the compartment. Even in the dim light, Tansil looked pleased—so pleased that Prasetyo, seeing him, at once demanded, "What have you found?"

He spoke in Indonesian, and Tansil replied in the same language. "We've located the Main Engineering spaces. We're clearing a path to the hatches now."

"Good news," Prasetyo said. "If we don't have the engines we don't have the ship. Make certain the men know that they shouldn't damage any of the gear down there. We'll need it later."

"Right you are," said Tansil. "I can—"

He never got the chance to finish. Another of Prasetyo's men appeared in the open doorway of Chiefs' Berthing. This man looked considerably less pleased than Tansil.

"We have a problem, boss," he said. "Those hatches going down to engineering—they're all closed, and we can't get them open."

"What do you mean," Prasetyo demanded, "you can't get them open?"

"We can't turn the handwheels on the scuttles."

"Unbolt them."

"We tried. We still can't get them open. I think they've been welded shut from below."

Prasetyo kept his face calm and his grip on the pistol unwavering. Of such appearances was a reputation made, and a good reputation was worth more than money.

"That *does* alter things," he said. He turned back to Stryker. With his free hand he gestured toward the compartment's sound powered phones. "Tell me," he said in English. "Who do those talk to?"

"Nobody."

The young man's voice was flat. He'd clearly thought better of his early moves toward cooperation, and had begun lying again. Prasetyo shook his head.

"My friend," he said, "this hero business gets old very fast. I'm not going to do the flamboyant threat thing. But you might seriously consider that pissing me off isn't a good lifestyle choice."

The woman spoke up again. "Where did you learn to speak English?"

"In school. But I got the finishing touches in Philadelphia."

She nodded, as if having a suspicion confirmed. "I thought I recognized the accent. What did you study—political science?"

"Business," Prasetyo said. "At the Wharton School. I'm a practical man . . . and this young man here should be, also. What spaces do the sound-powered phones connect with, Mr. Stryker?"

He considered striking the American sailor once or twice across the face for emphasis, but decided against it. He was rewarded for his restraint when the young man said sullenly, "It's the 2JZ line. Mostly nobody's there. The whole place is a mess."

"If I were to talk on it, would Engineering hear?"

"I dunno. This isn't my usual station."

Prasetyo shook his head. "Not a very promising start." He placed one earphone pad against his ear, held up the mouthpiece, pressed the silver button on top of it, and said, "Is anyone from Engineering on the line?"

A tinny and far-off sounding voice spoke up in reply. "This is Main. Who is it and whaddaya want?"

"I am a pirate," he said, "and I want your ship. Right now, I want you to open your hatches so that I can inspect your spaces."

"Not a chance."

"I have a number of hostages here," Prasetyo said. "As I have already made you aware. Would you like to talk to one of them?"

"Let me ask the Chief," came the answer from the other end.

"We're waiting."

"Chief says no dice," the phone talker in Main Control said a moment later.

"In that case, please stay away from your hatches. I'll be deploying explosives, and I wouldn't want anyone to be unnecessarily hurt when the charges go off."

Then he switched back to Indonesian and said to Tansil, "Stay here and watch them." He gestured toward the Tigers. "Don't kill them yet in case we need them later—live hostages can always be made dead later, but dead ones are hard to make alive. Meanwhile, I'm going to go take a look at that hatch."

24

The bodies of the dead intruders had yielded Master Chief Morrison two submachine guns and a pistol. The pistol was a 9mm, and had markings on it in Cyrillic. The submachine guns were Chinese AKs. Not much ammo, though—these guys seemed to have been spraying it around pretty generously. Unless they had a source, they'd run themselves out if they kept using it at this rate.

"They have to have supplies," Morrison said to himself, just as HT3 Vance reappeared from above, coming down the ladder from the main deck.

"Holy shit, Master Chief," Vance said, seeing the carnage and the bullet holes. "I was investigating the mess up by CIC. What happened down here?"

"Grab a weapon," Morrison said. "You're going to need one sooner or later." He pushed the submachine guns across the deck toward Vance. "Here, you can have both of these—one for you, one for your partner. There's the safety, it's off. You have a round chambered. Don't shoot unless you have a clear sight picture."

"Thanks, Master Chief," Vance said.

The investigator from Repair Two went up the ladder to the main deck—undogging the scuttle, then dogging it shut again behind him after his tender came through—and Morrison settled back again to wait.

Seven rounds left, he thought. *That's not going to go very far.*

The more he pondered it, the more he saw that someone was going to have to open *Cushing*'s armory and pass out weapons to the crew. The small arms locker on the main deck would be in unfriendly hands by now. The ship's armory, though, was located low and aft; maybe it was still safe. The Master Chief was acutely aware, however, that the key on his belt was one of only two keys on board that would open the lock on the armory door. GMGSN Stryker had the other key—but Morrison didn't have any idea where Stryker was.

He decided he'd better plan on getting to the armory himself. With the intruders holding the center of the ship, there wasn't any way for him to get to the armory directly. He'd have to go up and out onto the weather decks, then across and down, dodging intruders all the way. *If you're going to do it*, he told himself, *you'd better get up off your ass and do it now.*

USS *Nimitz*
85° 16' E/00° 08' S
0119 Local/2019 Zulu

Aboard *Nimitz*, the worsening weather conditions, and the awareness of time running out, combined to make Admiral Mayland even more irascible. He paced the Carrier's Bridge and scowled at Lieutenant Remey.

"Screw getting overflight permission," Mayland said at last. "If Indonesia wants to declare war on the United States over a humanitarian effort—trying to find one of our own ships in a storm, I ask you!—who's going to listen to them? What are they going to do? Refuse to export coconuts?"

"Isn't that a bit drastic, sir?"

"Yeah, well," said Mayland. "What's the Navy going to do to me—put me out to gardening that little bit earlier? If I lose that ship I'm fucked anyway."

"The weather isn't good for sending out high-performance jets at wavetop height," Remey pointed out. Deflecting a senior officer from a potentially disastrous course of action took skill and careful handling, but that was part of an aide's job. "Taking into account that wavetop height at the moment is about sixty feet and the wind speeds are pretty fierce."

"Well, what are we going to do then? I'm not going to lose anyone from my task force, not me."

"We've already sent one ship out to go looking for *Cushing*. And we won't be getting any helpful data from the satellites, either—the storm is blinding them. There's not really much else that we can do."

"You aren't thinking," Mayland snapped. "If we can't depend on getting intelligence from the fucking Airedales and we can't depend on getting any from the satellites, we'll have to go look for ourselves. Increase task force speed. Get me to the Strait."

"Yes sir. We do have some other fleet elements that we could draw on, if you're willing to get COMSUBPAC out of bed."

"Break my heart. Send him some Flash-precedence traffic. Find out if he has units ready to aid in a search."

"Most likely *Cushing* is doing just fine."

"If they aren't, then American bluejackets are clinging to floating trash out there. They don't want us tucking ourselves in saying 'most likely they're fine.' Get me a search pattern around *Cushing*'s last known posit, their assumed posit, and anything else you can think of."

Damage Control Deck, USS *Cushing*
Off Cape Buku, Indonesia
104° 10' 35" E/00° 47' S
0320 Local/2020 Zulu

The battle lanterns were burning dim, and the light was red and murky. Up ahead, Michael Prasetyo saw three bodies lying on the deck—dead, from the unresisting way they rolled back and forth with the ship's movement. They should have been *Cushing* sailors, but they weren't.

Three lost here. Three more with the hostages. That's six . . . maybe more.

He spoke into his handheld radio. "Fire teams, get going forward, leapfrog. All the way to the bow on this level. Then up a level, and sweep back. Anyone who isn't lying on the deck, get them on the deck. Concussion grenades are authorized. And get my demo guys down here with some plastique. I have a job for them."

"They're working the armory."

"Get them here, now."

"Where are you?"

"The nearest plate is 2-76-4-L," Prasetyo said.

"On our way."

Prasetyo did not like the way things had been going. His men should have taken control of the entire ship by now, and should have been well on the way to disposing of the destroyer's crew.

The presence of civilians aboard ship did present possibilities, however. The civilians had provided him with hostages, but the woman had spoken truthfully when she said that such a card could only be played once. If he judged the moment wrongly, he would accomplish nothing beyond convincing the doomed members of *Cushing*'s crew that surrender was out of the question.

Already, the civilians' existence had provoked more fighting than Prasetyo had anticipated. The situation in Chiefs' Berthing should not have deteriorated so badly that his own presence was required to bring it to order. It had cost three men who were needed elsewhere, as well as the man he'd had to detail to guard them— ten percent of his force in a battle where every man was crucial.

And now this, with the hatches leading to the engineering compartments . . . another delay, when swiftness was everything. The foul weather that sheltered the whole operation from satellite eyes in the sky, and from fighter planes off the distant American carrier, would not last forever. Prasetyo swore under his breath—levelly, and in English, so that his men, if they heard him, would not understand—as he followed his man through *Cushing*'s narrow passages down to the DC deck.

The DC deck was the lowest complete deck on the ship, and the one containing the hatches to Engineering. As he had feared, the hatches were not just stuck, but welded shut. There wouldn't be any quick way in, not even if *Cushing*'s crew members on the other side changed their minds and decided to let the pirates through. Somebody down in the engineering spaces, Prasetyo decided, was both quick-thinking and ruthless.

Sea King Mark 50A helicopter
Crossing the coast of Sumatra
105° 50' E/03° 45' S
0320 Local/2020 Zulu

The helicopter would have been cramped inside with half the number of men it currently held, not even counting their equipment. The helicopter's interior was lit by dim red lights that made its curving walls, under normal light a mustard green, look almost black.

In the red lighting, shadows lay dark as the void, and the men's pale faces floated ghostlike above their subdued uniforms. Each man had a rifle muzzle-down between his knees—muzzle-down because in a helicopter all the important stuff, the wiring and the hydraulics, go in the overhead. An accidental discharge downward had a smaller chance of taking down the bird and everyone in it.

The men leaned against the sides of the helicopter, trying to relax even while they were being buffeted all over the sky by the rising wind. Outside the night was still black, even though dawn was by now only a short while away.

Lieutenant Kerrie Burke could see out by turning her head to the left and looking between the pilots' seats through the windscreen. She was wearing one of the helmets with a microphone and headset combination. Major MacGillivray had another, as did the helicopter crew chief. Except for the pilots, no one else was on the circuit.

"So we find them," Lieutenant Burke said. Even with the headset and microphone, the noise made conversation difficult. The sound of the engines, coupled with the vibration of the helicopter, drowned out anything below a shout. "Then we land on them and do what?"

"We deal with the situation," the Major replied.

"And what if there *isn't* a situation? The Yanks aren't going to think that an armed invasion of their flight deck at zero-dark-thirty is a friendly act."

"Don't worry," said the Major. "I'll buy them all a beer, next port they come to. That should do it."

"Zero visibility," the pilot said. If the conversation between Lieutenant Burke and the Major had disconcerted him, it didn't show in his voice. Nothing showed on his face, either, concealed as it was by a full-face visor. "Coming up on bingo fuel."

Bingo fuel is the amount required to return to base. Lieutenant Burke said nothing, and waited for the Major to speak. He was in charge; the decision to go on or turn back was his.

"Keep on this bearing," MacGillivray said. "Use active radar and

FLIR to find an American destroyer that's probably running under EMCON. And watch for a nonhostile island to set us down on if we don't find them before our tanks have all run dry."

"Yes sir," the pilot said. "You know that's going to be hard to do."

"I didn't think there were many hostile islands here."

"It isn't the hostile part. It's the setting down in these weather conditions."

"Just get us within fifty feet of the ground," MacGillivray told him. "We're rigged to rappel."

"Yes sir," the pilot said. "Going active on radar. GEOS positioning on chart display. We're going to have a hard time identifying ships visually."

The Major looked at his watch. "Should be getting light soon."

"Lot of bloody good that'll do us," the other pilot said. "Rain, and clouds and fog right the way down to the deck."

"What do we do when we get there?" Lieutenant Burke asked again.

"We make sure that whatever is there doesn't threaten Australia," the Major said. "Using whatever degree of force is required to achieve that end. We are expendable. Melbourne isn't. Clear enough?"

"Ever so clear."

The men behind them on the canvas benches seemed to be taking all this in stride. Like experienced troops everywhere, they were catching sleep while they could. The rappelling ropes ran from ringbolts on the deck through rings on their harness, then coiled on their laps. The helicopter bobbed like a cork in the air.

"Looks like a radar return, ship of some kind," the right-hand pilot said, tapping his surface-search screen. "Going down for a closer look."

Lieutenant Burke couldn't see anything outside of the windows.

The eyes are the windows of the soul. She wished she could see Donnie's eyes right now.

The Sea King Mark 50A flew on, farther away from friendly land with every beat of its rotors.

25

Damage Control Deck, USS *Cushing*
Off Cape Buku, Indonesia
104° 10' 35" E/00° 47' S
0320 Local/2020 Zulu

On Prasetyo's orders, a pair of two-man fire teams took position, one against each bulkhead forward and aft. The first team sprayed automatic fire at the bulkhead, where a quick-acting watertight door pierced the thwartships passageway. The second team moved forward, past the ladder. One man looked up the ladder while the second man cracked the door, inserted the muzzle of his weapon, and let off a burst forward. Then the second man kicked the door the rest of the way open and sprayed more fire into the darkened passageway forward.

The first team moved past him, keeping well to port, staying out of the line of their friends' fire. The green-painted bulkhead on their left-hand side was the outer skin of the ship. Heavy iron I-beams—the frames that made up the ribs of the ship—divided the bulkhead into regular segments. Bullets that pierced the metal between the frames wouldn't sink the vessel even if they were below the waterline, but they might make things wet.

When the first team had moved forward to shelter in the angle irons of the next frame, the second team stopped and fired blindly forward into the shadows beyond. Without waiting, the first team moved forward, this time to starboard, moving stealthily but steadily, until they were ten feet ahead of the firing team. They stopped and fired, while the second team moved forward.

Machine guns, like mortars, are area weapons. HT3 Vance stood braced in the after inboard corner of the Engineering Office, portside forward, holding one of the submachine guns that Master Chief Morrison had given him. The Engineering Department kept all its many tech manuals on shelves in the office, out of the heat and moisture down in the holds. The Engineering Office was also the location of one of the two working Xerox machines onboard. Under normal circumstances, the snipes guarded that Xerox jealously. Now Vance hoped that the reams of paper in the tech manuals and the solid metal in the Xerox machine would help him out, providing protection from enemy fire.

The portside second deck passageway ran past the Engineering Office, and Vance had jammed a battle lantern into the angle irons on the other side of the passageway. Then he'd borrowed a marlinespike from his tender, Seaman Rivera, and used it to poke a hole through the painted one-eighth-inch aluminum of the office NT bulkhead, putting the hole in the center of the beam from the battle lantern in the passageway outside.

From his position inside the office, the hole in the bulkhead showed up as a dot of crimson light against the darkness. Even above the pounding of the waves on the side, Vance could hear small arms fire from aft, moving forward. He kept his eye on the crimson dot and waited. As soon as a moving body blocked out the light, he fired.

There's a John Wayne movie called *Rio Lobo*. It had been in the Fleet since before HT3 Vance was born. Pretty much everyone has seen it enough times to have it memorized. In it, John Wayne hands a shotgun to another man and says, "You don't have to be good; just willing." Vance still hadn't known, when he took the submachine gun from Master Chief Morrison, whether he would be willing. Turned out that he was.

The rounds from his submachine gun went straight through the aluminum bulkhead, making a stitchery of holes, like bent metal daisies all tending outward. From the darkened interior of the office Vance swept down the bulkhead once at chest level from forward aft, then from aft forward at deck level. The noise of his own gunfire deafened him and made his head ring. The battle lantern outside the office went out.

The submachine gun in Vance's hands stopped firing, its slide locked back. The captured weapon was empty.

Vance reached behind him to the tending line attached to the D-ring on his OBA and gave the line a single pull. In the forward inboard corner of the office, Seaman Rivera let out line. Vance walked across the deck to the NT door and hesitated, hand on the knob, afraid of what he might find. Suppose the shadows had been other sailors? *I'm an investigator*, he said to himself. *Investigating is what I do.* He pulled the door open. The battle lanterns from forward showed four men down on the deck. To Vance's relief, they weren't in uniform. One of them was still moving.

Vance looked at what he had done. Small arms wounds can be grotesque. He turned back into the Engineering Office and scribbled a note on his notepad: "Send Corpsman." He handed it to Rivera, held up four fingers, and gestured forward toward Repair 2.

Then he returned to the passageway. The scene there hadn't gotten any better. The white light on his helmet illuminated whatever he looked at, so not even dimness could save him. He leaned against the outboard bulkhead and puked.

"You okay?" Rivera shouted in his ear.

"Seasick," Vance said, "Get the Corpsman and"—he noticed that water was pouring in from where his bullets had pierced the skin of the ship—"and send the Plugging and Patching team." The tender vanished forward.

Vance turned to the casualties on deck. He went from man to man, and at each made a cross with his thumb on the man's forehead. "Into Thy hands I commend your spirit," he said at each one. But at each one he picked up the man's weapon and magazines. He might need them later.

Damage Control Deck, USS *Cushing*
Off Cape Buku, Indonesia
104° 10' 38" E/00° 47' 12" S
0330 Local/2030 Zulu

"Where's a sound-powered phone jack?" Prasetyo demanded.

The passageway here held admin offices.

At the engineering hatch, Prasetyo's demolition crew had set up a line of plastique all the way around the hatch combing. Prasetyo took the backpack of money—taken earlier from the ship's now-blasted-open safe—from the head demo man, then picked up a pair of working SP phones, and put them on.

"In Engineering," he said, pressing the button, "can you hear me?"

"Who is this?"

"I am the person currently in charge of this vessel," he said. "Put on your senior man."

"Wait one."

In a moment a new voice came back: "Lieutenant Commander Raymond. What do you want?"

"The hatches to the engineering spaces are welded closed."

"And?"

"I have hatch 2-76-6 wired with demolition charges." Prasetyo said. "Please have all of your men stand well away from it. There's a distinct possibility that when it goes, everyone in that compartment will be reduced to red jelly."

"Yeah, yeah. And?"

"There's also a chance that the engines will be so damaged that the ship won't maintain steerageway. You know that we're in a serious tropical storm—a typhoon, in fact. Without power, this ship turns broadside to the waves, capsizes, and sinks. Either way, you're dead."

Main Engineering, USS *Cushing*
Off Cape Buku, Indonesia
104° 10' 38" E/00° 47' 12" S
0330 Local/2030 Zulu

Down in the engine room, LCDR Raymond turned to Chief Otto. "What do you think?"

"I think the bastard'll do it."

"That's what I think, too. But if he does, he's going to have to do it the hard way, because I'm damned if I'm going to be the man who gives him the ship. So—can we burn a hole through from here to the after engine room?"

Otto thought for a moment. "Maybe. We can sure give it one hell of a try."

"All right, Chief. Make it happen."

"Yes, sir," said Otto, and set to work organizing the cutting team.

Raymond, meanwhile, turned to the other sailors. "All right, everyone—I want you to get as far away from the hatch as possible. Put your thumbs in your ears and your fingers over your eyes, and have your mouths open. Maybe the overpressure won't get you."

He turned to the man on the sound-powered phones. "Anything from the talkers?"

"Nada. Negative reports."

"Okay," Raymond said to the remaining sailors. "Looks like we're on our own for now. The intruders are going to be coming through here, so let's see about making this space fucking lethal. Look sharp, people. They should be coming through here any minute. And remember—I don't want to see any *minor* wounds."

Raymond paused and considered the sailors for a few seconds before singling out HT1 Simmons as the steadiest of the lot—not real imaginative, maybe, but that wasn't necessarily a bad thing right now.

"You," he said. He pointed to the overboard valve in the forward end of the engineering space. "Stand there."

He then pointed to a spot farther aft by the fresh water evaporators. "Any unfriendly gets over there, I want you to open this space to the sea and then knock off the handwheel. Open the sea cocks."

"Yes, sir," Simmons replied. He pulled a twenty-pound sledgehammer from its bulkhead mount. "Open the sea cocks, aye."

26

Chris and H. L. made their way steadily forward along the pas-sageway on the second deck. The only light was a glow somewhere ahead from a far-off battle lantern, its battery power dimming.

The seas were getting stronger and stronger, to the point where the ship was rolling through sixty degrees, from thirty port to thirty starboard, with each roll. Chris and H. L. trailed their hands on the bulkhead as they went, in an effort to balance themselves. All the same, at times they came closer to walking on the bulkheads instead of on the deck.

They came to a ladder and swung down it to the deck below. "This way," H. L. said, heading aft.

"But the armory's the other way—"

"We have someplace else to go first," H. L. said. She was counting non-tight doors. "If I remember the tour Daddy gave me, it should be"—she opened a door to port—"this one."

She felt about on the bulkhead inside the compartment until

she found the switch-operated battle lantern, and flipped it on. The lantern had a red lens, and filled the space with a ruddy glow.

"What have we got here?" asked Chris.

"Ship's laundry," H. L. said. She walked to a white canvas bag about four feet tall hanging from a hook on the far side. The bag had the words "First Division" stenciled on its side. She sniffed at it. "This one smells clean."

She dumped the bag onto the deck. A tumble of blue cloth poured out. She began scrambling among the pile of chambray shirts and dungaree trousers.

"Find yourself something that fits," she said over her shoulder to Chris. "As soon as our people get weapons, anyone who doesn't look like a *Cushing* sailor is going to be a target. Under the circumstances—"

"Got it," said Chris. He began pawing through the heap of loose clothing himself. "Under the circumstances, it behooves us to look as much like *Cushing* sailors as possible."

"Not that you're going to get real close to it, with that hair." She held a shirt up against her torso to judge the size. Good enough, she decided; she stripped off her own wet shirt and slipped on the uniform garment.

"I'll just have to concentrate on looking as Anglo as possible," Chris said. "I think the barbershop is closed right now."

"Whatever—but hurry up." As she spoke, she slipped out of her shorts and into a pair of dungarees. "We have places to be."

Chris found a shirt-and-dungarees combination that more or less fit him, and changed clothes as quickly and discreetly as possible. He knew that H. L. was watching him, and was glad that the red light of the battle lantern would hide any blushes.

"There," he said when he was ready. "Do you still have the keys?"

"Yes," she said.

"Then let's get on with it."

"Right," she said. "Arms Dealers R Us."

She took the red-lensed battle lantern down from its bulkhead bracket and switched it off, leaving the space in darkness. Then together she and Chris headed forward in the direction of the weapons locker.

Main Deck, USS *Cushing*
Off Cape Jabur, Indonesia
104° 30' E/00° 58' S
0430 Local/2130 Zulu

Up on the fantail of USS *Cushing*, deafened by the roaring wind and soaked to the skin by the driving rain, a small group of sailors huddled in the lee of Gun Mount 52. They had ended up here, most of them, after hearing gunfire en route to their General Quarters stations—those of them who had not themselves been hit by gunfire, or found dead sailors blocking their way.

Cushing's Executive Officer was among them. Fire and smoke had blocked Flandry's efforts to make it to his GQ station on the Bridge.

"Sir?" said one of the sailors. The XO didn't recognize the voice, and in the grey pre-dawn light he couldn't make out the name on the man's uniform shirt. "What are we going to do now, sir?"

"Whatever needs to be done," the XO said. To himself, but not aloud, he added, *Just as soon as I figure out what that is.*

"Sir, who do you think—" the speaker began.

"Shut up, Harris," somebody else said. This time Flandry recognized the speaker: Boatswain's Mate 1st Class Merrick from Deck department. "I thought I heard something."

The huddle of men fell silent, waiting for another momentary lull in the wind. A few minutes later, it came. The noise of the storm lessened for an instant, dropping off just enough that they could hear a distant *whup-whup* sound above the steady pounding of the waves.

"You hear it, sir?" BM1 Merrick asked.

"I hear it," Flandry said.

"Sounds like a broken pendant to me," said the sailor who'd first spoken.

"No, you idiot," said Merrick. "It's a chopper."

"You're kidding," another sailor cut in. "Nobody in their right mind would fly birds in this weather."

"Nobody in their right mind would attack a US warship in this weather, either," Merrick said. "And somebody's gone and done just that."

"Do you think whoever's in the chopper is friends with whoever's been shooting at us?"

"I don't think so," the XO said, after a few moments' consideration. "If they were expecting reinforcements to arrive by helicopter, they'd have made a push to take the landing pad first thing. My guess is that we got off a signal somehow, and these guys are the cavalry riding over the hill to the rescue."

That thought led to another one. If the new arrivals on the helicopter were indeed friends, they would need guidance in order to land safely. If his guess was wrong, though, he might be helping more of the enemy to come aboard.

No-risk procedures are for wimps, he told himself. He squared his shoulders and pitched his voice to carry over the renewed howling of the wind.

"Okay, everybody—Smokelight Procedure!"

The sailors abandoned their shelter—such as it was—in the lee of the gun mount, and braved the wind and the heaving deck to grab smoke floats from the racks on the aft end of *Cushing*'s superstructure. Smoke floats are cylindrical canisters, painted white, about three feet long by eight inches in diameter. One end has a pull ring that, when released, removes the tape cover from a pair of holes in the canister. When the smoke float is tossed into the water, salt water goes into the open holes and starts a reaction, causing flames and smoke to shoot out of the top. The canister bobs upright in the water; once it burns all the way out, it fills with water and sinks.

The sailors hauled the smoke floats back to the taffrail.

"On my mark," said the XO. "Now."

The first of the smoke floats went over the side. The XO squinted through the sheets of rain at the luminous dial of his wrist-watch, waiting for the sweep second hand to go around once.

"Two," he said, and sixty seconds later, "Three."

He kept on counting as the sailors threw floats over the side at one minute intervals, pulling rings and tossing canisters until the stock in the ready service locker was expended. It didn't take long— no more than six minutes by Flandry's watch—before a line of flares stretched out across the storm-tossed ocean, leading up to the ship like a path of fire. A helicopter flying low across the water could pick up the trail and follow it home, even under conditions of radio silence and bad visibility.

Flandry had another thought. Flares would be good, if they had any, to illuminate the pitching and rolling deck and the helo landing pad. "Anyone here have the keys to the pyro locker?"

A few moments of mumbling and whispering, and BM1 Merrick reported, "That's a negat, sir."

"Our friends'll just have to do without them, then," Flandry said.

At that moment the sound of the helicopter returned. The chopper—a Sea King Mark 50A, nearly canted on its side to fight the wind—emerged from the clouds, then came up the string of floatlights and across the landing pad.

As it crossed the flight deck, lines fell from the side of the heli-copter, and men in combat fatigues came sliding down the ropes.

Each man wore a backpack and carried an assault rifle. The last man to come out wore a flight suit and a helmet.

The pilot, thought Flandry. *That means nobody's—*

Before he could finish the thought, he saw that the helicopter was already drifting away, only a few feet above the waves and no longer held steady by a living hand at the controls. Then the wind took it. It spun completely on its side, hit the water, and sank.

One of the shadowy newcomers landed near the group of sailors on the fantail. He sprang to his feet in a quick, catlike movement, and said, "All right, then—which one of you is in charge?"

"I am," Flandry said.

"The Major'll be wanting to talk with you, then," the man said.

"The Major?"

Another newcomer stepped forward. "MacGillivray, Special Air Service. What's the situation?"

"Unknown number of intruders aboard," Flandry said. "Any time we stick our noses inside the skin of the ship, we get shot at."

"Any nukes on board?"

"I can neither confirm nor deny the presence or absence of special weapons or forces aboard this ship."

"I'll take that as a yes. Anything else I need to know?"

"We have civilians on board," Flandry said. "If they aren't all dead, we may be looking at a hostage situation."

"Oh, bloody. Well, Her Britannic Majesty will be glad to return your ship to you expeditiously. In the meantime, I'll need people who know their way around your vessel as guides." He turned to his men and said, "Split up, groups of three—team one goes below and team two goes up the ladder to the upper weather levels, and team three goes to the door into the main deckhouse. There are civilian friendlies on board. Rules of engagement: Only armed non-American males are targets."

Flandry stared at him. *Of all the high-handed* . . . "Major, I can't let you do this!"

"You haven't done such a bloody brilliant job of defending the ship yourself. I'll let you know when you're back in charge. Right, then, where are my guides? You, you, and you, come with us."

27

Michael Prasetyo waited, pistol in hand, as his demolitions
expert finished work on the hatch. Acting under the demo expert's
instructions, the pirates had attached a chain to the handwheel of
the hatch and run a thin cord of plastique around the hatch itself,
at the lip. Now the expert affixed the detonator and the det cord,
then looked over at Prasetyo.

Prasetyo nodded. "Do it."

The sound of the explosion was deafening in the enclosed space.
The high-brisiance plastique cut away the metal at the edges of the
hatch with its shattering effect.

At another nod from Prasetyo, the pirates pulled on the chain
attached to the handwheel, and the hatch lifted. The opening led
down into pitch darkness. A throb and rumble of laboring machinery rose up from the engineering compartment below, loud enough
to penetrate even ears dulled by the detonation of the plastique.

"Flashlights," said Prasetyo, turning on his own light as he spoke.

The other pirates switched on their flashlights as well, and the first man started down the ladder. He had his pistol in his right hand and the flashlight in his left, and braced himself with his hip on the handrail against the rolling of the ship.

At the first step the pirate cried out in dismay and slid abruptly downward, dropping out of sight in the blackness. His pistol went *whang* against some unseen metal projection, and his flashlight went out.

"Hey!" shouted the man closest to the open hatch. "Are you all right?"

No answer came back from below. The man who'd called out looked over at Prasetyo.

"You next," Prasetyo said, and pointed at the open hatch. "Go."

The man started down the ladder—only to vanish like the first, his hands flying up over his head and his skull knocking against the edges of the metal rungs with an unmistakable noise. Prasetyo heard a clang as his flashlight hit the metal deckplates. The beam of white light danced about crazily for a few seconds as the flashlight rolled and spun. Then it blinked out, leaving only darkness and the sound of the engines.

They've greased the treads, Prasetyo thought.

"Get me a line!" he shouted to his remaining men. "There, that fire hose! Lower yourselves. Get down there."

He tucked his pistol back into its holster and grasped the handrail. But even knowing about the greased treads didn't help him when *Cushing* took another severe roll. His feet came out from under him in a rush and he slid downward, landing on the metal catwalk and continuing to slide. He grabbed the narrow sides of the catwalk to stop himself—letting go his flashlight to do so, the beam of light tumbling away and vanishing with a splash into the bilges—then pulled out his pistol and pointed it ahead of him into the dark.

He rolled over onto his hands and knees without getting up—the catwalk was covered with lubricant like the steps had been, and he didn't want to risk falling into the bilges after his flashlight. The noise of the engines was everywhere, a steady vibration in the air and metal all around him, and the whole compartment was hot as the inside of an oven. The air stank of oil and bilge water.

A voice shouted down the hatch after him. "Boss! You all right?"

"I'm all right!" Prasetyo shouted back. "Now get on down here!"

He squirmed forward a bit as he spoke. The fire hose he'd pointed out to his men a few moments earlier fell down through the hatch behind him. One by one the remaining pirates climbed through the hatch and descended the ladder, holding onto the hose as they went. Their flashlights illuminated a space full of dark shapes of hulking machinery, beneath an overhead marked by unlit fluorescent tubes and incandescent globes in explosive-atmosphere mountings.

"Spread out," Prasetyo ordered. "We have to secure this space."

He worked his way aft, sliding belly-down on the catwalk with his pistol in front of him. No one behind him was standing; they'd followed his lead and were sliding too. A few feet more, and they finally came to a section of catwalk where the metal wasn't as slippery.

Prasetyo got his feet under him and pushed himself up to a standing position, holding onto a stanchion for balance. The deck heaved and rolled under his feet.

The catwalk divided here, running thwartships around a piece of machinery too high for Prasetyo to see over. Two more of his men stood up and came to join him, holding weapons and flashlights.

"Find the switch and get some light down here," Prasetyo said. "Don't damage the machinery."

"Right, boss." One of the men turned to starboard—gripping a handhold with his right hand, with his weapon in his left and his flashlight clipped to his belt—and took a sliding step, testing the deck for slipperiness. He put down one foot before lifting the other, then moved farther to starboard, looking sharply around.

Another step and the man fell, suddenly headless. Blood spurted upward in a red fountain, splattering the metal and machinery.

Prasetyo trained the beam of his flashlight upward and to starboard. He spotted something in the air—a mist, a shape—a disk that seemed somehow solider than mere air, but still near-transparent. It was a piece of wire, or perhaps light chain, attached to a rotating shaft, spinning, invisible as an electric fan, until a man walked into it.

Ruthless indeed, thought Prasetyo, not without some admiration. To his men, he said, "Stay low—there are booby traps. If you see an American, shoot him."

Two more men slid past Prasetyo, one to right, one to left, and pushed away into the darkness. Prasetyo followed, to starboard. The presence of a trap suggested that something of high value lay in this direction.

The diamond tread of the catwalks gave way to a lattice of metal, gleaming silver in the flashlights. A bulkhead loomed ahead, marked with a large yellow and black safety sign that read: DANGER.

Right, Prasetyo said to himself. *Care to be more specific?*

He pushed past the corpse of his man. Part of his mind was doing arithmetic again, the same kind of cold and unblinking sums he'd done at the very beginning, when his contacts had first come to him with the proposal for this operation. Three men down since entering this space alone—and he'd lost too many already. He'd boarded *Cushing* with a small, elite force, counting on the advantage of surprise. Now he'd lost half of his men and didn't even have the ship yet.

The sound of machinery was louder here, and the sound of the waves pounding the skin of the ship was stronger. He could feel the shock as each wave hit. The man ahead of him turned aft again as the openwork catwalk followed the skin of the ship around another of the great machines. The engines were painted gray, and the pipes coming in and out of them were covered with thick white insulation. Black arrows along the length of the pipes showed the direction of flow. The pipe directly overhead was labeled "LP Steam."

At the corner, Prasetyo looked back. His men were moving through the space. It couldn't be that big—just the darkness and unfamiliarity made it seem so.

Without warning, the man just aft of him screamed. Prasetyo felt a blast of heat, and a moment later, a wetness, as a jet of live steam came from under the openwork and took his man, cooking the tissues of the pirate's lungs and windpipe even as he struggled to draw breath.

Prasetyo groped for his handheld and keyed it on. "Everybody freeze! They're watching us. Fire three rounds into every shadow you see. Ready, fire!"

He too took his pistol and shot—one, two, three—into what he hoped were lurking places. With luck, nothing he did here would cripple the ship. Even so, he didn't dare continue in this direction. That steam could come again any time anyone went by. He pushed back, still staying low, to try the other side.

"Did you have any luck?" he asked his second at the juncture of the catwalks.

The man shook his head. "We lost two more on the port side. You couldn't make it down the starboard side?"

"No," said Prasetyo. "It's time to get those civilians down here from Chiefs' Berthing. They can walk ahead of our people and clear the way."

Main Deck, USS *Cushing*
Off Cape Jabur, Indonesia
104° 32' E/01° S
0445 Local/2145 Zulu

"We're going up and over the superstructure, starboard side," the leader of Fire Team Two said into his handheld radio. He had luminous dots on the back of his black balaclava, so that the other team members would know who and where he was. "Looking for a way in."

Major MacGillivray's voice came back over the handheld. "Get to the Bridge, then sweep back from there. Meet up with Team One midships, main deck. They're sweeping forward portside."

"Roger, moving up."

The Australians had a US sailor with them, Yeoman Second Class Charski. He pointed to the right, where a ladder went up from the main deck to the 01 level.

"That way," he said. "Then forward, past the boat deck."

The leader of Fire Team Two waved his hand and started across the deck toward the ladder. The rest of the team followed him, leapfrogging—one man advancing, then pausing to let the man behind him go past, then advancing again in turn—and covering each other as they went.

Their progress was made more difficult, though not halted, by the continuing storm. The rain soaked their clothes and their gear, and the heavy seas made the deck tilt and shift unexpectedly beneath their feet.

Low clouds obscured the early morning sky; everything was grey and shadowed, which—combined with the rain—made for poor visibility. Flashes of lightning lit up the sky almost continuously, their blue-white flicker breaking up observed motion into a series of stark vignettes, and thunder crashed and rumbled over the noise of the wind and the sea.

The Australians and YN2 Charski continued up the ladder and forward, heading toward Secondary Conn. The SASR troopers exercised as much caution as possible, moving from one bit of cover to another, but there was no way they could avoid open areas completely. It was during the crossing of one such area, when their dark-uniformed shapes stood out in brief contrast to the haze grey paint of the superstructure, that the pirates' submachine gun opened fire.

Muzzle flashes like quick bursts of white light, coming from beside the destroyer's stack, showed where the pirate gunner was hiding. His initial burst took out YN2 Charski, bringing the American sailor down with his dungarees plastered to his body by rain and blood. One of the Australians fell an instant later.

The rest of the SAS team hit the deck and returned fire. Then a second submachine gun opened up from high up in the after mast, catching the Australians in a crossfire—but not for long. The after man in the fire team turned and fired his shotgun, a South African Street Sweeper, in the direction of the second gunner. The shotgun's Jurassic bellow resounded even over the tumult of the storm. Seconds later, a dazzle of lightning lit up the stop-motion image of the machine gunner falling from *Cushing*'s mast.

The gunfire ceased, leaving nothing but the wind and the rain. Only the last of the Australians—the team leader, with his shotgun—remained standing. He lifted his handheld radio to key it on, but the sharp report of a .45 pistol put an end to anything he might have said, and then he was standing no longer.

28

Outside the broken windows on *Cushing*'s Bridge, the sky had gone from solid black to a cloud-smeared gray. The storm, however, had not eased off with the coming dawn. Rain slashed in through gaps in the shattered glass of the windows, and flashes of lightning came and went like strobe lights at a wild party. The captain's chair was smoke-blackened and partly melted, its orange vinyl seat covers cracked and torn. Warner could feel the material complaining every time he shifted position.

He was alone on the Bridge. The dead and injured had been moved away.

Warner thought about the distance to the nearest shore. He'd intended to keep *Cushing* well out of dangerous waters during the storm, but the pirates might not take any such precautions.

Oh, well. Some questions, at least, had answers. He flicked the switch to Main Control. "How much water do we have under the keel?"

"Excess of 200 fathoms, sir."

So far, so good.

"What's the pit log showing?"

"Twelve knots."

Warner relaxed a little, but not much. *Cushing* might not be going aground inside the next half hour or so, but that didn't take away his other problems.

He spoke to Main Control again. "Any luck on getting to Radio Central?"

"Investigators from Repair Three say it's wasted."

That wasn't good. A ship without communications could meet with disaster and no one would ever know, except to add one more name to the centuries-long list of mysterious disappearances at sea.

Warner asked Main Control, "You have contact with Repair Three?"

"That's a Flag Charlie."

"Report from aft?"

"We hold aft." The talker paused. "Just got a weird report."

As if the words had been a cue, Warner heard the sudden slash of automatic fire—one submachine gun speaking, then a second—coming from somewhere aft.

"What's that?" he demanded.

"We have a helo just dropped off troops."

"Say *what?*"

"Investigator from Repair Three says there's a load of troops, speaking English with Brit accents, just jumped off a bird back near the fantail."

Brit accents? In these waters, more likely Aussies, Warner thought. *But whoever they are, it probably isn't Greenpeace, and I* know *it's not Davy Mayland. Whether or not they're friendlies . . .*

"Who else is back there?" he asked as the roar of a shotgun entered the sounds of the firefight. "Do you have comms with the XO?"

"Negative."

An idea was beginning to take shape in his head—a dangerous idea, but one infinitely preferable to sitting and doing nothing. "Very well. Pass to Chief Engineer: You have the load. I'm going into the skin of the ship."

He got out of his chair and stood for a moment amid the water and wreckage of the Bridge. *Cushing*'s Tigers were still his responsibility—as were the destroyer's Special Weapons in their cradles down in the forward deep mag. He picked up a portable battle lantern, and used it to light the way down the passage to his cabin.

Outside the Bridge, the firefighting team had gone and the door to CIC stood open. The air still smelled nasty and acrid, full of smoke and steam. Warner ignored CIC this time and went on to his sea cabin.

His locker was still shut. Warner opened it and pulled out one of the Hawaiian shirts—this one patterned with loud blue, white, and green flowers—that he kept for wearing on liberty.

Warner pulled off his khaki shirt with the silver eagles of his rank and put on the gaudy Hawaiian number. He tucked the .45 into the waistband of his trousers at the back, where the shirt covered it; the rifle he'd carried from the Bridge he left behind, somewhat regretfully, on the bunk. Then he headed aft, looking—he hoped—like a civilian.

Rather than going down the ladder, he made his way through the wreckage of CIC and what was left of Sonar Control. From there he took the midships aft ladder down past the 01 level to the main deck. The lights were out down here, too, though there wasn't much in the way of damage. Warner shut off his battle lantern. If he couldn't find his way around his own ship by Braille, he wasn't fit for command.

The Tigers should all be in Chiefs' Berthing—assuming they'd made it to their GQ station at all. The goat locker was one more deck down, with who-knew-what blocking the way.

That didn't matter. A metal ship has lots of air pipes and ven-
tilation shafts, some of them big enough to take a full-grown man,
and Warner knew where all of *Cushing*'s scuttles and access plates
were. Specifically, in this case, he knew about the scuttle that gave
access to the air plenum chamber on the second deck. Warner
turned the wheel, opened the scuttle, and swung down.

The plenum chamber was small, but it had a door on this deck,
right across the passageway and just forward from the Chiefs' Pantry. Warner opened the door cautiously, hoping that this wasn't his
day for any more bad luck than he'd had already.

The passage was empty, at least for the moment. A pause, a
dash across the open space, and he was inside the pantry, looking
out through the side of the fold-down cover over the serving line.

The Tigers were there, a small huddle of pale and bedraggled
civilians, their tired faces and dirty clothing illuminated by the fading red and white glow of the battle lanterns. Everyone was silent,
watching the man who stood guard over them with a pistol in his
hand. He was slender and muscular—probably Indonesian—and
wore cammies and a tee shirt rather than a formal uniform.

One of the pirates, clearly. Warner, hidden in the shadows,
studied him intently. Not regular military—even in less developed
countries, there was a certain look that the man didn't have. Practiced, though, and confident.

The handheld radio at the man's hip began speaking in Indonesian. The pirate keyed on the radio and replied in the same language, then said in English to the Tigers, "It's time you made
yourselves useful. Come with me."

For a brief instant Warner thought that the Tigers would refuse, but the 9mm seemed to decide for them. One of the Bailey
twins opened his mouth to talk. Chief Willis's father quieted him
with a gruff word.

The Tigers started moving forward. Warner slipped out of the
shadows and entered the queue himself. He worked his way unob-

trusively forward to stand beside Laura, then reached down and squeezed her hand. She glanced over at him and looked startled, but said nothing.

Only after he'd successfully made contact did he realize that Chris wasn't part of the group. And neither was H. L. Morrison.

Main Deck, USS *Cushing*
Off Cape Jabur, Indonesia
104° 32' E/01° S
0445 Local/2145 Zulu

Chris followed H. L. down the passageway in what he hoped was still the general direction of the weapons locker. The all-around darkness, combined with the constant motion of the ship, had thoroughly scrambled his own mental map of the vessel's interior layout. When H. L. came to an abrupt stop, he almost ran into her again.

"Here," she said. She pointed at the oblong hatch set into the deckplates near her feet. "I think this is the right one."

"Are you sure?"

"Reasonably," she said. "At least, I'm not *more* sure about any other way down to the next level, if that's what you want to know."

"Close enough. Let's open it up and see what happens."

Working together, they undogged the hatch, then raised the hatch cover and set the stanchions in place to hold it up. Chris more than half expected armed intruders to come boiling up from the deck below like ants—but when, after a nervous interval, he chanced a look, no one stood before the door to the armory, alone at the bottom of its own ladder well.

Cautiously, Chris and H. L. descended the ladder and stood looking at the closed door, and the big Greenleaf and Sergeant lock with the armored shackle. H. L. switched on the battle lantern she'd carried with her from the ship's laundry, and handed it to Chris.

"Shine this on the door," she said.

She fumbled in the pockets of her borrowed dungarees and brought out the key ring that Stryker had tossed over to her back in Chiefs' Berthing. The ring held a number of different keys. Chris did his best to keep the light steady while H. L. fumbled with the lock, trying to find the right key by experiment while the ship rolled and tossed.

The first key she tried didn't fit at all. The next two fit the lock, but wouldn't turn. Then one fit, turned, and the lock fell open.

The inside of the armory was even darker than the ladder well outside, with no light at all reflected down from the dying battle lanterns on the higher decks. When Chris shone the portable battle lantern into the space, its red light played across racks full of weapons, each rack fitted with its own padlock.

"Here we are," he said. "Your one-stop neighborhood discount weapons shop."

"Very funny," H. L. said. "Let's get going."

"Okay." Chris set the battle lantern down on the armory workbench, where it promptly fell off due to the ship's motion. He picked it up and wedged it securely in place. "What's next?"

"Now you take the keys and I stand guard," H. L. said. She had already braced herself in the corner of the armory, covering the door with the weapon she'd recovered earlier. Once Chris had the key ring, she nodded toward the rows of weapons. "Over there. The shotgun rack."

Chris started fiddling with keys, while H. L. braced and waited.

"Here we go," he said finally. The lock fell away, and Chris lifted the bar that restrained the Model 870s.

"Great," H. L. said. "Ammo's in the cabinets under the bench. Start loading them up."

"Small problem there," said Chris. "I don't know how."

"You *what*?"

"You're the gun nut, remember? I'm just a nature photographer."

29

The handful of civilian hostages, and Captain Warner, made their way unsteadily down the rolling, tilting passageways toward Main Control, under the watchful eye—and the 9mm pistol—of their captor. As they went, Warner made his way unobtrusively to the head of the ragged line, closer and closer to the pirate. He had a bad moment when a heavy roll sent one of the Bailey twins—he couldn't tell if it was Kyle or Tyson—stumbling into him, and the boy's eyes went wide with recognition.

Don't say anything, he thought, and moved his lips soundlessly on the words. *I'm not here.*

It wasn't going to work—he could see the muscles of the boy's throat and face tightening for a shout of surprise—but rescue came unexpectedly. Before the boy could cry out, the relative quiet of the passageway was ripped in two by a wail from his twin.

"Daddy! *Daddy!*"

LTJG Bailey lay sprawled on the deck of the passageway in a

dark puddle of blood. The twin who'd cried out tried to run forward, but Laura grabbed and held him in spite of his struggles to break away. His brother, the one who'd recognized the Captain, could only stand and stare at the crumpled body.

Cushing took another heavy roll, and Warner knew that he had only a brief moment in which to take advantage of the opening that Bailey had, through the time and place of his death, unknowingly provided.

"I feel sick," he said in a loud and—he hoped—queasy-sounding voice. He put his hand over his mouth and made heavy retching noises, doubling over as he did so as if he were heaving up his guts.

The pirate was not sympathetic. Pistol in hand, he moved closer to Warner.

"Come on, you!" he said. Warner straightened, reached out, and pushed him as hard as possible.

The pirate skidded on the metal deckplates and sat down hard. Warner followed him down, as did the nearest of the older Tigers.

Warner felt a hard thump against his ribs. He grabbed the pirate's clothing, pushed hard, and slammed the pirate up against the bulkhead with his shoulder in the middle of the man's chest. The machine pistol in the pirate's hand went off, chattering. Warner pushed his left forearm against the pirate's throat, forcing the man's head back. Pain shot up the captain's leg—the man had stomped on his foot.

A hand—Willis's—punched past Warner's head into the pirate's face. Warner reached into his waistband, pulled the pistol, and slammed its butt against the pirate's skull. He drew back his hand and smashed it down again. The man went limp. Warner stepped back. The man fell. Warner stood and shot the man once.

"Follow me," Warner said to the Tigers, once the pirate was dead. "I'll get you back to the fantail."

But Laura said, "Wait—Chris and H. L. have the keys to the armory. They might have it open by now."

"Now *that*," Warner said, "is a good point. The armory is just down two ladders from here, almost directly below us. You and you"—he looked at Willis and Dellamonica—"are you with me?"

The two retired sailors both nodded, and Warner turned to Laura. "I'll need you to take the two boys back to the goat locker and stand fast there. One way or the other, this should all be over soon."

"I certainly hope so," Laura said. She was tired and disheveled and splattered all over with other people's blood, but the smile that she gave him worked better than bourbon or strong coffee. "I've promised myself a nice cool drink at the O Club in Yokosuka, and you're the one who's going to buy it for me."

"It's a date," Warner said. "The rest of you—come with me."

He picked up the pirate's hand-held radio and 9mm pistol. *Now*, he thought grimly, *there's no one alive among the intruders who can say, if things go wrong, that Laura was part of the counterattack.*

Armory, USS *Cushing*
Off Cape Jabur, Indonesia
104° 32' E/01° S
0450 Local/2150 Zulu

H. L. unlocked the ammo locker and pulled out a package of shotgun shells, red double-ought buck. She pushed them into the first shotgun's magazine tube until it was full, pushed the release, pumped a shell into the chamber, and pushed one more into the extended magazine. She slung the first weapon over her shoulder and loaded a second, then filled a canvas bag with loose shells and put it over her other shoulder.

Then she turned to the rack of .45 pistols. She drew two, sticking them into her waistband, then picked up a box of bullets and started stuffing magazines with rounds.

"I'm being a bad girl," she remarked to Chris as she worked.

"You're only supposed to put five rounds in each mag, to save the follower spring, but I'm filling them up all the way."

"How many is 'all the way?'" Chris asked.

"Eight 230 grain copper jacketed rounds each—good stuff."

After she'd filled a dozen magazines, she turned to the rack of M16 rifles. Again she loaded two, and filled six more magazines with 5.56mm rifle bullets.

"Okay, Nature Boy," she said when she was done. "We are about to go hunting. So listen up."

She picked up a .45, and pointed. "This is your basic pistol. The thumb safety is here, the grip safety is here. The slide lock is here. I'm not going to get into half-cock or anything else. With the slide in the rear position like this, you insert a magazine like so. The pointy ends of the bullets go forward."

"I know *that*," he said.

"Shut up and listen. With the magazine fully inserted, you trip the slide release with your thumb like so, and allow the slide to fly forward. That chambers a round. When you have emptied the magazine, the slide will again lock in the rear position. You drop the expended magazine by pressing this round button on the side of the grip, slide in a new one, and continue firing. Questions?"

"Where should I aim?"

"Center of body mass," she said. "Don't get fancy. Now your basic M16 rifle is similar. Here is where the magazine goes. You then pull back on the charging handle and let it fly forward to load the first round. This is the safety. You'll notice three positions: safe, semi-auto, and full auto. Since I don't have time to train you in the employment of full-auto fire, leave this in the semi-auto position. Mine will be set to Rock 'n' Roll."

"Comforting."

"It should be. Now, when the mag is expended, here's the button for dropping it. Insert a new magazine, and continue as above. Last is your shotgun. Pull the trigger, it goes off, that releases the pump so you can rack another shell. The safety is here. Don't put it on safe. That'll just waste time."

"How about those?" Chris asked, pointing to a rack of M60 machine guns.

"Too heavy. Now stay behind me, and try not to shoot me in the back when things get exciting. Any sailors we find, tell 'em the armory's open. Let's go find some intruders and ruin their day."

The heavy metallic rattle of feet coming down the ladder interrupted her monologue. In the red light, the shadows in the ladder well were deep, but not deep enough to make a good disguise. Whoever was coming down was dressed in civvies and carrying a weapon.

H. L. raised her shotgun. She drew a breath and let it out again gently—but before she could pull the trigger, Chris Warner slammed into her and knocked the weapon aside. The shotgun went off with a deafening roar, filling the air in the enclosed space with bad-smelling vapors.

"You idiot!" she shouted at Chris, struggling to pull her weapon back into line.

Then Captain Warner stepped into the space, and she fell silent. But Chris Warner was grinning in the red light of the portable battle lantern.

"Hey, Dad," he said. "I'd recognize that ugly-ass Hawaiian shirt anywhere."

"So would any crewmember," Warner replied. "Let's start rounding up stragglers and handing weapons around. I'm going to take back my ship."

Damage Control Deck, USS *Cushing*
Off Cape Jabur, Indonesia
104° 32' E/01° 2' S
0500 Local/2200 Zulu

Up on the DC deck once again, Captain Warner and the volunteer Tigers took position, some of them covering the passageway forward and others watching aft. They'd found five sailors as they moved up and forward, survivors of the fighting around the repair lockers, or men prevented from going to their GQ stations by fires or intruders. They'd taken cover, to await the arrival of an officer who could give them orders. Now the Captain was there, and orders weren't lacking. Warner used them all. Some of he placed covering the passageway; and others he set watching aft, as the group started forward toward the engineering spaces. So far they had not encountered any of the intruders.

"Now to see where things stand," Warner said. He opened the door to the admin office. H. L. and Chris followed him, weapons ready. Picking up the SP phone handset, he turned the selector to Main Control and larrupped the crank.

A moment later, a voice answered up, "Main."

"This is the Captain," Warner said. "Interrogative sitrep?"

"Situation sucks, sir. We have intruders in the space. Holding them aft of the donkey boiler, but don't know how much longer we can do that. Lost comms with everything aft of the Mess Decks when they blew the hatch."

"Pass to Chief Engineer, I have the midships passage, second deck. Hold what you have, I'll be taking them from the rear."

"Roger. Be advised, entering the main spaces is bad for your health."

"Roger that," said Warner. "And don't any of you guys stick your heads up until I give the all clear."

"Aye aye."

Warner went back out into the passage. "Okay, people," he said. "Here's what we're going to do. One M60 team stays here. Anyone comes up the passage who isn't in a US uniform, you shoot 'em. Anyone shoots at you, you shoot 'em. You get a bad attack of the what-the-hells, you pop off half a belt. One shotgun man stands behind you, providing cover to the machine gun. Everyone else, we're going forward to Main Control."

He turned and led the way up the passage. The hatch leading downward to Main Control lay up ahead to port. As soon as the hatch was in sight, Warner had a second M60 team set up, the weapon placed to put rounds about two inches over the hatch combing. Then he keyed on the radio he'd taken from the guard.

"Attention, pirates," he said. "This is *Cushing*. Surrender or die. How copy. Over."

The two men weren't standing more than a dozen feet apart, measured vertically, separated only by the armored DC deck. At Warner's signal, the machine gunner squeezed off a burst of five rounds with the M60—a distinctive sound unlike that of any weapon anyone else had been using, its full-throated roar far deeper and louder than the ripping noise of the submachine guns.

"Attention, *Cushing*," came back a voice after a moment. "I have your bilges wired with explosives. Allow me and my men to withdraw with their weapons, or I'll blow the bottom out of your boat."

"How many men?" Warner asked.

"I'll tell you when we're all out," the voice said.

"You have two minutes to get up out of my Engineering spaces before I come in and kill you all."

"A man of direct action. I like that."

A few moments passed. Up the hatch from below came a hand, grasping for purchase. Then a man followed. He stood, leaning against the bulkhead for balance on the rolling deck, a weapon in his hand.

"Shall I shoot him?" H. L. asked.

"Nah, let him go," said Warner. "I want them off my ship. If they think there's no way out they might just blow the rest of their demo charges out of sheer cussedness." He'd never expected that the Master Chief's adored baby daughter would turn out to be a blonde Amazon with an itchy trigger finger, but that was the turn of the millennium for you.

One by one eight more men came out, each one heading up the

ladder, no more than two men at a time ever in sight. Just as the last of the eight men emerged, the M60 Warner had left aft with Willis and Dellamonica opened up, answered by a collection of other small arms fire.

The distant machine gun fired bursts of three, then five, then another two. Then the shotgun added its distinctive roar. The last sounds were of US weapons. The gunner on Warner's forward M60 didn't hesitate, but let loose a burst of his own, and the two departing pirates fell.

2nd Deck Aft, Portside, USS *Cushing*
Off Cape Jabur, Indonesia
104° 32' E/01° 2' S
0504 Local/2204 Zulu

The group of Tigers Warner had left in ambush aft on the second deck waited in the darkness. A battle lantern glimmered, low on batteries, farther aft.

A burst of automatic fire came from aft. It was answered from closer by. A flash-and-bang rolled forward, and its glare illuminated a group of men dressed all in black, with tight-fitting balaclavas, just like movie terrorists. They were firing behind them at some unseen foe.

"Not US uniforms," Willis said. He fired a burst down the center of the passageway. The battle lantern went out. Return fire came pelting toward him. Dellamonica let loose with a blast from his shotgun into the dark.

Willis pulled his trigger and swept the muzzle from side to side of the passageway. A moment later, Dellamonica stopped firing, out of shells.

"What happened?" Willis shouted.

"We're still alive," Dellamonica said. "Reload."

Damage Control Deck, USS *Cushing*
Off Cape Jabur, Indonesia
104° 32' E/01° 2' S
0505 Local/2205 Zulu

"Truce is over," Warner said into the handheld. "Whoever you sent around the stern is down."

No answer came over the radio. Warner stepped forward to the hatch, and shouted down the ladder well, "In Main, this is the Captain, secure your space and report."

Then he turned to his own machine gunner and said, "Don't let anyone up until I say so."

With that, he headed aft, Chris and H. L. with him. The after passage when they got there was still in the hands of the Tigers. A bit farther aft they came on a set of three men dressed in black, with black balaclavas, holding submachine guns. They were down and lying still. An American sailor, equally motionless, lay near them.

"Damn," Warner said. He pulled off the balaclava from the head of the nearest body. The dead man was a blond of European descent. "It's the guys from the helo. This game looks like it's going to go into extra innings."

At that moment he felt a shock through the deck plates. An explosion. The ship bucked as it was taken by the wind; the rolls increased. A moment later, the ship heeled hard to starboard as it pulled into a screaming right turn. "Fuck," Warner said, forgetting both his reserve as Captain and that there were young civilians present. "What now?" He turned to the man on the SP phones. "If there are any investigators alive, get 'em out there, now. Forward and topside."

Then he turned to the other Tigers. "Proceed slowly aft. When you find sailors, turn over your weapons to them, and tell them to proceed to their GQ stations. Message to any officer: I'll be on the Bridge."

30

Master Chief Morrison came out from the shadows behind a reel of five-inch mooring line. He stuck his now-empty .45 into his belt and made his way across the heaving deck to the man he'd just shot. The last of the armed intruders on this part of the 01 level was down and not moving, and Morrison needed more weapons and ammo if he wanted to have a hope of making it all the way across and down to the ship's armory.

He spotted the man's handheld radio lying on the deck, picked it up, and keyed it on.

"I don't care who you are," he said. "You picked the wrong ship."

Then he heard the sound of a pistol firing, and felt the impact of a bullet slamming into him and knocking him down.

He lay on the deckplates, unable to move, and watched the man who'd shot him come up the external ladder onto the weather deck.

With one hand the man held onto the railing to keep his balance; in the other he held a 9mm pistol. He stood looking down at Morrison for a moment, and thoughts moved darkly behind his eyes.

A squawk from the handheld radio interrupted the man's calculations: a voice, Australian-accented, demanding, "Who is this? Teams, report!"

The man bent and picked up the handheld, still keeping his 9mm trained on Morrison. "I have control of this ship. Whom do I have the honor of addressing?"

"Major Donald MacGillivray, SASR," the radio said. "All teams, sec freq, now."

The radio went silent.

Main Deck, USS *Cushing*
104° 32' E/01° 2' S
0506 Local/2206 Zulu

Lieutenant Kerrie Burke stood with Major Donald Mac-Gillivray on *Cushing*'s rain-lashed deck forward on the 01 level. No one else was in sight. The sky was growing lighter as the morning wore on, but the rain and wind had not slacked off any since the Australians had ditched their helicopter, and the motion of the waves had not eased. She had to hold on to a stanchion to keep her balance, and the driving rain soaked her clothing and stung against her exposed skin.

MacGillivray was speaking urgently into his handheld radio. "Report! Report!" he demanded, but the handheld remained silent. The Major scowled at it. "Damn."

"That makes three teams down," Lieutenant Burke said. The noise of the storm caught the words from her mouth and blew them away, forcing her to shout in order to be heard. "Presumed lost, no comms. Time to activate the second set of orders?"

MacGillivray shook his head. "Not yet. There are still a couple of things to try."

"Look around, Donnie," said Lieutenant Burke. "We're all there is. One of Prasetyo's snipers could blow your head off in the next two minutes, and then there'd be nobody left to do the job but me. I don't have your training and experience."

"Right then. Second set. We are to prevent nuclear weapons from falling into unfriendly hands by any means necessary. This ship is in unfriendly hands right now. Down she goes."

Considering the probable fate of the three SASR teams, and the deadly efficiency shown by the pirates so far, Lieutenant Burke wasn't inclined to disagree. "That's how it adds up for me, too. Now, as to the means?"

"I have a duffel full of plastique and detonators. Is that meaningful enough for you?"

"It'll do for something brief but intense."

"My favorite kind of encounter," MacGillivray said. "We need to get low, below the waterline. Let's get going."

And with that, he ghosted forward over the weather decks. Lieutenant Burke followed close behind.

Forward Missile Control, USS *Cushing*
104° 32' E/01° 2' S
0509 Local/2209 Zulu

Lieutenant Ernie Gilano lay under the ladderback next to For-ward Missile, his back against the bulkhead and the M14 rifle in his lap. The starboard bulkhead here, painted white, formed part of the skin of the ship, below the waterline. The iron of the frames wasn't lagged. Bare metal under paint, it throbbed with the power of the storm.

The space itself, saving his presence, held nothing except a yellow-painted tag identifying the space and who was responsible for it, a bulkhead-mounted Damage Control list of all the fittings in the space, and a battle lantern—its battery-powered light faded down to a dull yellow glow—still shining at the base of the ladder.

Gilano had pushed the safety on the M14 forward out of the trigger guard some time ago. He wasn't sure how long, because his mind and body had conspired with the pain of his injuries to stretch and compress the flow of time in confusing ways.

The journey from *Cushing*'s Bridge to his GQ station had been a slow crawl through hell, and he no longer entirely trusted his own senses. Even the increased pitching of the ship felt strange and dubious to him. He couldn't be sure how much of the motion he experienced was the ship and how much was the result of his own altered perceptions.

When the two black-clad figures—one carrying a loaded duffel and the other carrying a submachine gun—came down the ladder into the space, he thought at first that he had begun to hallucinate. Especially since the one with the submachine gun had a woman's shape under the dark, rain-soaked garments.

Nevertheless, he stilled his breath when the man with the duffel glanced his way, and tried to keep his eyes half-closed and unblinking.

"Another dead one," the man said. He spoke English with a Crocodile Dundee accent, which argued for his unreality. Gilano couldn't think of any reason outside of a nightmare for English-speaking pirates to attack *Cushing*. "Time to set the charges and get out of here."

"Glad to hear that getting out is on the agenda." The second speaker, if she was real, was definitely a woman. Her voice was a husky alto, and under different circumstances Gilano might have found it sexy. "*Dulce et decorum est pro patria mori* and all of that, but I'd just as soon leave the dying to somebody else for as long as possible."

"Right, then. No argument there," the man said. "It's up the ladder and head for a life raft as soon as I pull the detonator."

Working rapidly, the speaker began placing bricks of plastic explosive in the angles of the frames that defined the space. Lieutenant Gilano watched the procedure with growing alarm. His mind was hazy, and reality was fading in and out with the throbbing of his broken leg—but if the man in black and his female companion weren't just the products of his own pain-wracked imagination, then *Cushing* looked to be in even worse trouble than before.

Slowly, carefully, Gilano pushed the selector switch of the M14 from semi to full automatic. The pounding of the seas and the creaking of strained metal from the ship's strength members drowned the low click as it popped into place. Then he pulled the trigger, and let the natural rise of the weapon stitch a line of shots up the man's body.

The man in black fell to the deck, pulling the detonator as he went down. Gilano already had his M14 coming to bear on the woman when she fired at him in response. Bullets ricocheted around the enclosed space like maddened, metallic bees. Gilano couldn't tell whether the bullets that brought down the woman were his or some of her own. Neither could he say who had fired the rounds that slammed into him.

Pain blurred Gilano's vision, but he could still see, dimly, the fuse that led from the pull-type detonator to the demolition blocks. How long, he wondered, did *Cushing* have before everything blew? The man who'd rigged the charges had spoken of making an escape . . . long enough for a person to scramble up the ladder, at least. Maybe that would be long enough for Gilano to try cutting . . .

"The red wire or the blue wire?" he said aloud. Neither of the two dead intruders answered him. "Hell, why not all the wires?"

He dropped his rifle and began to pull himself forward, clawing his way across the heaving deck until he reached the fuse. He grabbed hold of the fuse and pulled. It tore free of the demo blocks, dragging the crimped-on blasting caps with it.

If the pain of moving had left him with any breath to spare, Gilano would have cursed. In an enclosed space like this one, if the blasting caps went they might not need direct contact to set off the demo blocks.

Through the fog of pain, he glared at the body of the man who'd rigged the charges. *This is all your fault, you son of a bitch.*

Then an idea struck him, and even through the pain and haze, Gilano smiled.

Your fault, and you can help fix it.

He dropped the bundle of fuses and detonators on top of the man's body. Then, moving as rapidly as he could—his body was losing strength fast, and he felt like he had to tell each individual muscle when to twitch and contract, and fewer and fewer of them seemed to be listening—he dragged over the body of the man's female confederate. *A pity*, he thought. *She really did have nice tits.* He stretched her out across the fuses and detonators like the top half of a grotesque sandwich, then lay down himself across the top of the pile. After that, he didn't have the energy left to do anything except wait.

He didn't have to wait long. He felt the blasting charges go, their concussive effect muffled by the dead flesh surrounding them, but a moment later—when it became clear that the demo blocks themselves remained whole and undetonated—he no longer had the strength left to feel anything.

31

Prasetyo climbed the ladder to Secondary Conn. In the end, he'd left the American sailor to lie wounded on the deck, less out of mercy than out of a recognition that shooting the man a second time would do no particular good.

Hearing the voice of an Australian SASR Major coming over the handheld had startled him. Clearly, though, someone aboard *Cushing* had made a distress signal—he'd have to figure out the trick later, when he had the time—and the Australians had responded.

An Australian presence aboard would complicate things, but not for long. Prasetyo had already made up his mind to quit the ship. All his life, numbers had spoken to him: profit and loss, minimax equations, cost and earning. When he was tired, the lessons learned in all-nighters at Wharton flashed crystalline to the fore. If the mission was lost, all hope of profit gone, then each bullet was an expense with no recompense, and not worth firing.

Down in the engineering spaces, he'd found himself caught between live steam and an M60 machine gun, with twenty-three effectives left from his original force and only nine with him in Engineering and under his direct control. The numbers had spoken, and what they said to him was that it was time to cut his losses and get out.

He hadn't expected, after his brief negotiations with *Cushing*'s Captain, to meet with an attack from behind. Now he had only five men, and not a lot of options. His threat to rig explosives in *Cushing*'s bilges had been a bluff—the last of his few demo charges were up here in Secondary Conn.

"Stand by," he said to his remaining handful of men. He took his radio and called the vessel which had been guiding them by its lights ahead. "Come up alongside, starboard side. We're going to go home."

Then he turned back to his men. "Time to leave our American friends a good-bye present."

He pointed at the remaining demo charges, then at *Cushing*'s wheel and binnacle. "Blow it. Without steering, they're dead." In a storm like this the ship would turn broadside to the waves, capsize and sink.

And a US Navy warship that never comes home, he thought, *will make an impressive story to tell prospective backers. Otherwise, this is nothing but a failed operation . . . and nobody wants to back a failure.*

By now the escort vessel was drifting back alongside *Cushing*.

"Rappelling rig in place," Prasetyo said. "Stand by—here they come—go, go, go!"

On his command, the few remaining pirates leapt over the starboard rail to the deck of the wildly heaving 80-footer below. Prasetyo followed them, and his craft turned off its lights and peeled away to starboard. Seconds later the demo blocks on Secondary Conn blew up, painting the storm clouds with a lurid glow.

A moment later, *Cushing*'s head fell off to port as the destroyer came about, no longer under command, coming broadside into the heavy seas.

After Steering, USS *Cushing*
104° 32' E/01° 2' S
0510 Local/2210 Zulu

In After Steering, Fireman Raveneau stirred uneasily.

Something bad had just happened—he wasn't sure what. But he could feel the ship coming about, and the change in her motion as the waves hit her.

Then he remembered Lieutenant Commander Raymond's order: *If you lose communications with Main Control, I want you to two-block the tiller hard right and leave it there until I personally tell you different.*

He could do that from down here, no matter who held the Bridge or Secondary Conn. All that would be needed would be to use the trick wheel to put the tiller as far right as it could go, setting the ship turning in a tight circle. She wouldn't go anywhere that way, but neither would she be lying broadside to the waves and in danger of capsizing.

The gyro repeater was drifting in a slow circle right now. And it wasn't anything that could be explained by steering, either; Raveneau could see that the rudders weren't moving.

That meant the gyro had tumbled, or was off line—and *that* meant that IC Central was gone. And IC was right next to Main.

"Main, After Steering," he said into the phones. "Main, After Steering. Answer up."

No reply.

"Any station, After Steering, come on, guys, where the fuck are you?"

Nothing.

A sudden metallic noise coming from above him made Raveneau jerk his head back and look upward. Someone was fooling with the handwheel on the hatch.

The wheel spun until it caught on the dogging wrench that Raveneau had jammed into its spokes. The wheel backed off a fraction, then tried to turn again. Whoever was up there was trying to get down into After Steering. With him.

"Oh, fuck me," Raveneau said.

He was short—his time left in the service was measured in weeks rather than months. Overhearing the conversation back in Engineering berthing had confirmed what he should have known all along: His Chief had already put in the paperwork to have him shitcanned. As soon as they got back to Hawaii he was going to be getting on that big silver bird for the mainland with a Convenience of the Government discharge in his hand. He'd had enough adventure; he was going to get a job.

"I do not fucking need this right now."

He reached over to the switches that controlled the steering cables and rotated them to the straight-up neutral position, engaged the trick wheel, and spun it to the right, as far as it would go. Behind him the steering motors whined as the rudder posts came up against the stops.

The deck heeled to starboard as the ship went into a screaming right turn. He walked back to the steering motors and switched them off, so the bearings wouldn't burn out. Then he braced himself back in the frames, phones on his head, and awaited developments.

Main deck, USS *Cushing*
104° 50' 2" E/01° 12' 30" S
0512 Local/2212 Zulu

Captain Warner was halfway up the ladder from the second deck to the main deck when he felt the ship heel over hard to starboard. He held on to the handrails until the motion steadied, then continued to climb.

Once, naval regulations stated that in battle the Captain's station was on the quarterdeck. This led to at least one unfortunate court-martial and conviction during the War of 1812, when a man who was not on the quarterdeck became Captain while away from that area by virtue of having every officer senior to him killed in action within five minutes.

Later, the Captain's station was defined as being on the Bridge. This seemed reasonable, since the Bridge was the center of command and control, where the Engine Order Telegraphs and the wheel were located. High on the superstructure, the Bridge also gave better visual information than other places on board.

Then came the ascendancy of radio and radar. Now more information was flowing into the Combat Information Center than onto the Bridge, so the Captain's station was defined as being in CIC. Still later, reality set in, as much as it ever does in the Navy, and the Captain's station was defined as "where he can best fight his ship."

While still allowing the power and glory of the Fleet to punish a commander who avoids personal danger to the detriment of his command, now if in the Captain's judgment he can best take the war to the enemy while he himself is standing knee deep in the bilges, then in the bilges you can find him.

Captain Warner, for his part, had chosen to stand amidships, against the forward railing of *Cushing*'s Signal Bridge, just forward of the signal shelter.

The seas were still mountainous. The howling wind lashed the spray from their tops, mixing it with the rain to form drifting grey sheets. As *Cushing*'s head fell off, the waves struck more and more to the side, and the ship's roll increased. Warner braced his legs and held on to the teak rail atop the bulwark forward of Sigs.

Then the seas were on the quarter—the pitching grew even

worse—and then from the stern. Wave on wave crashed aft, the weight of the water sending shudders through the deckplates.

Warner picked up the sound-powered phone chest set from its storage box on the Signal Bridge, and plugged it into the 1JV—primary maneuvering and docking—jack. He pressed the silver button on top of the mouthpiece.

"All stations, Sigs, report."

The ship was turning. She'd been stuck in a hard right for a while now, alternately pounding, rolling, and in danger of getting pooped. The door aft past the crew's berthing was shut, dogged from the far side, and the surviving BAF members—now sweeping the ship for any remaining intruders—reported that there were still unfriendlies in the space beyond. No way to get to After Steering through there—not without a cutting torch and some time.

"Sigs, After Steering, aye," came the reply.

"Who's back there?" Warner asked.

"Who's asking?"

"Raveneau! Is that you?"

"Yeah. Who's that?"

"This is the Captain. Listen, is there a problem with the steering motors?"

There was a long pause. Raveneau was not, Warner recalled, the world's fastest thinker even under the best of circumstances. "How do I know it's you?"

"You've heard my voice enough times."

"Maybe someone has a gun at your head."

"Raveneau," Warner said, "why did you choose this morning to get smart, instead of doing it before you stole that baseball trophy?"

Another long pause. "Okay, sir, yeah, I guess it's you. No, nothing wrong with the steering gear."

"Then come to amidships, and stand by for rudder orders."

"But Mr. Raymond said not to do that, unless he told me personally."

"Raveneau, you've never obeyed an order in your life. You've picked a hell of a time to start."

"Will I get in trouble with Mr. Raymond?"

"Not with him."

"Okay, I've got the steering motors switched back on. Let me see if we're frozen." The line clicked off as Raveneu took his hand off the silver press-to-talk button on his mouthpiece, then clicked on again. "The motors are okay. Listen, sir . . . if you could upgrade my discharge?"

"General, under honorable conditions, do it?"

"Yes sir, thank you, sir."

"Sigs, After Steering, standing by to answer the helm."

"Very well. Left standard rudder."

Warner brought the ship to a place where the waves were breaking on the port bow—about the most comfortable ride they could find, given the seas. "Rudder amidships. Steady as you go."

"Captain," Raveneau said, "I don't have any gyro back here. And I'm worried about the guys in Main. Why don't they answer up?"

"IC got wiped. They're off line, but most of the snipes are okay. We'll straighten it all out later when we get a chance to hold a muster. Right now we're still in a fight. You with me?"

"With you, Captain."

"Right five degrees rudder."

"Right five degrees aye. My rudder is right five degrees."

"Very well. Just hang in there, Raveneau. I can see the way home."

"I sure hope so, sir, 'cause I sure want to get there."

Warner looked out at the sea ahead. Through his binoculars, he could still see the fleeing pirate ship. A man stood on the stern of the 80-footer. It could only have been the pirate leader. Warner gave the engine order: "Warp factor four."

With that word, *Cushing*'s gas turbines were set to the maximum. The ship increased in speed through the water, overtaking the waves, the bow pitching up, then tilting down as the ship slid down the face of each wave in turn, burying the bow under the sea as it plunged, the green water coming as far back as the base of Gun Mount 51.

Then the ship pitched up, the bow rising, the water sluicing off each side in a welter of foam. With each impact, the rail slapped Warner's hands where he held on to the wood.

"Left standard rudder."

The swing of the ship stopped. Now he was bearing straight down on the fleeing black craft.

Cushing's bow tilted up, leaving only sky visible ahead for anyone on the main deck. Then the ship again crested the wave and slid forward. The target was closer now. At least with the wind astern, the signal shack cut the flying scud.

"Main, Captain," Warner said. "Give me liberty turns. Wire down the safeties if you have to. And get everyone out of the sonar spaces forward. We may lose the sonar dome."

"Captain, just what do you have in mind?"

Prasetyo's 80-footer was growing closer, but its relative bearing hadn't changed against the mark on *Cushing*'s rail.

"An improved *Spruance* is one of the finest naval weapon systems in the world," Warner said. "I intend to use it. On my signal, sound the collision alarm."

The black boat was nearer now. He could see the white water of its wake, and then the froth curling under its bow as it started to drift right against the rail.

"After Steering, Captain, right five degrees rudder." The 80-footer's drift slowed, then stopped. "Rudder amidships."

"Captain, Main, ahead four."

A moment later: "Very well. Raise the pit sword."

The pit sword sticks out below a vessel's keel in order to measure speed through the water. Warner's order raised *Cushing*'s pit sword into a protective well on the bottom of the ship.

Now Warner didn't need to use binoculars to make out figures on the boat he was pursuing. "He's going to turn left," he said to himself. "After Steering, Captain, left full rudder."

"My rudder is left full," came back the reply.

"Increase your rudder to left hard."

"Increase my rudder to left hard, aye. My rudder is left hard."

As Warner had predicted, Prasetyo had come left. Thanks to Warner's order a moment before, the 80-footer's bearing didn't change. *Cushing* had perhaps a ten-knot speed advantage, and the destroyer was still gaining.

"Shift your rudder," Warner ordered. "Steady as you go."

"Steady as I go aye," After Steering answered up.

Now the pirate craft was close and plainly visible, pounding up and down through the storm-driven swells, rolling wildly as it fled. On the stern, Prasetyo stood, a machine pistol in hand. He pointed it up at the onrushing destroyer and fired a long, futile burst.

Warner didn't move, standing and watching, and talking on his SP phone. This was his ship, and he gave the *Cushing* her orders as easily as a man telling his own hand to make a fist.

"Right hard." *Put the rudder to the right as far as it will go.*

"Meet her." *This is the course I want. Use the rudder as you please to keep us on it.*

"Starboard stop." *Stop the starboard engines, making the ship twist to the right.*

"Port ahead flank." *The port engines now go ahead as fast as they can, making the ship turn to the right even faster.*

"Starboard back full." *Reverse the starboard screw. The ship will now be twisting about, making a right turn within its own length.*

"All stop." *Stop all engines.*

"Left full rudder." *Put the rudder to the left, but not as far as Hard.*

"Midships." *Put the rudder straight back.*

Then, finally, he said, "Sound collision. All ahead full," and the pirate craft ship vanished beneath *Cushing*'s stem with a sound of rending wood that Warner could hear even above the wind. Men in the machinery spaces heard a thumping pass along the keel beneath them.

Astern in the rain-lashed sea, a calm patch appeared, the oil on the waters. A few broken pieces of flotsam bobbed nearby. *Cushing* sailed onward undisturbed, into the wind-driven waves.

"Main, Captain," Warner said. "I'm returning to my quarters. See if anyone can find the XO and get a fix. I'd like to get back into the channel and onto track as soon as I can. Going off now."

Bridge, USS *Cushing*
104° 50' 3" E/01° 12' 34" S
1508 Local/0808 Zulu

Ten hours later, with the storm at last abating, a *Ticonderoga*-class cruiser, *Vincennes*, came over the horizon. With *Cushing*'s radios out, the cruiser had to send its message by flashing light: *Do you require assistance?*

For the reply, Warner himself took the handle of the signal lamp: *Not anymore I don't.*

32

Captain Warner sat at the table in the wardroom, drinking his first uninterrupted cup of coffee since the pirates' attack. Laura was with him. She'd managed to wash off the dirt and blood from the mess in Chiefs' Berthing, and had put on fresh clothes. Just looking at her did a lot for Andrew Warner's sense that all was once again right with the world.

Mostly right, anyhow; he was still going to have to do all of the paperwork. Some of it was going to be interesting. So far, the Australian government was denying any knowledge of, or responsibility for, the presence of what appeared to have been SASR troopers attempting to sink USS *Cushing*. Warner supposed that Canberra would come up with a not-too-ludicrous cover story eventually, so that all the bodies could get directed to the right quarters for burial.

Eight pirates had been left behind aboard *Cushing* when their leader attempted his escape. They'd still been trying to break into After Steering when the SAT/BAF showed up, but they'd given up without a fight when they learned how things stood: no food, no water, limited ammo, their leader had bugged out, and there was no way to get out of that compartment that didn't involve sticking your head out of a hatch.

The pirates were now housed as prisoners in After O. The Indonesian government would, without doubt, condemn their actions, while at the same time demanding their release. The United States, meanwhile, would probably stall long enough for American intelligence to wring them dry, then hand them over to the Indonesian authorities.

None of that, fortunately, was Captain Warner's problem. All he had to do was keep the prisoners fed and healthy until somebody in authority showed up to take them off his ship.

There also remained, less happily, the task of writing letters to the next-of-kin of those *Cushing* crew members who had died in the line of duty during the pirate attack. There were far too many of those: ET2 Harness; LTJG Bailey; the crew members in Repair 5; Lieutenant Ernie Gilano and most of the sailors who'd been on the Bridge when the missiles hit; and a sad list of others who had been, fatally, in the wrong place at the wrong time.

Some people had turned out lucky, though—like HT2 Charley Ross, who'd survived both the firefight in Repair 5 and the second firefight in Chiefs' Berthing.

Master Chief Morrison was another of the lucky ones. The 9mm bullet he'd taken in his chest was going to keep him out of action for quite a while, but—as *Cushing*'s Corpsman had said—if it hadn't killed him yet it probably wasn't going to. GMGSN Stryker would be back on his feet, and up for promotion, a great deal sooner.

Chris, now, and H. L. Morrison . . . "The kids did all right," Warner said.

"Chris takes after you," said Laura. "It never showed much before, but he does."

"You're no slouch in a crisis yourself."

She gave him a tired smile. "Yes, but I don't *enjoy* a crisis the way you do. Chris does."

"So does H. L.," Warner said. *Cushing*'s Master Chief didn't know yet that his baby girl had been running around menacing pirates with an automatic rifle. There was probably going to be quite a scene when he found out. "She and Chris make a hell of a couple."

"I give them until Yokosuka," said Laura. "A couple of days in the real world, and . . ."

"Maybe," Warner said. "Or maybe not. I know a shrink and a sailor who still get along after all these years."

She reached out and took his right hand—the left one was still bruised and aching from the fall he'd taken when the missiles hit. "It hasn't been dull, I'll give you that."

"You don't mind?"

She smiled at him—the same smile he'd seen come over her face when *McCloy* pulled into the yards at Puget Sound, all those years ago. "If I'd wanted a dull life, I could have had one. I wanted you instead. I haven't changed my mind."

01 Level, USS *Cushing*
104° 50' 2" E/01° 12' 30" S
1523 Local/0823 Zulu

GMGSN Stryker—somewhat surprised to find himself still alive—was in *Cushing*'s unused helicopter hangar on the 01 level, awaiting transfer to USS *Vincennes* along with Master Chief Morrison. Charley Ross had already been flown over, as had several of the most seriously wounded; Stryker and Morrison, not being in immediate danger of dying, had to wait their turn. Both men lay in Stokes baskets—international-orange stretchers with flotation devices at either end, rigged to swing beneath a helicopter.

"Hard to believe it's over," Stryker said. He paused. "Is it true what I heard, Master Chief?"

Morrison turned his head sideways with some effort and looked at Stryker. "Depends on what you heard."

"I heard that not all of the guys who came aboard us during the storm were pirates."

"You heard wrong, then."

The Master Chief's voice was sharp despite his injuries. Stryker thought about the implications of Morrison's denial for a moment, then said, "Yes, Master Chief. I guess I must have."

"Hold that thought."

"Yes, Master Chief. What do you think happens now?"

"We spend some time in the hospital getting fussed over by the nurses," Morrison said. "And then we get some convalescent leave."

"No, I mean with the ship. Is the Captain going to be in trouble when we get back to port?"

"In the long run?" Morrison said. "Probably not. A bunch of bad shit happened on his watch, but he had it all under control by the time the Tico showed up."

"That's good," Stryker said. He liked Captain Warner, or at least, liked him as much as a lowly GMGSN could be presumed to like a distant authority figure.

"Yeah," Morrison said. "Tommy J. Raveneau's getting himself an Honorable Discharge out of it, too, for hanging on in After Steering when things got tough."

"No kidding? I owe him, then. I had a buck on an Honorable in the Rat Boot pool."

Morrison chuckled—or rather, he tried to chuckle, and thought better of it. "How did you figure out he was going to pull it off?"

"I didn't," Stryker admitted. "It just didn't seem right that nobody at all had money on an Honorable, and I had a buck on me when I heard about it, so—" He shrugged, then winced as the shift in position made his injured leg start throbbing again.

"From what the Captain says," Morrison told him, "you didn't do too badly yourself."

"It wasn't . . . things needed to get done, is all."

"So you did them. They call that 'leadership and initiative.' " The Master Chief paused again, then said casually, "Are you planning to re-up at the end of your hitch?"

"I was thinking about it," Stryker said. "I figure by that time I might have a good shot at making Third Class if I study hard."

"You might want to think about going for officer instead."

"I thought they only wanted college graduates."

"What they want is good officers. And there's ways to take care of the college part of it, like the NESEP program."

"What's NESEP?"

"Navy Enlisted Science Education Program," Morrison said. "They send you to college for four years on Uncle's dime, while you wear civvies and pull down your regular paycheck every month. Plus about as much social life as you can handle."

" 'Social life?' "

"Some people say that NESEP stands for Never Ending Supply of Erotic Pleasure." Morrison chuckled weakly again. "Not that I'm saying you'd let a consideration like that influence your mind."

Quick, firm footsteps sounded outside the helicopter hangar as he spoke, and a few seconds later H. L. Morrison came in. She knelt by Morrison's stretcher and gave him a careful hug.

"Daddy!" she said. "I came to keep you company until the helicopter takes you over to that other ship."

"You don't have to do that, honey. I'll be fine."

"Yes, I do have to," she said. "Mamma's going to ask me how you're doing, and there's no way I'm going to tell her that I don't know."

Stryker had been watching H. L. ever since she came on. She

was a college girl, definitely; and he'd have to be blind not to see that she was currently an officers-only boyfriend type. But if there were any others like her back on campus . . .

"You know, Chief," he said, "that program you were talking about sounds like a great idea. I'll give it a look as soon as I'm back on my feet."

Main Deck, USS *Cushing*
104° 50' 2" E/01° 12' 30" S
1523 Local/0823 Zulu

Chris and H. L. stood together at the rail of the ship, looking out across the ocean. The sunlit waves sparkled blue and golden under a sky so clean-scrubbed and cloudless there might as well never have been a storm. Only the missile damage to the destroyer's superstructure remained as visible testimony to what had happened during the long, storm-wracked night.

"You aren't taking pictures," H. L. said—half question, half statement.

"Not for a while yet."

"Why not? I thought taking pictures was what you did."

"Yeah, well." He watched the flight of a seabird against the blue sky for a few seconds, then said, "I kind of feel like letting my head settle down a bit first, if you know what I mean. And besides, I don't want to accidentally take a picture of something that would only make humorless authority figures try to violate my civil rights later when I go to get it printed."

"Good idea."

"I think so," he said. "Save my luck in case I ever need to do something like that on purpose."

After a while, she said, "You're still planning on being a pho-tographer, then."

"It's what I'm good at. You're still planning on taking the political world by storm?"

"One little piece of it at a time," she said. She smiled. "Starting with the bits closest to home. Can you *imagine* how jealous the guys at school are going to be?"

"Because you got shot at over vacation, and they didn't?" Chris shook his head. "Amazing. I hope you're not planning to date any of those people."

"Are you kidding? It took me most of my first year to convince them that I *didn't* want to do anything like that with them."

"Good."

She stared at him. "What do you mean, 'good'?"

"If you aren't dating any of them, then maybe you'll be interested in dating somebody else."

"Uh-huh. Like who, Nature Boy?"

"Like me, maybe, if I happen to wind up in Virginia for some reason."

"And just how likely is that? I thought you were a West Coast kind of guy."

He shrugged. "Once I graduate, I have to look for work somewhere. And Virginia's as good a place to look for it as anyplace else."

"Yes," she said, starting to smile again—at him, this time, and with surprising warmth. "Yes, I suppose that it is."

EPILOGUE

All in all, Nuril Salladien felt pleased at the events of the past few days. True, Operation Tigerclaw had not been successful, as success had been originally defined. But much insult and inconvenience had been given to an arrogant superpower, which was always to the good. It served to demonstrate that no country was invincible.

And Prasetyo was dead, which was even better. The pirate leader had become an uncomfortably sharp tool, one which threatened to turn and cut the hand of anyone who used it—and one which Salladien did not dare to let go. Captain Andrew Warner and USS *Cushing* had solved the problem of ending the relationship.

Salladien was not expecting, therefore, to enter his downtown office and find a dead man waiting there for him. The pirate had one arm in a sling, and an ugly red gash across his forehead was just starting to heal, but he was clearly still alive.

Prasetyo had his good hand in the pocket of his tailored white suit. Before Salladien could say anything, he brought the hand out, and the pistol with it.

The office had excellent soundproofing; the three shots Prasetyo fired in quick succession—two into Salladien's chest, and one into his head—were not heard anywhere outside of its walls. Prasetyo put the pistol back into his pocket and stood looking down at the body.

All of the remaining members of his crew had died when *Cushing* broke the back of his 80-footer and drove the pieces under. Prasetyo himself had nearly drowned, and had expected to die more than once in the next few days afterward. But he had survived the collision at sea, and survived his injuries and the storm, and survived the trek back to civilization from the deserted island beach where the waves had taken him.

He might as well have been born a new man, coming up that way out of the water. Only Salladien had recognized him since then. And with Salladien dead, there was no one left who could say for sure that this new man was the pirate leader who had tried to capture a United States destroyer, and who had failed.

The man who very soon now would not be Michael Prasetyo any longer smiled to himself. His old bank accounts were still within his reach; he had set them up that way from the beginning, so that he could access them using any one of a number of different names. With that much front money, he could buy himself a fast boat and recruit another crew. And after that . . .

After that, the Strait was always full of ships.

1312